Additional Praise for Linda L. Richards and
Death Was the Other Woman

"With crackling dialogue, a tommy-gun plot, and bang-on authenticity, *Death Was the Other Woman* engrossed me in a terrific, compelling mystery. With memorable characters and settings, Richards manages to dig beneath the surface of Prohibition-era Los Angeles and give a sense of its historical context. A great read!"

—Daniel Kalla, author of *Pandemic* and *Blood Lies*

"Sharp, vibrant, and crackling. One chapter in to Linda L. Richards's sparkling 1930s Los Angeles mystery, *Death Was the Other Woman,* and we'd follow her smart, resourceful, spirited heroine, Kitty Pangborn, down any dark alley, any mean street."

—Megan Abbott, author of *The Song Is You* and *Queenpin*

"Kitty Pangborn, the narrator of Linda Richards's winning new mystery, *Death Was the Other Woman,* is just what every underachieving, over-imbibing, minimally employed, and maximally hard-boiled PI needs: that is, a decent secretary . . . *Death Was the Other Woman* is a first-rate, rousing new take on the Southern California detective novel. Let's hope it's the beginning of a long series."

—Dylan Schaffer, author of *I Right the Wrongs*

"Linda L. Richards can grab her readers better than a slap in the puss or a slug from a forty-five. She breathes new life into the L.A. noir genre with an array of fresh characters and stylishly seedy neon-lit dives. More important, she moves the gritty crime genre on in the form of Kitty Pangborn, a well-brought-up young lady who gets a crash course in the dark underbelly of the City of Angels. She may be a long-suffering PA to a less-than-successful PI, but Kitty is no kitten. She's the broad with the brains, and readers will be left clamoring for more."

—Brendan Foley, author of *Under the Wire* and director of *The Riddle*

DEATH WAS

THE OTHER WOMAN

DEATH WAS

THE OTHER WOMAN

LINDA L. RICHARDS

———

THOMAS DUNNE BOOKS

St. Martin's Minotaur 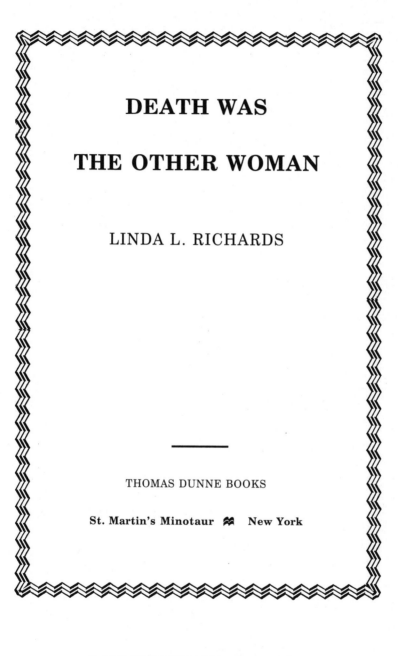 **New York**

THOMAS DUNNE BOOKS.
An imprint of St. Martin's Press.

www.thomasdunnebooks.com
www.minotaurbooks.com

Book design by Abby Kagan

Library of Congress Cataloging-in-Publication Data

Richards, Linda, 1960–
    Death was the other woman / Linda L. Richards.—1st ed.
        p.   cm.
    ISBN-13: 978-0-312-37770-0
    ISBN-10: 0-312-37770-3
    1. Private investigators—California—Los Angeles—Fiction.   2. Adultery—Fiction.   3. Depressions—1929—California—Los Angeles—Fiction.   4. Los Angeles (Calif.)—Fiction.   I. Title.
    PR9199.4.R5226D43   2008
    813'.6—dc22   2007038734

First Edition: January 2008

10   9   8   7   6   5   4   3   2   1

DEDICATED TO THE MEMORY OF MY FATHER,

KARL HUBER,

WHO TAUGHT ME ABOUT ZOOT SUITS,

AND SO MUCH MORE

ACKNOWLEDGMENTS

You begin with a hint of something; a whisper, maybe even a dream. You toss it up ever so lightly to see if the wind fills it with life. And if you're lucky and your timing is right, others will step up and stand in and offer bits of themselves to this thing you are creating. At this point, some of "I" becomes "we" and you have to look around and give thanks where they're due. And here I am.

Peter Joseph is the editor authors dream about: everything he touches ends up better than it was. Thank you, Peter.

Amy Moore-Benson is more than my agent; Amy is cheerleader, friend, and a force of nature. It's lovely to have her in my corner.

My partner David Middleton is generous with his time, advice, and prodigious knowledge of *everything*. Always. My son, the actor Michael Karl Richards, continues to push me to my creative best. He will not accept anything less of either of us. My brother Peter Huber offers unflinching, unblinking, unwavering support. I've said it before but will say it again here: most women consider themselves lucky to have a strong, sensitive, caring man in their lives. I'm more than lucky, I have three.

Thank you to Michéle Denis, Andrew Heard, Carolyn Withers-Heard, Laura-Jean Kelly, Jackie Leidl, Patricia McLean, Betty Middleton, Linda Murray, Debbie Warmerdam, and Carrie Wheeler. Your input and support keep me going; warms my heart.

Thanks to the Los Angeles Conservancy (www.laconservancy.org) for struggling to save representative bits of the city's rich and beautiful history. There are only vestiges of Kitty Pangborn's Los Angeles left in the twenty-first century. I can't imagine a modern city whose physical history is more threatened. This is partly due to the fact that L.A. is such a young city, and her periods of growth have often been dramatic to the point of violence. All that paving of Paradise. The Los Angeles Conservancy is the largest member-based organization for historic preservation in the United States. Not only have they been able to establish a solid long-term plan, saving several important landmarks along the way, they also do an admirable job of bringing the past to life for modern Angelenos.

CHAPTER ONE

HE'S DRESSED WELL, the dying man. Sharply, one would say. He's wearing a good suit. Dark, and of a wool so fine it would feel soft to the touch. The suit has a pale pinstripe; it's barely discernible. And he's wearing the suit well—he wore it well—except for the dying part.

He's standing there, his lifeblood draining from him, the look on his face showing surprise as much as horror. He hadn't planned on dying today. Had, in fact, planned on being the one doing the killing. Killing is part of his job. Not dying. There's not enough money in L.A.—or the world for that matter—to get a man to give up his life as easily as that.

The man is standing. I can see him as clearly as if I were there, though of course I was not. But I understand things now. Things I had no hope of understanding at the time. I can re-create them in my mind and know what the details mean.

His hat is fashionable, well shaped, well made, and for the moment, it's worn at a good angle. His features are as well cut as his suit. Dark like the suit as well. He'd be handsome if he weren't presently concerned about the end he can see so clearly.

Another man is there, similarly dressed, but the look on his face is different. No surprise. No pain. He's in control. He's always in control. The gun in his hand tells that story.

The woman is barely in the room, but she doesn't look away. That shocks me somehow. She shouldn't watch. Why would she watch? What profit will her witness bring?

She's exquisite. That shocks me as well. Her shoulders are broad and smooth. Her legs long and well defined. Her hair, her features, soft and lovely. And the look on her face . . . that shocks me most of all. Not pleasure, no. But not distress either. To her, this scene is correct. The only proper conclusion to a story she helped write.

But all of this is later. Much later. It makes sense to me now. But then? Not then. At the time I found him, it made no sense at all.

CHAPTER TWO

DEX IS TALL AND DREAMY. Oh, sure, he's a mook, but he's the kind of mook that can heat a girl's socks, if you follow my drift. The kind that can get your lipstick melting.

It's never going to happen for me and Dex. Most days I don't really want it to anyway. Dex is my boss, first and foremost. The work is easy, and most weeks Dex remembers to cut me a check. That's important; a girl's gotta eat. And there are worse ways to make a living. A lot worse.

Take Rita Heppelwaite, for instance. I had her figured before she even settled down in the chair across from my desk. It's just a little space, and when no one is listening Dex and I call it our waiting room. It's a joke because Dex isn't the busiest P.I. in L.A., and that's no understatement. And anyway, to be a waiting room it would have to be a room, and that little space between my desk and the door to the office is more like a steamer trunk without all the legroom.

So Rita Heppelwaite breezes into the office nice as you please, the scent of violets following her like a mob. She looks haughty, like she thinks I don't know what she does for a living. Like Dex hadn't already spilled his guts about everything he knows. Though to be honest, at that point he didn't know much.

Rita, Dex had told me, was a "lady of the night," which was his attempt at polite talk "in front of the kid"—which is me—for saying that what Rita does for a living, she does on her back. From the looks of her, she probably gets paid a damned sight better than I do. Probably doesn't have to answer the phone or bring coffee either.

The first thing I notice is her coat. It's a pretty hard thing not to notice. Even in October, Los Angeles just doesn't get that kind of cold, so a fur coat hits you right off. And this was one you'd mark in any room, at any time of the year. Anywhere. Black lamb's wool, all curly and fine, and a jaunty little hat to match, perched on her head just so. I wouldn't have hated her just for the coat though. I've never been a girl who dreamed about furs.

There were other reasons to hate her. The dark red hair that poured over her shoulders, for starters. Dusky flames that seemed to make her lips even redder. Her eyes were the color of the ocean at midnight. A green so dark you'd swear it was black until the light shifted; then you had to look again. She was beautiful enough that you might have taken her for a movie star. Until you looked into those eyes. Then you saw something else.

"Mr. Theroux will be with you in a moment," I told her, when she showed up five minutes ahead of their appointment. "Please have a seat and I'll let him know you're here."

She settled into the "waiting room" chair so meekly, I should have suspected a trick, but I just didn't see it coming. Who would have thought anyone in heels that high could be so quiet?

So when I opened Dex's door to let myself in, I didn't expect her to follow right behind me, catching Dex kicked back in his chair before he could stuff the sports pages and his usual glass of whiskey into the top drawer of his desk.

I expected a curt word from him. Dex doesn't like it when clients barge into his office before I have a chance to announce them. He says it's unseemly. And I mostly agree. I like it when my paychecks aren't made of rubber, and I've discovered that the best way to avoid that is to do everything I can to keep Dex's clients from running in the other direction when they first get a load of him.

Like I said, Dex is kind of dreamy. But the way I figure it, seeing a detective hitting the sauce before noon and greeting you with bleary eyes and not a lot of other customers lined up in front of you isn't the most inspiring thing in the world. There's gotten to be a lot of detectives in the city. Most of them better at it than my boss.

So I expected Dex to bawl me out for letting this broad sail into his office like nobody's business. But one look at his face gawping at Rita Heppelwaite told me that wasn't going to happen. I glanced back at her to see what he was seeing, and I understood.

She stood framed in the doorway, doing her best damsel-in-distress. Her coat was open, and the dress beneath it was as red and tight as the skin on an apple. Did she practice all that bosom heaving in front of a mirror? I figured she'd have to. If I tried a stunt like that, I'd look like I had just run a block to catch a bus. And the sight of me wouldn't cause Dex Theroux's jaw to go all slack and his eyes to lose focus either. As things were, I wanted to cross the room and slap some sense into him. What kind of client, I wondered, would want to hire a detective who looked at her the way a dog looks at meat?

I didn't slap him though. Instead I just said, "Let me know if you need anything, Boss." Then I breezed past Rita, who was now leaving the doorway and taking a seat, uninvited, in front of Dex's desk.

As I closed the door, I heard her say, "Thank you for seeing me on such short notice, Mr. Theroux." A smoky voice, filled with experience and promise. A combination that startled. And another reason to hate her.

The time seemed to pass real slow while Miss Heppelwaite had her meeting with Dex. I think the phone rang a few times—bill collectors who I politely told that Dex was out of town on a job.

I remembered to shove a blank piece of paper into the typewriter and make a lot of clacking every once in a while. Dex asked me to do that when he's with a potential client. He figures that because you can hear the echo of the clacking in his office even with the door closed, a new client will realize how busy and important he is and cough up the required dough more easily.

Actually, what Dex asked me to do while he's with a new client was, "Be sure to catch up on the typing." But really? There's never anything to catch up on. It's not like there's much to type even when he's on a case. And when he's not? What would I type? Some ode to rye whiskey that my boss mumbles when he's dancing with the sauce? I don't think so. So I mostly clack pointlessly. It gets the job done.

I was happily clacking when half an hour or so later, Dex escorted Rita Heppelwaite out of the office. That was my first clue that the meeting had gone well. When Dex actually escorts a client past my desk, it means some cash has been choked up for him, or promised for the immediate future. But if potential clients come out in a huff and slam the door behind them, it means I might have to wait for my paycheck. So I was glad to see Dex escorting the Heppelwaite dame, even though it meant I got an extra look at her apple-skin-tight dress while she dragged her fur coat behind her and batted her eyes up at my boss.

I closed my brain to the scent of violets and kept clacking.

"Well, whaddaya think of that?" Dex sauntered up to my desk once the office door closed and we could hear the tapping of Rita's heels receding down the hallway toward the elevator. Dex plunked himself on the corner of my desk, balanced himself on his behind, and crossed his long legs at the ankles.

"That coat looks hot," I said dryly, without looking up, leaving it to Dex to figure out if I meant Rita's fur looked stolen or was too warm for the day. Either way, he would get the idea it wasn't a compliment.

I was still clacking away, by now with a bit of venom. And more pointlessly than ever. It's not like there were any clients in the office that Dex needed to impress.

"Heh-heh." His laugh had a lecherous sound that I figured I understood. I was wrong. "Look what she gave me." He spread the cash between my eyes and the typewriter, a nice big fan of green. I stopped typing. Dex was holding out a couple of twenties, three sawbucks, a fin, and a mitt full of singles, all so bright and unlined that—if her manicure hadn't been so perfect—I would have suspected the Heppelwaite broad had made them in her garage that morning.

"That's gotta be like, what? Eighty bucks?" I said, surprised. "What for?"

"Eighty-three," he corrected. "It's my retainer," Dex said smugly.

"I figured that part, wise guy. I mean, you know, for how long? And for what?"

"I told her my daily rate was twenty-five bucks." I issued forth an appreciative whistle and flushed when Dex grinned at me approvingly. "Plus expenses. You know."

I nodded. "Sure. What's she want you to do?"

"You could probably guess, kiddo. She's got a boyfriend. . . ."

I rolled my eyes at the euphemism. Dex caught it and grinned again.

"Well, what else would you call it? Anyway, she's afraid the boyfriend is stepping out. She wants me to follow him for a few days and give her a report."

"The usual stuff."

Dex smiled and stretched, then eased himself off my desk. "Precisely, my dear. The usual stuff. So I'll need a new bottle of Jack and a good car. Can you make that happen?"

"Can't you just take a Red Car?" I asked, knowing full well that managing a tail from a streetcar was asking a bit much. And if I hadn't known, Dex's look would have set me straight.

"Let me know when the car is ready to roll," he said. "Meanwhile, I've got some paperwork to do in my office."

Paperwork, I thought, when Dex's door closed behind him.

That would be his version of pointless clacking. And what it really meant was the heel of the bottle of bourbon in his office—now that he had some loot, he wouldn't need to hoard his stash—and maybe forty winks while I got things ready.

I groused a little about the car, but only to myself. We'd been a while between clients, and I always thought about expenses, even if Dex seldom did. Still, as soon as the door clicked shut, I got on the blower.

"Hey, Mustard," I said, when he answered the phone. "Dex just bought a case. He needs a decent heap for a tail."

I've known Mustard as long as I've known Dex, which is to say about two years. Word is, they were in the army together, though neither of them has told me so. The other thing no one has told me is why he's called Mustard. Is it his name? I mean, it *could* be. I think "Mustard" can be a name. What confuses me is that his hair is a sort of dirty ginger color. When pressed, I think you could say his hair is the color of mustard.

And Mustard smokes a lot of cigarettes. In fact, he smokes them end to end. As a result, the index and middle finger of his left hand are—you guessed it—mostly the color of mustard. And I've never actually seen him eat, but it may well be that he just loves the condiment so much that he puts it on everything.

I do know that Mustard is as sunny as Dex is dour. Dex calls Mustard a fixer. I'm not entirely sure what he fixes, though I suspect it has something to do with horses and dogs and maybe bootleg whiskey. For Dex though, Mustard fixes everything. Like today, Dex needed a car, so Mustard was the man to call. He'd fix it.

"Couldn't convince him to do it in a Red Car, eh?" I could hear the laughter in Mustard's voice. He knows all about the back-and-forth Dex and I do about spending money.

"It's for a *tail,* Mustard. He needs a car."

"OK. Sure," he said, humoring me. "You want me to have it dropped by the office, or will Dex swing over and pick it up?"

I considered briefly. Having it dropped off would mean an extra charge. However, considering the amount of whiskey Dex had already consumed on this cold but sunny morning, plus the amount he was now consuming in celebration of getting another job, I figured I'd better have the car dropped off. No sense in taking the chance of Dex getting waylaid on the way to the garage.

"Have it dropped off, please. And if it wouldn't be too much trouble, it would be great if there was a new bottle of Jack Daniel's on the passenger seat."

Mustard didn't bother hiding the laugh this time—he knew what all of that meant—but he promised the car would be waiting downstairs by midafternoon.

Now understand, my boss isn't just a pointless lush. As much as I watch out for him and sometimes even baby him, he can be a capable guy, though he has some very real challenges.

Like a lot of boys, Dex went off to war when he was eighteen. The Great One. Unlike a lot of those boys though, Dex came back. There's something in that combination that's made him not right. Something that's damaged him, like a shiny Ford that's been fixed after a fender bender. It might look OK on the outside, but it never works in quite the same way again.

For a while after the War he went back to Canada, to the small town on the Ontario border where he's from. Things didn't work out at home, so he slid over to Buffalo, where he got a job as some kind of deputy. He's never told me the whole story, but I've been piecing things together. Things between him and Mustard. Things I hear when Dex is on the phone. Even things he tells me when he's been into the sauce and is waiting for a job. He talks at times like those, but he talks in half thoughts, as though to himself. I have to put two and two together then. It's possible that sometimes I come up with six.

From being in the War, Dex knew how to handle a gun, knew how to use it on a man. He knew how to wait real quiet for a long time in order to get a job done. And he knew—and this part is important—he knew how to stay alive. Police work seemed like the only kind of thing he could do. Somehow—and I don't really know how—that didn't work out. So he came out to L.A. at the same time a lot of other people were coming here, and he hung up his shingle: Dexter J. Theroux, Private Investigator.

A little over two years ago he caught a big case that, as near as I can figure, he concluded quickly and almost by accident. But that led to a lot of work, which led him to hire me to answer his phones and do his paperwork. And we've been getting along pretty well ever since.

About half past three, Mustard's guy showed up with the heap. The kid gave me the keys and smiled on his way out the door when I tipped him a quarter.

I poked my head into the office after the kid had gone. "Your car's ready," I said. Dex was sitting behind his desk, not even pretending to read the newspaper. His expression was morose, and the glass on his desk was empty but for the ice I'd picked up for him on my way to the office in the morning. Disappointment on the rocks.

"What is it?" His eyes focused on me slowly and he didn't get up. He was clearly half cut. Maybe more than half.

"What is it?" I repeated. "It's a car. What do you think?"

"No, I meant is it a Ford? Or a Packard? Or what?"

"Geez, Dex, I don't know. It's a car. I guess it'll be black. Whaddaya want?"

He grunted and lapsed back into looking morose, having hit a high of mildly interested for about thirty seconds.

"So what's the plan?" I asked.

It took him a few seconds to refocus.

"Plan?" he said, looking honestly confused. I choked back a stub of impatience.

"Yeah. Remember? Rita Heppelwaite? The boyfriend? You wanted a car. And there's someplace you're supposed to be. You didn't tell me where."

He pulled himself out of his slouch and took a stab at sitting upright. He ran his hands through his hair and sighed deeply, as though something was causing him pain. I knew, however, that it was not actual pain. I'd been down this road before. I breathed a small sigh of my own and took a step back to watch.

As expected, a minute or so later Dex hauled himself up, straightened his tie, popped his fedora onto his head at almost the usual angle, put on his jacket, rummaged around a bit for his piece, gave it up, and headed out the door.

I followed fairly closely behind him, pausing only to grab my hat, coat, and handbag, grab his holstered gun off the coatrack in his office, and lock the door behind me before I scurried down the hall as quickly as my sensible-but-still-ladylike heels could carry me.

Though we rode down in the elevator together, Dex didn't say anything to me, not even when I passed him his gun. I held his jacket while he put on the holster, but he continued to seem lost in whatever dark thoughts he'd been wrestling with in the office.

When we located the car Mustard had dropped off, I broke the silence. "You know I'm driving, right?"

He looked at me—bemused or annoyed, I couldn't quite tell—then said very succinctly, "I did not know that," while he shook his head. "What gave you that idea?"

"Well . . ." I smiled, shrugged, and held up a fob. "I've got the keys, for one thing."

"Ah," he said thoughtfully.

"Right, Dex. Which confirms why I'm driving. You didn't even realize you didn't have the keys 'til right this second, did you?"

"I don't need a babysitter, Kitty."

I did not correct him on the name, just this once. Though I've always disliked being called Kitty.

"You don't need a babysitter," I agreed, "but you *do* need a chauffeur."

"Can you even drive?"

I looked at him with more patience than I felt.

"Dex, you taught me."

"Right. Well . . . well . . . who's gonna answer the phones?"

"You mean, who's gonna tell your bill collectors you're in Chicago?"

That sigh again. "Get in," he said finally, walking around to the passenger side.

"Where we going anyway?" I asked, as I started up the huge black car.

"Lafayette Square."

"You didn't need a car to go to Lafayette Square. A Red Car would have gotten you there easily."

"Thanks, Mom," he said dryly, something that was especially funny since he's a lot older than I am. "We're starting at Lafayette Square. Buckingham Road and Saint Charles Place, to be precise. From there, I'm not sure. But it's gonna take a car. Now pipe down already. If you're gonna drive, drive. Otherwise I'll take it from here."

"As you wish, sire," I quipped, as I started the car and got it rolling. "We're on our way."

CHAPTER THREE

I WAS NOT RAISED TO WORK in an office. Quite frankly, I wasn't raised for commerce at all. For the first two decades of my life I had more delicate concerns. My mother died when I was very young, and my father instructed those charged with my care that I was to be brought up to be the mistress of a large house, hostess to the dinners that would further my someday husband's business concerns, and needless to say, to be the mother of this same mysterious husband's children.

My father was from a different era. Sometimes I thought his expectations for me weren't modern at all: more 1830s than 1930s. Not that I ever said anything. Not that I would ever have dared, which is sort of the point, if you follow.

I was carefully schooled and gently reared, as they say, and from the age of seventeen to the very end of my father's life, I seldom saw my childhood home on Bunker Hill.

I was in San Francisco in my final year at Mrs. Beeson's Finishing School for Young Ladies when I got the news that I'd become an orphan. I was twenty-one at the time, and feeling very much as though my wings had grown beyond the point where the small school could contain them. My best friend, Morgana Cleverly, and I had applied to go to Vassar in the next school year. Morgana's mother was a Vassar girl, and my father liked the fact that Morgana had family in the Hudson Valley, near campus. It had made him feel more receptive to the idea of my living on the other side of the country.

I didn't think that having a country between us would change things very much: there were times when San Francisco may as well have been the moon. I'd seen little of my father in the three years I'd been at Mrs. Beeson's, often spend-ing weekends and even some holidays with Morgana's family in Pacific Heights. And my increasingly infrequent trips home had become less and less comfortable. When I saw him, Father was preoccupied, distant. He always seemed to have a lot on his mind.

I wonder now, should I have pressed him in those days? I have a good mind, and Mrs. Beeson's was the best school of its kind in the West. "Nimble" was what Mrs. Beeson called my mind, and though it wasn't always a compliment, I knew it meant I was anything but stupid.

So what if I had pressed Father? Would he have allowed me to help him? And if he didn't let me help him, would seeing how much I cared have changed the outcome? Would he have seen something in me—something different—that would have altered the course of events, the course he ultimately chose? Those are not good questions, I know, if one wants to go for-ward with a clear heart. Sometimes it's difficult to turn your mind away. Your good mind. Your nimble mind. And some-times it hurts your heart. And it's moot, of course, because I didn't do any of those things. Maybe I should have had some kind of foresight. But I did not.

It was October 29 and I was in Mrs. Sedgewick's music class. It was Elvira Cheswell's turn at the bench, and I was helping her practice the scales. A big part of the curriculum for senior girls at Mrs. Beeson's was working with the younger ones. Mrs. Beeson said it straightened our backs, got us ready for the idea of giving of ourselves, something she felt was im-portant for young women of our station. A philanthropic spirit would be necessary, she told us repeatedly, both for women of position and for our likely role as mothers. When Mrs. Beeson wasn't around, the older girls teased that what she really had in mind was cutting her own expenses: with what was in essence a whole class of teaching assistants, she was likely required to fill several fewer places on her staff.

On that October day, Mrs. Beeson herself came to the door of the music room and asked to have a word with me. The look on her face put me in mind of all kinds of things. What had I done? Some report not handed in? Some weekend misadventure with my friends that had gotten back to her ears? Yet there had been nothing so significant that even its discovery would cause a personal interview.

So, lesson one: we make these things be about ourselves. In truth, it had nothing at all to do with me. Though what she told me changed my life.

"It's your father," Mrs. Beeson said, once I was seated in her office.

"My father?" Nothing she said could have surprised me more. Or so I thought.

"Yes, my dear. Your father." She cleared her throat delicately. The throat clearing and that quiet "my dear" put me on sudden alert. "Miss Pangborn, I just don't know how else to say this, dear. Your father . . . your father has passed to the world beyond."

It took me a full minute to understand what she'd said. A minute when she said nothing at all to me, just sat primly behind her desk with her hands in her lap and watched as I sorted through her words for the sense beneath them.

The world beyond.

At first I was envisioning some sort of business trip—perhaps to the Far East—but I couldn't recall him telling me about anything like that. And then, of course, it hit me. She'd told me in a ridiculous way, but how else should she have said it? "He exited this world by attempting to fly out of a window from the top floor of the Pangborn Building"? Or "He could not face what he'd created"? Or, really, a lot of other things. All of them would have been true. Bottom line: the stock market crash of 1929 was more than a crash for me; it was the day I lost, in a certain way, my innocence, and—and this leads me back to Dex—the day when phrases like "financial reality" would begin to have meaning for me, because they certainly never had before.

It's uncharitable of me, but I'm still angry with my father. It was not very good planning on his part. In so many ways. For instance, how could he wager everything on one bad bet? Didn't he ever hear about too many eggs and a single basket? Most important, of course, how could he make this decision? How could he decide that no father at all was better than one who was a financial failure? My biggest fear: that the reality of his fatherhood didn't enter his mind at all.

He lost everything. You'll have gathered that already. The Pangborn Building—all eight stories of beaux arts beauty—was gone in a heartbeat and renamed almost as quickly. All of the companies that had fueled the need for a Pangborn Building? Gone. The automobiles, the cottage in Malibu, the motor yacht, and of course, all the money needed to do things like buy food and pay for private girls' schools, all gone, gone, gone.

Later I found out that my father must have had some kind of inkling, because he had done one tiny thing to protect me. At least I tell myself it was to protect me; it's possible he had other reasons. I try not to think about that.

Unbeknownst to anyone other than his lawyers, he'd transferred the title of the house on Bunker Hill to Marcus and Marjorie Oleg, the husband-and-wife chauffeur and housekeeper who had been with us as long as I could remember. He'd done it a full year before he died. I hope he did it to ensure I'd at least always have a roof: he knew very well that Marcus and Marjorie wouldn't turn me out.

And they didn't: they let me keep my old room with the private bathroom Father had installed when I became a "young

lady" and needed my privacy. But there was no money for anyone. And suddenly even Marcus and Marjorie were out of jobs,
and things were very difficult. Like some weirdly arranged family though, we've all worked together to get through. The two of
them have taken in boarders—it's a big house—and I con-
tribute what I can when Dex remembers to pay me. It's really
not a bad life, but as I said, it's not the life I ever envisioned
when I was at Mrs. Beeson's. Not the one that was envisioned
for me. And Vassar, of course, was suddenly out of the question.

It was while I was selling Mother's jewelry at a scary little
pawnshop at First and Alameda that I met Mustard. He did
not work at the pawnbroker's, of course. He was just there, no
doubt fixing something, when he overheard the part of my
plight I could bring myself to tell the man pawing at Mother's
things. I was hoping to get enough to at least pay for my father's coffin. I must have been quite pathetic.

"For crissakes, Lou." It was Mustard, behind me. I hadn't
noticed him before. His suit was well made and dark, with a
fine stripe that was even darker. He wasn't a tall man, but he
had a solid look about him. Not fat, but you got the idea he
hadn't missed a lot of meals either. "She just told you her father died, and she's trying to scratch enough together to buy
him a proper funeral. You can give her more than *that*."

"Yeah, well." Behind his wicket, Lou scratched at himself. I
could see that all that scratching had rimmed his nails in
black. "These days *everyone*'s got a dyin' dad, Mustard. You
can't believe every sob story you hear, y'know."

"Look at her, Lou. She's just a kid. What are you? Seventeen?"

I pulled myself to my full height. "I'm twenty-one," I said
truthfully, though I saw the look of doubt in his eyes.

"Aw, never mind. It looks like nice stuff." Then to me, he
said, "Is it good stuff?"

"I . . . I don't know, honestly, sir. I would imagine so. My mother was from a good Baltimore family, or so my father always told me."

"Your mother's dead, too? Ker-riste, Lou! Sorry, miss. Listen, Lou, what were you offerin'?"

"Fifty bucks," Lou said defensively, scratching again. "For the lot."

"And how much is the funeral?" Mustard asked, looking at me.

"One *hundred* and fifty." I think by then I was probably close to tears.

"Listen, kid, Lou's going to give you two hundred." I gasped, and if I wasn't mistaken, Lou gasped too. "But you keep this ring." Mustard slid a piece that I knew had belonged to my grandmother toward me. It was ebony and emerald set in white gold. "It doesn't look like it's worth much anyway," though he kind of grinned when he said it.

"That's just crazy," Lou snorted from behind his window. "I ain't gonna do that."

"What's crazy, Lou?" Mustard looked straight at the pawnbroker. I would have sworn I saw Lou shrivel slightly.

"Nothing," he muttered, opening his cash register and counting out the money, then writing out the pawn slip. He did it with ill grace, but he did it. "You owe me for this one, Mustard."

My savior smiled while he watched me stuff the cash into my handbag. "Come on, kid, I'll buy you a coffee," he said, when the transaction was complete. He walked toward the door and held it open for me. I must have hesitated. "Don't worry, I ain't gonna bite. I've got a proposition for you." Another hesitation. He laughed. "It's not that kind of proposition. You'll see. C'mon."

In truth, I felt inclined to trust the man, though I didn't have to work hard to imagine Mrs. Beeson's face as I preceded him out the door. He was definitely *not* our sort of people, was what she would have said. Though, in my new world, I was no longer sure who "our sort of people" were.

The coffee shop was clean, and the coffee good, if stronger than I was used to. It was just after noon and I hadn't had breakfast, so when my companion offered me a bowl of soup, perhaps I didn't hesitate as long as I should have. He didn't order anything to eat, but when mine came, I started right to work on the chicken-and-noodle concoction, the cook's special of the day.

Mustard sat back and smoked while he watched me eat, a grin all but hidden on his face. He didn't say much about my obvious hunger except, "For a skinny kid, you sure can pack it away. I like to see a broad eat."

I put the spoon down neatly on the plate under the bowl and looked fully into his gold-rimmed gray eyes. "I'm not a broad," I said, tightly but with, I hoped, some authority.

He raised his eyebrows and just looked at me for a full ten seconds that might have been a minute. Then he laughed, and I could tell he wasn't laughing at me. "You know, you're right, kid. I'm sorry. You're not a broad at all. What's your name?"

"Kate . . . Katherine. Katherine Pangborn."

He sat back in the booth and whistled, the cigarette he'd put down in the ashtray forgotten for the moment. "No kiddin'? Are you *that* Pangborn?"

I shrugged. Nodded. I probably was. "William Pangborn was my father."

He whistled again, then reapplied himself to his previously neglected cigarette. "Sheesh." For a moment he seemed lost in thought. "Sad times," he said, exhaling a column of smoke at the ceiling, then crushing his cigarette in the ashtray.

I nodded again, then went back to my soup. It was delicious, and I honestly didn't know when I'd see food this good again. Marjorie did the best with what she had for our meals, but she usually didn't have much. Things were that tight.

Mustard waited until every speck of the delicious soup was gone before he told me what was on his mind.

"Look, a buddy of mine—a shamus, see?—his business is doing real well, and he could use a secretary."

"Shamus?"

"P.I., you know. Peeper. Gumshoe," he explained.

I looked at him cautiously and waited.

"You think you could do that?"

"Do what?" I said, honestly perplexed.

"You know . . . secretarify."

I shrugged.

"Do you type?"

I shook my head.

"Take shorthand, maybe?"

Another shake. I wasn't even exactly sure what shorthand was, but I knew I couldn't take it, and if I could, I didn't know where I'd take it to.

He looked surprised. "Well, what *can* you do?"

I laughed. A gentle laugh but heartfelt. There was a lot I could do, really. In a flash I realized how useless all of it had become. "I can play the piano. I can make a soufflé. I can organize a dinner party for twenty-four and ensure there are no conflicts in the seating arrangements." I paused and contemplated my nails before I went on. "I can do needlepoint. I can crochet. I can ride a horse. And I can knit when called upon." I looked at my companion and smiled. "But knitting is certainly *not* my strong point. I know what clothes to wear for every situation . . ." Then I added, almost as an afterthought, "And I know what sort of clothes *you* should wear, as well."

He laughed and I hoped I didn't detect a note of pity in that laugh. Then he surprised me by touching my hand very gently and squeezing it so softly I might not have felt it at all. His hand was back to his side of the table and lighting yet another cigarette so quickly, I almost doubted my recollection.

"Listen, kid." He reached inside his breast pocket and pulled out a creamy business card, which he handed to me. "Bury your father," he said kindly. "Do what you need to do. But like I said, my friend needs a secretary. And I figure maybe you need a job. A smart girl like you—who knows how to do needle-point *and* make a soufflé—should have no trouble answering his phones and figuring out how to type. Call me next week if you're interested."

And then he was gone. I looked at the card. MUSTARD, it said in raised black letters. And underneath: CLinton 2519. I figured maybe I'd call.

CHAPTER FOUR

I'VE GOT A SPECIAL AFFECTION for Lafayette Square. By rights it should have been my neighborhood. George Crenshaw and my father had some business interests together at the time Crenshaw developed the Square. Right around then, Bunker Hill was starting to get a bit shabby, and the apartment buildings that have begun to take it over were starting to go up.

Crenshaw worked and worked on Father to be one of the first people to buy a lot at Lafayette and build a big house there. Father actually gave in and bought one on Victoria Park Drive, then hired the architect Paul Williams to design a house.

I remember driving out there with Father when I was a little girl, walking around on the lot with him and Mr. Williams while they waved plans around and talked about what would be where: the garden here, the summer kitchen there, and so on. Even a reflecting pool, which I was very excited about because I thought it meant we'd have frogs and lily pads. Maybe we would have too. I've thought about that on occasion.

When it came time to break ground though, my father found he didn't want to leave our home, increasingly shabby neighborhood or not. I suspected his reluctance had something to do with my mother. They had envisioned raising their family there, in the beautiful house my father built for her on Bunker Hill. My mother had died, but I suspect that some of the dreams they'd shared lingered on in the home they'd created. And so we stayed put.

All of that meant I knew where Lafayette Square was. And I knew my way around, at least a little bit.

I didn't have much trouble finding the address Rita Heppel-waite had given to Dex. He motioned for me to keep driving past the house—a low-slung pile with a lot of white plaster that looked more like a plantation house than a Los Angeles mansion. I looked at Dex questioningly, but did what he asked, strong-arming the big car slowly back around the Square. About a half block before we reached the house again, he indicated with a flick of one elegant index finger that I should pull over. I did.

"Now what?" I asked.

"Now nothin'," he said, cracking his shiny new bottle of Jack and taking a pull that he chased with a sigh. He offered the bottle across to me, out of politeness I guess, though I figure he'd maybe remember the look I gave him and think twice before he offered the booze again. I do *not* drink bourbon. I'm not opposed to it for any moral reasons, and like a lot of people, I think Prohibition is a bit silly and not long for this world. But to me bourbon tastes an awful lot like gasoline, which is another substance I don't drink. And if I *were* to drink bourbon—or gasoline, for that matter—it wouldn't be straight out of the bottle. A girl has to have limits, has to know where they are.

When I prodded him, Dex told me that the house we were sitting more or less in front of belonged to one Harrison Dempsey, the "boyfriend" the Heppelwaite broad had talked about. She'd told Dex that she suspected ol' Harry was stepping out. She wanted my boss to spend a few days tailing this Dempsey character, then report back to her. Where did he go? What did he do? And most importantly, who did he see? All pretty much one-two-three for a shamus. Tailing unfaithful lovers is the bread and butter of most private investigators' business.

From Rita, Dex had Harrison Dempsey's address, a description of his heap—a '29 Packard, of a green so dark it was the color of the head of a duck—and the address of his office in the Banks-Huntley Building downtown.

Dex said Dempsey was a real estate developer and general deal maker, which I knew could mean a lot of things. But whatever it was Dempsey did, I figured he was good at it because both his girlfriend and his house looked expensive.

We could see the green Packard parked sort of willy-nilly in front of the house, like the guy who drove it had been in a hurry. Or maybe like he just didn't care.

Dex told me we'd settle here until Dempsey got in motion. "Rita said he goes to the Zebra Room in the Town House Hotel on Wilshire every evening at eight without fail. So we know he'll leave a little ahead of that, maybe sooner."

"Why not go straight to the Zebra Room and wait for him there?"

"We could," Dex agreed, "but then that wouldn't be tailing him, would it? She wants me to find out what he does, who he sees. Best place to figure that out from is here."

"And it's five now. If we know he doesn't go to the Zebra Room until eight, why not just show up here at seven-thirty and follow him then?"

Dex looked at me in a way that let me know I was trying his patience, but when he spoke, his tone was unchanged. "My instructions weren't to follow him to the Zebra Room, Kitty. My instructions were just to follow him. Period. I don't know what he does before he goes to the Zebra Room, or that he goes straight there or what. I only knew he'd be here at this time . . . and then he'd be there. Everything else is a mystery, which is why she needed to hire me, get it?"

"So what do we do, Dex? Just sit here until then?"

Dex smiled. "Pretty much, kiddo. Hey, you're the one who wanted to come along. If you're bored with our little picnic, pack up your basket and go."

I didn't say anything, nor did I point out to Dex that it wasn't so much that I'd wanted to come along, but that I hadn't been sure he was in any condition to drive. And I knew he'd been kidding about the picnic, but now that he'd mentioned it—and it looked like we might be camping out here for some time—I figured a picnic would have been a pretty good idea. I made a mental note that next time I followed Dex on a stakeout, I should pack a lunch.

It was October, but it was warm enough that we didn't need the heater running to stay warm, even without a fur coat. We didn't have a lot to talk about one-on-one, Dex and me. Anyway, he had his new friend Jack to talk to, and they were getting better acquainted by the minute.

We sat there, silent for a while. I wasn't aware of any traffic noise floating over from Crenshaw Boulevard, and the neighborhood itself was silent, almost dead. The only sound for a while was the easy rhythm of Dex's breathing and his regular swigs from the bottle. When after maybe half an hour Dex spoke, his voice startled me.

"You remind me of her sometimes, you know. Have I told you that before?"

I looked across the car at him, taking in his red-rimmed eyes, the slight shake of the hand that held the bottle. I knew he was at least slightly drunk. But I also knew I had nothing to fear. Dex could occasionally be a maudlin drunk, but I'd never seen him dangerous.

I shook my head. "You've never said that. Who? Who do I remind you of?"

I might not have spoken. "She was as young as you are now when we met. Younger maybe. But it's not just that. Something in the tilt of your head. And now and then, the sound of your voice."

"Who?" I repeated. Softly this time.

"Zoë," he said, just as softly. He wasn't looking at me, but at some point above my head. I knew he was looking back. "Zoë," he said again. "My wife."

I blinked at him without saying anything. Once, twice, three times perhaps. I must have done, because I didn't have words. It was the first time I'd heard even a whisper about a wife.

"Your wife?" I said, still softly, not wanting to shatter his talkative mood.

Another swig from the bottle. Another hand over the growing bristle on his chin. "I met her when I was in France. During the war." He was quiet so long I thought he might not say anything else. Just as I was about to give him a gentle prod, he spoke again. "I was injured pretty much as soon as I got off the boat." He gave a small laugh, but I could hear something more. "I was at the Battle of Neuve Chapelle, the first one, in nineteen fifteen. Have you heard about it?"

I shook my head.

"It was the first battle of the war for the Canadians. The Americans weren't there yet. They wouldn't be, either, for another couple of years. It was . . ." Here his voice drifted away, as though he were struggling for words or managing his thoughts; I couldn't tell which.

"I was injured," he said finally, indicating his thigh. "Took a bayonet right there. Went clean through my leg." I could feel myself grimace, but I didn't say anything. "I was lucky too," he went on. "Like I said, it was early. We didn't understand the scale of the thing then. We didn't know what it would be. So many men died that day. Good men. Bad men. They all died the same."

Dex told me that Zoë's family had a farm near the little town of Neuve Chapelle. It was here that the Allied forces brought their injured, and Zoë's family had pitched in to help. What else, she asked in her labored English, could you do when war broke out almost in your backyard?

Comparatively speaking, Dex's injury had been slight. Within a few days he was hobbling around behind Zoë, helping her help.

I had some trouble with this image at first. Dex as the doting helper, that is. But then I mentally shaved fifteen years off him, trimming away the jaded air along with the lines. I imagined him fresh off the boat and probably scared as hell. The tall, gawky, smooth-faced young man, not much more than a kid, trailing behind an earnest and beautiful young woman like a pup.

"Every leave I had, I'd come back to her. To Zoë. I was just a kid—just nineteen. But we fell in love." He spread his hands as though this had been an inevitable thing. Inescapable. "We were married at a church near her home early in nineteen sixteen. Didn't have much of a honeymoon. All of Artois was pretty torn up by then. It was a crazy thing to do, marriage in that dangerous time. But I loved her, Kitty. I would have done anything for her. I would have laid down my life for her."

The sound of my name startled me. I hadn't even been sure Dex was aware I was still there. His voice was hypnotic, or hypnotizing; I'm not sure which. But it was as though the world outside the big black car had ceased to exist, and the torn-up French countryside was more real to me—perhaps to both of us—than the upholstered seat we shared.

"There was a small house on her family's farm . . ." Here his voice broke slightly. I looked at him quickly, but I could see no sign of it on his face; only the slight unevenness in his tone betrayed emotion. "After Zoë and I were married, her father gave me a good price on renting the land from him . . . Do you want to hear this?" he said suddenly, breaking the spell. "I can stop now if you like. I don't even know why I'm telling you."

I hadn't spoken for so long that I needed to clear my throat before I could answer. Or maybe emotion held me back. "No, please," I said, when I found my voice, "go on."

He looked at me a long moment before he continued. Another swig. Another hand through unruly hair. He seemed to debate with himself before he continued, but continue he did. By now I knew it was more for his own sake than for mine.

He took a long pull from the bottle and turned to face out the window. I had the feeling he didn't want me to see whatever might be in his eyes.

"My son was born in the summer of nineteen sixteen." Now there was joy splashed in with the pain. "I wasn't there. It was around the time of the Battle of the Somme. We called our child Raymond, because it was a name we thought would work in both languages—English and French—and I knew someday I'd want him to see my home. It would be part of him. Raymond."

A son, I thought. Born in 1916. He would be around fifteen now. An adolescent. Surely the age when a son needed his father most. I waited for the rest of the story. I waited for a long while. There had been long pauses already in Dex's tale. I gave him the space he needed to think about it all, to pull out the last painful bit. I had no doubt that it *would* be painful, that Dex's story didn't have a happy ending. It would explain a lot. The hurt I'd heard in his voice as he told the story. And all those tortured days slumped in his chair in the office. Everything was a little clearer, or so it seemed at the time. So I waited quietly, feeling as though an answer was at hand.

After a while though, I realized that the end of the story wasn't going to come. At least not today. Dex's head slumped forward slightly, and his breathing evened out. There were no more painful pulls on the bottle. I wanted the end of the story— so badly, I wanted it, you can't imagine—but a part of me was glad. For the moment, for Dex, there was no more pain.

I didn't have the feeling of falling asleep. I was aware of Dex's even breathing and the heavy smell of bourbon in the closed car. I thought about the things Dex had told me, and while I did, it felt as though I turned some mental corner and was transported.

CHAPTER FIVE

I WAS RUNNING THROUGH a vineyard in France. It was beautiful. I was aware of colors—the vivid greens of the vines, the intense brown hues of the earth, the bright blue canopy of the sky—and I even felt the sun on the back of my neck, on my hair.

I turned a corner and I saw a boy—a beautiful boy—ahead of me on the path. He looked over his shoulder at me, and the light danced in his eyes. He laughed and he ran faster. I laughed then too. That was the sound that woke me: my own real laughter piercing my dream, calling me back.

When I opened my eyes it was dark. Dex was still on the passenger seat next to me, one hand on his precious bottle—half empty or half full, depending on your perspective. His head was lolling back at an angle I knew would give him hell when he woke up. Or sobered up. I wasn't ready yet to find out which it would be.

As I tried to shake some life into my legs, I saw a car leave Harrison Dempsey's driveway. Fast. I thought maybe the car had awakened me as much as the laugh. The sound of the motor or the lights coming on, or both. It wasn't the green Packard though. That was still parked willy-nilly, just as it had been before. The car that left was all black, which didn't exactly make it a rarity. And I couldn't see the driver and I didn't think to get the plate.

I lifted Dex's arm to get a glimpse of his watch. Half past ten. I tried not to think about how long we'd been sitting there. Hours. Hours and hours. The big house was in darkness. It didn't look like anyone was around. According to Dex, it was well beyond the time Dempsey would normally have been at the Zebra Room.

"Dex." I said his name, softly at first. Then repeated it a little more loudly. "Dex!" I shook him gently. All I heard from him was a muffled "Mrrph." It didn't feel like he was going to wake up anytime soon.

I sat back deeply in the driver's seat, contemplating our options. Or really *my* options, because I knew I wasn't going to get any big ideas from Dex.

We were supposed to be tailing this Dempsey guy. But in all likelihood, we'd blown our chance on making good on the job by falling asleep—quite literally—at the wheel. I figured Dempsey had probably hooked a ride with some pal, and through all the shut-eye, we'd missed seeing him leave in the car that had just left his place. I figured that the sensible thing to do was go check out the house, make sure it was as empty as it looked, then maybe drive over to Wilshire. By then Dex would be sober enough to put one foot in front of the other into the Zebra Room and make like the big shamus he was supposed to be.

Like I said, that's what I figured. And it all seemed like a good idea at the time. But once out of the car, I felt desperately alone. Traffic was light here, but I could hear more of it echoing over from Crenshaw. Los Angeles sometimes snoozes, but it never really sleeps.

In the car with Dex I'd felt safe, even slightly cozy. The sound of Dex's light snores and the angel's share of the bourbon drifting through the interior of the car. And here's the thing: my boss was currently inebriated. Some would argue that he was flat-out drunk. But he was carrying a gun, and he knew how to use it. In a pinch I figured his instincts would kick right in.

Outside the car though, I felt exposed, like some small rodent or maybe a bug. I don't know what I was afraid of exactly.

But some secret part of me knew there was something of which to be afraid. Call it a feeling in my bones.

My bones. As I got closer to the house, I thought I could hear them creak. I don't know why silence seemed important to me then, but it did. As though I should be creeping up on the house. As though it might see me or feel me and somehow fend me off. Ridiculous imaginings, I know. But it was late, it was dark, and I felt completely alone.

I trotted up the front walkway cautiously, careful not to step on any crack. A goofy precaution, but you can't be too careful in situations involving the unknown.

There was no porch light on, so I couldn't see a doorbell or even determine if there was one. I reached out, intending to deliver a firm knock, but the door swung open to my touch.

I stood there for a couple of minutes. At least it felt that long to me. I stood on the front step with the door open, listening to the cicadas call and catching the ripe, sweet scent of honeysuckle and a whiff of the distant sea.

Right inside the door was a big marble-floored foyer framed by a couple of elegant winding staircases. A half dozen hallways led from the foyer to adjacent rooms. I could see all of this just by the illumination of the streetlights, because there didn't seem to be a light on in the whole place.

"Hullo?" I called out. I didn't think anyone was there, but it seemed like the thing to do. "Hullo?"

There was no answer, but for the tiniest echo of my own voice off the marble. And then it came to me, maybe it was even the reason I'd engineered this trip from the car to the house: after drinking coffee all day at the office, followed by all those hours of sitting in a car, I really, really needed to find a powder room.

One more try: "Hullo?" And when there was still no reply, I put a tentative foot onto the marble. And then another. The place was so quiet, I could hear my steps echoing around me. It was as though I was in a museum.

"Hullo?" My voice was a little weaker now. A little less confident. Standing in the middle of the foyer, I felt more exposed than I had in the open doorway, when everything inside the house was mere possibility.

Faced with half a dozen openings veering off in different directions, I had a choice to make. I knew I didn't want to spend all night touring the house while I looked for the powder room. On the other hand, finding it felt like an increasingly good idea.

I became aware of the scent of a woman's perfume, lingering but still present. I couldn't place it, but it struck me as deep and rich and faintly cloying. I ignored it and moved on.

"Hullo?"

All six of the hallways leading off the foyer were dark. I could have turned on a light. But somehow scuttling around looking for a place to relieve myself seemed like violation enough without adding the glare of electricity. Also, in the semidark I felt slightly invisible, like a little kid playing hide-and-go-seek who closes her eyes and thinks she can't be seen.

I don't know how it happened that I picked one dark hallway over another, because from where I was standing those hallways all looked pretty much alike. Still, I reasoned, they were all bound to lead to a bathroom eventually. And lacking a sign with an arrow that said, "Ladies Room, 26 Steps to the Right," I'd just have to take my chances on a shot in the dark.

I wasn't quite sure when I became aware of the smell. And unlike the lingering perfume in the foyer, it wasn't an odor I could put my finger on, not right away. Not on any conscious level. On some other level—from some deep, instinctive place— I knew what it was from the first second.

It smelled metallic. It smelled dark. And as I put one foot carefully in front of the other on the highly polished wood floor of my chosen hallway, I tried to both identify the smell and block it out. It would have been a neat trick if it had worked. But it didn't.

When I found the bathroom, I was too frightened to use the facilities in the continued dark. I snapped the light on pretty much as I headed for the commode, illuminating a large, beautifully appointed bathroom done in delicate shades of rose and champagne.

The light brought a sliver of comfort, but only a sliver. It was an odd feeling: relief and fear seemed to become one emotion, the first spurring the second and back again.

I washed my hands in the echo of the flush, then went to dry them on a towel that was hanging on a bar. I looked at my hands in confusion as I tried to dry them. Confusion because what I saw there made no sense. Where my hands had been wet with water, they were now the sticky red of drying blood.

I screamed then. I screamed as I turned and looked for the first time toward the bathtub at the other side of the room. No longer blinded by the needs of my body, I saw what I hadn't noticed before. The heavy opaque shower curtain was pulled shut. Not odd in itself, but there was an oddness to the way the curtain lay against the inside edge of the tub. As though it were leaning against something. I couldn't guess what that something might be, but I was pretty sure it was not the edge of the tub.

Every instinct instructed me to get out of that big, echoey, empty house. In fact, my feet started doing just that, all on their own heading toward the door. I grabbed the edge of the sink to stop myself, turning on the tap and letting warm water shoot over my hands. If I'd had any doubt before, I didn't now. The pale pink that swooshed from my hands and down the drain was blood, sure as anything. A woman knows.

Unwilling to go back to the blood-spattered towel I'd dropped on the floor, I dried my hands on the edge of my skirt, not even bothering to check if any residual blood might stain the pale fabric. Not even caring in that moment, truth be told. I was intent on the shower curtain. On the bulge in the shower curtain. It still hadn't moved.

Before I pulled it back, I stood with my hand high up on the curtain, steeling myself. Yet when I pulled it back I was not surprised. Shocked perhaps. Certainly weak in the stomach and in the knees, but at some level I'd known what I would find. It seemed so cliché, I could have laughed. But I did not.

There was a man in the bathtub. Not old, perhaps in his middle thirties. He was wearing a dark suit of some shiny fabric, a tie with a dull maroon pattern, and a white shirt, though the front of the shirt was streaked with blood. I could see that he'd been shot in the chest. A good shot, I guess, because he was as dead as could be. I didn't check his pulse; didn't have to. His mouth was open, as were his eyes. The emptiness there was immense. And he was pale. So pale. I hope never again to see a human so completely lacking in color. I didn't need a doctor to tell me: this guy had checked out.

I managed to see all of this, to note all the details, because my feet were, quite simply, rooted to the spot. It was as though I were attached to the cool tiles of the bathroom floor. A part of my brain instructed, "C'mon, get the lead out. The dead guy in the tub means danger isn't far off." But my body responded not at all.

I heard a noise nearby, and at the same time, the invisible roots released their hold. I would have run, but between the bathroom door on one side of me and the grisly inhabitant of the tub on the other, there was no place to go.

While I considered my options, my heart fluttered in my chest like a frightened bird. As I stood there trying to calm myself, I heard footsteps. And they were getting closer.

And then I heard a sound I'd never thought would almost make me cry out in relief.

"Kitty?" And then more insistently and blessedly even closer: "Kitty!"

"I'm here." My voice had ceased working and I stopped to clear my throat. "I'm here, Dex, right here."

Dexter J. Theroux was miraculously restored when he entered the bathroom. I couldn't see the day's hard drinking on him, but for some extra creases around his eyes and a puffiness in his jowls. His step was steady and the hand on his gun looked firm. When he saw me, the relief in his eyes was obvious. I could tell he'd feared the worst.

"I thought I heard you scream," he said simply.

"You did," I replied, then motioned to the body in the tub.

Dex let out a clear low whistle. It came out of him as though pulled from deep inside. "What have we here?" he asked, while he holstered his gun.

"He's . . . he's dead, Dex."

"Yes, Kitty. I do believe you're right. It doesn't look like he stopped off for a bubble bath."

He leaned over the body and pulled out a billfold, drawing out the man's driver's license and checking his name.

"Looks like you were right, kiddo," Dex said. He settled back on his haunches while he struck a match on the grout between tiles and lit up a cigarette. He looked at the corpse in the tub thoughtfully while he exhaled a tight plume of smoke.

"I was right? How's that?" I asked.

"We won't need to be tailing Harrison Dempsey," he said, holstering his gun. "I could have done this job in a Red Car after all."

CHAPTER SIX

DEX FINISHED HIS SMOKE in what looked like a leisurely fashion, but I could see the wheels turning while he puffed. After he was done, he tossed the spent cigarette into the toilet, took out his handkerchief, and started wiping down every surface either of us might feasibly have touched.

"What are you doing?" Even while I asked, I knew it was a silly question. It was fairly obvious Dex was erasing all signs of our visit.

Dex just looked at me, cocked one eyebrow, then went back to his wiping. It didn't take long.

I stood in a corner of the bathroom—the corner farthest from the place where Dex worked—trying to take in everything that had happened.

"We didn't do it," I pointed out. "Aren't you afraid that you're erasing evidence that might help the police find the killer?"

He looked at me as though I were a child, and not a particularly bright one at that.

"Listen, Kitty," he said, as he finished up. "Whoever did this doesn't care about evidence, even if they left any. Which they probably didn't. Look at him," he said, forcing my attention back to the corpse. "He didn't slip in the shower, kiddo. He was chilled, neat and sweet. And it doesn't look like it was amateur night, any way you slice it." He popped his hanky back into his pocket and pushed me out the door ahead of him. I noticed that as we left the bathroom he didn't bother stopping to turn off the lights.

"You touch anything else?" he asked. I shook my head. "What about the front door?"

"I touched the door and it opened," I replied.

The hanky was out and the door wiped down so quickly, you would have thought Dex did cleanup for a living. Then he ushered me back to the car, popping me, unprotesting, into the passenger seat and taking the wheel himself.

I didn't ask where we were going. Frankly, at that moment I didn't care. "I still don't think cleaning everything up was the right thing to do," I insisted as we drove, not liking the petulant note in my voice but beyond caring. "The police would believe us, I think. We didn't have any reason to kill him."

"It's not so much the cops I'm worried about, Kitty. Like I told you back there: whoever croaked him wasn't an amateur. This guy's got friends you don't want to play with. This just smells like something we shouldn't get mixed up in."

Though my conscience wanted to argue, I could see the sense in his words, and I lapsed into thoughtful silence.

As we moved deeper into the city, the distant scent of the ocean was replaced with the ever-present odor of Los Angeles: the smell of the oil that the derricks all over the region pumped out of the ground twenty-four hours of every day. It was a hard smell to define. Dark and ancient. The smell of a prehistoric era. And modern wealth, but not a clean wealth somehow. You got used to it after a while.

"One thing bothers me about all this, Dex," I said, when we'd traveled a few miles.

"*One* thing."

"Seriously. What was he doing in the bathtub?"

"He wasn't soaking his bunions," Dex pointed out.

"Exactly," I agreed. "But did he die there? Did someone get him to step into the tub at gunpoint and then execute him? If so, why?"

"I see where you're going," Dex said. "Because if they *didn't* kill him in the tub, why put him there?"

I nodded. "It's tidy," I said thoughtfully.

"Hmm?"

"Well, easy to clean up, right? It's a bathroom. Water and everything."

"What are you saying?"

"Well, if you were going to execute someone but you didn't want to leave a mess, the bathroom would be a good place to do it because it'd be easy to clean up afterward."

"That's true," Dex agreed. "But they didn't clean up, did they? Not really. They left the body in the bathtub. That's pretty much a mess."

"But the towel, Dex. The one I used. It was folded up, all tidy like. Someone used it—I guess to clean up some blood—then put it back carefully. If I hadn't had to dry my hands, I wouldn't have seen the blood at all."

We passed ideas around for the balance of the ride downtown. Dex felt it likely someone had gone to the house with the idea of killing Dempsey and had executed him in his own tub. I suggested there might have been a fracas that ended up with Dempsey killed and the killer stuffing the body into the tub in order to get it out of the way. But that scenario asked more questions than it answered. Why would a hired gun care if the corpse was in a bathtub or sprawled on a divan or . . . why would some gunsel care where the body ended up?

We hadn't reached any conclusions by the time Dex dropped me off on Bunker Hill. We realized it was possible we'd never have answers to the questions we were asking. But when all was said and done, it didn't matter anymore, not to us. With the subject Dex had been hired to tail now dead, there was no reason to pursue the matter. And Dex groused a bit when I suggested he give back at least part of the retainer, but we both knew he'd do the right thing in the end.

CHAPTER SEVEN

I DIDN'T SLEEP WELL. No big surprise. For one thing, I didn't need much sleep, having had an extended nap in the car. More than that though, despite what Dex had said, I felt an acute sense of guilt for having played a part—however small—in tampering with the scene of a crime.

I tossed and turned for a while after I went to bed. Then I got up and straightened the bedclothes, plumped up my pillows, and hopped back in to toss and turn some more.

Sleep finally claimed me, but it was not the peaceful sleep of the innocent, or so I told myself in the morning. Things chased me in and out of sleep. And none of those things were beautiful boys in French vineyards.

Dark shapes chased me and I . . . I chased them. A long-legged woman stood nearby, laughing. She had glorious flame-colored hair, and her full body was sheathed in a silk so fine it might have been made of spun clouds.

I woke in full dark, a fine sweat covering my body though the night was cool. I lay there panting for a moment, catching my breath and making a conscious effort to keep the night shapes from following me out of my dream.

Though the dream had been filled with abstracts, I didn't have to work very hard to decipher what my subconscious was trying to tell me. Despite the inglorious end my father came to, I was raised with a certain moral code. There is right, my father taught me from the time I could understand such concepts. And there is wrong. What's in between doesn't stand thinking about. If there was one single theme in my upbringing, it's that you must live with a clear heart and a clean conscience, and if

you tell the truth, everything will come out right in the end.
They were words my father had lived if not died by, and they
had colored my view of the world.

At the breakfast table in the morning, Marjorie took one
look at my face and asked what was wrong. I compounded
things by not telling her. How could I? And even if I could, what
could I have said? The truth seemed too awful to say out loud.

Marjorie suspected I was coming down with something and
tried to push an extra piece of toast on me. I declined. I knew
we could ill afford to squander bread that one of the boarders
might eat. In any case, I could hardly stomach the piece I'd
taken, let alone the soft-boiled egg she placed alongside it. We
couldn't waste perfectly good food though, so I dipped the corners of my single piece of toast into my egg and managed them
both with my morning tea. And felt better for it, but only
slightly.

My head was still so filled with grisly thoughts that it de-
tracted from my usual pleasure at the clean swoop Angels
Flight cut between Bunker Hill and downtown. On most days I
loved everything about the ride on the little tramcar that was
part of "the shortest paying railway in the world." I loved the
luxury of sitting when I would have been walking—and always
for free on the way down. I liked the rumbling feeling beneath
me as the car got going. It gave me a sense of anticipation, like
I was going on a big trip, not just downtown. And I loved the
split second when the little car seemed almost to hover on
the crest of the hill, before it began the descent in earnest and
you got a sense of the city spreading almost beneath your feet.

On most days I loved all of that. But on this day I barely
saw it. I gave the ride on Angels Flight no more attention than
I would have had it been a Red Car; then I trudged the few
blocks to the office barely noticing my surroundings, stopping
only to get Dex's ice.

The door to the office was still locked when I got there.

I wasn't surprised to find myself in ahead of Dex. As sober as he'd looked when he dropped me off, he'd done a fair piece of drinking during the day. I thought he'd probably have something to sleep off, and there was no reason for him to rush into the office just now: his single case had disappeared like the smoke from one of Mustard's cigarettes.

I unlocked the door and closed it behind me, popping my hat and light coat on the rack and my purse on my desk as I came in. In my haste to follow Dex out the day before, I'd not closed the office for the night with my usual precision, and the place smelled like a tavern.

In Dex's office, the jade green ashtray was overflowing. His whiskey glass was empty, of course, but unwashed. When I went to the window and threw it open, I stood there for a moment watching the traffic on Spring Street. Traffic was light a few hours before noon. Even so, cars and trucks moved down the street, and pedestrians hurried about their business.

I could see one couple moving more slowly than the others. They walked arm in arm, her hatted head turned up to his much taller one. She seemed to be listening carefully to what he was saying. I couldn't quite make out the details of their faces, but I imagined that she was beautiful and he was exotically handsome and that both of them were looking forward to a stolen hour—brunch perhaps—in the Palm Court of the Alexandria Hotel just a block away.

When they were out of sight, I pulled myself back inside, instantly missing the warm touch of the sun on my skin. I didn't have any work to do and the phone wasn't ringing, but I had plenty to think about, and think I did. After I tidied the office, I sat at my desk primly for maybe half an hour, one eye on the phone and the other on the door, waiting for any sign of Dex.

The phone didn't ring, but I couldn't stop thinking about it. There was a call I could make. A single call. And I knew that if I made it, some of the horror I felt would start to dissipate. I would feel better, I told myself, because I would have done the right thing.

I waited another half hour, but when at ten o'clock there was still no sign of Dex, I figured I'd better make that call or else forget about it altogether. Once Dex finally got to the office—and I knew he would eventually—it would no longer be an option.

And I was right: I felt better afterward. A surprisingly simple operation, considering the grief I put myself through about it. I gave the police the name of the dead man and the address where he could be found. And when the officer I spoke with asked for my name and asked how I knew, I replaced the receiver calmly in the cradle. Then I sat there with my hand still on the phone while my pulse raced like a frightened rabbit and I contemplated what I'd done.

I told myself that there was no way the call could be traced to me or to Dex. And nothing at the house on Lafayette Square would tell the police we'd been there; Dex had seen to that. It was possible that the unknown hatchetman had seen us when he'd left in a big hurry, but I didn't think so. And if he had, it didn't seem likely he'd be telling the police.

As soon as I was off the phone, the face of the dead man in the bathtub became more indistinct in my mind, and the grimness of the night before started to recede. Before long, I was prepared to put the whole business behind me for well and good, and I felt more lighthearted than I had since I'd placed a single foot into that house on Lafayette Square.

I hadn't come to this conclusion long before Dex came in, aiming his usual morning smile at me. "What's cooking?" he asked cheerfully, no trace of the previous night's adventure on his recently shaved face.

"Absolutely nothing," I said, matching his tone.

He had the morning paper tucked under one arm and a familiar-looking brown bag under the other.

"Well, then, I've got some business to take care of. Got my ice? Good, good. You know where I am if you need me," he said, closing the door to his office behind him and settling in for his day.

Unlike Dex, who seemed to have his itinerary all laid out, I had no plans for the day, which was the only part of the job I didn't like.

When Dex was on a case—and especially at those rare times when he was working two or even three at the same time—there could be a fair amount for me to do. The phones would be ringing, and there'd be calls for me to place or people he had asked me to track down, and time would speed by.

The last few months though, things had slowed down. I figured it was a sign of the times. No matter what the newspapers said, things were tough and looked to be getting tougher. For a lot of people, choosing between paying the rent and hiring a shamus wasn't much of a decision.

Even so, I knew there were P.I.'s in town who were still making a decent living, but in a business like ours, a lot of work comes by referral. Dex could be the most charming guy alive when he cared to. Most of the time though, he just didn't care. Maybe he'd told one too many customers off—or just told off the wrong ones—or maybe he'd not delivered on a job once too often. Or maybe I was just whistling "Dixie," but I knew one thing was true: the phone didn't ring as much as it used to.

This was a problem for me. Not only did it make me worry about getting paid; it also made it tough to fill up my time at the office. On days when we didn't have much going on and the hours dragged slowly, I'd twiddle my thumbs or practice my typing. Both of those activities provided a limited amount of entertainment.

Seeing my plight—and perhaps suspecting how flush I wasn't—Mustard had taken to bringing me books every now and then. I could see they'd been read before I got them, but I never asked if Mustard was the one doing the reading. He didn't volunteer the information, but it really didn't matter. I took his offerings greedily. Reading offered escape as well as a pleasing way to get through the slow-moving office days that didn't have a lot of work in them.

The book Mustard had dropped off most recently, *Revolt in the Desert*, was an exciting account of T. E. Lawrence's adventures in Arabia. It was proving to be a magical transportation from my life in the city, concerned as I was with things that to me seemed everyday. "The march became rather splendid and barbaric," I read. I could almost smell sun on sand, feel the particles of dust in my hair. "First rode Feisal in white, then Sharraf at his right in red head-cloth and henna-dyed tunic and cloak, myself on his left in white and scarlet, behind us three banners of faded crimson silk with gilt spikes, behind them the drummers playing a march, and behind them again the wild mass of twelve hundred bouncing camels of the bodyguard, packed as closely as they could move, the men in every variety of coloured clothes and the camels nearly as brilliant in their trappings. We filled the valley to its banks with our flashing stream."

I read away the balance of the morning, lost in rivers of camels and streams of brightly colored silk, then put the book aside at noon and went out into the sunshine to find a bench on which to eat the sandwich Marjorie had prepared for me—sardines today, I noticed with distaste while I ate—and stretch my legs.

Los Angeles at street level is a series of contradictions. Just within sight of the bench I'd chosen near the corner of Spring and Fourth, I could see girders on three different buildings. A casual glance would show that the growth of Los Angeles continued apace. Yet the careful eye could see the difference. The crews on the buildings were smaller than they'd been even a few years ago, and the crowd of men who came to line up in the morning—the men wanting work—seemed to swell every day, as did the number who were unsuccessful and trudged unhappily away when a handful of their rank were chosen. "You, you, and you. Not you."

I'd seen the selection process when I'd come to the office early one morning. Perhaps twenty or thirty of the assembled men were chosen to do rough labor. Four or even five times that many were turned away. You could feel the desperation pouring off them in waves. I imagined that many of the men would have families somewhere nearby, hoping that this threadbare head of house would manage to come up with enough from his day's labor for a bit of bread and perhaps some milk. More would be disappointed than not.

Yet the party line was clear: we were above the Depression in Los Angeles. Other less golden regions might have to deal with it, but not us. Not here. And the *Los Angeles Times* trumpeted freely that the Depression that had so affected other parts of the country had not touched us and was not expected. Our eyes told a different story.

At street level you could feel the difference. From above and from a distance you couldn't see the details, and everything looked just as it always had.

You could, as I had this morning, see what looked to be a beautiful, happy couple and imagine they were heading for some romantic hour. Now, on my bench, I saw that couple again. They walked right past me, in the direction opposite the one I'd seen them travel a few hours earlier.

Up close, everything about them told a different story. I could see his shoes were down at the heels, and her dress had been washed so often, the colors were no longer bright. And the movements I'd seen pass between them—his sheltering presence, the laughter sent up to him—were quite different up close as well.

I don't know where they'd been—I'll never know where

they'd been—but at close range I could see it had not been the Palm Court at the Alex, as I'd hoped and supposed at first glance. The Los Angeles Trust and Savings Bank was just up the street from the hotel. From the looks of this pair, that's where they'd been. And things had not gone well.

Just as I'd seen this morning, he leaned over her, as though protecting her, as they walked. She looked up to him, but not in laughter. What I saw in her face was a desperation so raw, I had to turn away.

As I watched, he leaned down to her, said something softly in her ear. He might have been offering her something reassuring, but whatever it was, I figured it was probably a lie. Nothing would ever be the same again.

CHAPTER EIGHT

BY ONE O'CLOCK I was back at my desk with my nose pushed firmly into my book. I heard the elevator arrive at our floor a little after one, but figured its occupant must be visiting the accountancy firm down the hall. I was wrong.

Dex doesn't care if I read at my desk when there's nothing much doing, but he doesn't like it when clients see me doing it. I just managed to get the book into my desk drawer when Rita Heppelwaite sailed into the office unannounced.

Her arrival was a repeat of the performance from the day before, but today's dress was lilac, with about a million tiny buttons down the front and a froth of lace at the neck and the sleeves. I figured it would have taken me about a year to get into that dress or out of it, a hardship she seemed to have skirted by leaving more of the buttons undone—top and bottom—than I would have thought appropriate. She was the image of a woman intent on toppling the men on the high iron from their girders.

Today the fur coat was nowhere to be seen, but I figured that was because it was a few degrees warmer. Too warm for a fur coat, even if you were set to show it off.

Aside from her outfit, Rita Heppelwaite herself seemed different today. I couldn't quite put my finger on the why, but I knew it was more than the coat. When she asked for Dex, there seemed to me to be something false and foreign about her, though she smiled and seemed affable enough. Maybe that was part of it: "affable" wouldn't have been a word I would have used to describe her the day before.

I got a little more suspicious when I asked her to take a seat in the waiting room and she not only complied, but stayed put.

I went into Dex's office, careful to close the door behind me. I hadn't checked on him since before lunch, so I was thankful to see him not only sitting upright, but looking reasonably tidy and acceptably clear. He'd probably had only a couple of drinks so far.

"Rita Heppelwaite is here to see you," I said softly, more aware than anyone that voices from Dex's office could carry if pitched just so.

"How does she look?" Dex asked.

I considered briefly. "Trampy. And she's dressed in lilac today. No sign of the coat."

Dex shook his head. "I don't need a fashion report, bright eyes. I don't care what she's wearing. I was just wondering—you know—does she seem upset?"

I considered the question, surprised I hadn't thought of it myself. "You know, Dex, she doesn't. Not so's I can tell, anyway. She just seems a little . . ." I thought about it again. "She seems a little bright. A little . . . brittle. Why?"

"I'm just wondering if she knows about Dempsey. I'm figuring it's possible she doesn't. That she's just here for a report."

"I don't know, boss. You're the detective. And you're probably right. Should I send her in?"

He considered briefly. "Naw," he said, "I'll come out. If she's gonna make a scene, I'd rather she do it out there."

"Thanks," I said dryly. "A floor show is just what I need. You gonna tell her?" Because thus far Dex had seemed disinclined to tell anyone anything.

"Sure," he said, getting up and running a hand through his hair. "She's the client. She's got a right to know."

"You want me to type while you're telling her?" I knew he didn't want me to make myself scarce. If he'd wanted to talk to Rita Heppelwaite in private, he would have had me send her into his office.

"Naw, too noisy. Maybe file," he suggested helpfully.

I told him I'd see what I could do.

"Miss Heppelwaite," he said, when he saw her. "It's good to see you again so soon." I busied myself with the files, moving N's to M and vice versa, trying to look occupied while not making too much of a mess. Trying to look busy, as Dex had suggested, while keeping the pair of them in plain view.

"Mr. Theroux, it's good of you to see me again on such short notice," she said as she rose. I looked at her closely when she said this, but if there was irony in her voice when she uttered the words, I didn't hear it. I entertained the possibility that we'd been doing such a good job covering it up that no one knew how busy Dex wasn't. The thought gave me an odd glimmer of pride.

"Not at all, Miss Heppelwaite." He indicated she should take a chair there in the waiting room, and he pulled the other chair out slightly, so he was facing her. If she wondered why he didn't invite her into his office, she gave no sign. "I guess you're here for a report?"

She nodded. The light reflected off her lavender dress, adding a cool glow to her skin.

"Then I'm afraid I have some disturbing news for you. And there's just no way easy way to tell it." I could see that Dex regretted this. He would have softened it if he could. "I'm sorry to have to inform you that Mr. Dempsey is dead."

I saw her eyes go all wide, as though it would help her hear better, help her comprehend. At the same time, she let out a little gasp, something that came out sounding a little like "Oh," and her hand flew to her mouth, as though to stop the word from escaping.

"Dead," she repeated. Her hand left her mouth and fluttered to her throat. She touched the small bones there, at the base of her neck. An unconscious gesture. She touched them carefully, one by one, as though for luck or perhaps for strength; I wouldn't have bet money either way. "Please, Mr. Theroux," she said at length. "Go on."

"Not much to tell really," Dex said, not without sympathy. "I staked out the place on Lafayette Square, just as you asked. I intended to follow Dempsey, but he never came out. Near eleven o'clock last night, I thought it best to go and investigate. I found his—sorry, Miss Heppelwaite—I found his body in the bathtub. It looked to me like it might have been a professional job."

I liked this version of things. First of all, I liked how neatly I'd been left out of it. My reasons for liking it were probably different than Dex's reasons for leaving me out, but I liked it just the same.

Also, I appreciated how he actually managed to tell the truth, while at the same time avoiding any mention of the fact that he'd been asleep at a time when he should have been awake. The story didn't suffer from the absence of these facts: the Heppelwaite broad got the information she needed, while Dex got to leave out the little detail of his complete incompetence.

Rita herself looked gunshot when the news sunk in, as though someone had pulled a rug out from under her feet, as though the world had shifted. I watched her closely from behind my filing, and if she was acting, she should have won an award.

When she started to cry, it took both Dex and me by surprise. Maybe we'd figured that her arrangement with Dempsey had a business core and that her heart wasn't engaged or terribly involved. Her apparent grief put a lie to this. Dexter fished a white linen handkerchief from his jacket pocket and handed it to her. I hoped it was a clean one, and not the hanky he'd used to wipe our fingerprints up the night before.

"Did you . . . did you see anything?" she asked after a while.

"Ma'am?" Dex said.

She blew her nose then. Delicately. It sounded like a kitten sneezing. "Well, you were watching the house last night, weren't you? I thought you might have seen something."

Dex shook his head. "It was over by the time I got there," he told her. I noticed him run a hand over his smooth jaw. Probably no one but me would have spotted this as one of his tells: no one but me would have known he wasn't quite telling the truth.

He offered to return part of the retainer she'd given him the day before, but she waved the money away. I saw Dex's eyes slide over to mine, and he sent me a self-satisfied wink. "See," he seemed to be saying, "I *tried* to do the right thing. But it looks like you'll get a paycheck after all."

I shrugged back at him imperceptibly, relieved but a little disturbed. If I was reading things right, Rita Heppelwaite's meal ticket had just disappeared. Either she wasn't thinking clearly or she really didn't need the money, which struck me as odd in a way I found hard to put my finger on.

"Thank you for your help, Mr. Theroux," she sniffled, dabbing once again at her eyes. Then her shoulders heaved, and she was crying in earnest. Dex looked helpless, as men often do when faced with a woman's tears. He looked as though he wished he could be anywhere else.

"There, there, Miss Heppelwaite," he said, kind of patting her shoulder as though hoping this might be comforting. It was odd seeing Dexter, usually so confident in any situation, not knowing quite what to do with himself. "Please let me know if there's anything I can do. . . ."

"But you've been so helpful already," she said, lifting tear-filled eyes up to his and batting them furiously. "I can't imagine what I would have done without you." He patted her reassuringly some more, but I wondered what—aside from patting her shoulders—she really thought he'd done.

Before long she pulled herself together enough to take her leave.

"Please, Miss Heppelwaite," Dex said, as he walked her to the door. "As I said, if you think of anything at all . . ."

"Thank you," she sniffed. "I'll keep that in mind."

When the door had closed behind her, I realized there were two things about the scene that had bothered me. Rita's distress had seemed genuine, and the tears had looked real, but neither had left a mark on her beautiful face.

There are women who can cry in that way: I've read about them in books. When *I* cry, the tears leave their mark. My eyes get puffy and rimmed with red, my nose runs, my skin gets all blotchy. When I cry, it's not a pretty sight.

Rita Heppelwaite had cried like a fictional beauty on the edge of a breakdown. She'd poured out her emotion and soaked in Dex's sympathy. And when she'd left, none of it had marred her face in the slightest.

The other thing that didn't sit right had been her immediate reaction when Dex told her Dempsey was dead. She'd taken it all in and she'd cried—sure, she'd cried. But she hadn't asked how her lover had died. I went back over Dex's conversation with her in my mind, but no, he hadn't mentioned the how, only the when and the where.

"She took my handkerchief," Dex noted bemusedly after she'd gone.

A small price to pay to see the last of her, I thought but did not say. It wouldn't have mattered, because I was wrong.

CHAPTER NINE

I WENT BACK TO MY BOOK. Dex went back to whatever demons he'd been chasing—or whatever drink he'd been nursing—before Rita Heppelwaite interrupted the rhythm of our day.

The afternoon was endless. The day had gotten progressively warmer, and by midafternoon it felt like high summer, not the middle of fall. We were on the fifth floor, but even so, in the new heat you could smell the garbage ripening at street level. It seemed to roll itself up in the exhaust of a hundred motorcars and waft up to us in heat-soaked packages. I daydreamed about Angels Flight: about the little railcar lifting me out of the dirt and stink of downtown, to the cleaner air of residential Bunker Hill.

At four o'clock I'd had enough. I decided to pack it in early. I'd long since put all the files back where they belonged and tidied my office and the waiting area. The day was almost done, and we'd had our bit of excitement with Rita's visit. The phone hadn't rung even once—not even the usual cadre of bill collectors—and I had a strong feeling it wasn't going to. There didn't seem to be any reason for me to hang around.

I was just giving my desk a final tidy, intending to go in and say good-night to Dex before grabbing my purse and heading out the door, when we got our second unannounced visit of the day. It made me wonder why we even had a phone.

I didn't know the two men who came in the door, but I didn't have to. I knew they were the law before either of them had even opened their mouths. One was tall and dark; the other, short and florid. Both had the buttoned-down but messy look that seems to be part of the training to wear a detective's badge in Los Angeles these days. You had to wonder about it. Sometimes I think you could take a perfectly good, clean suit and drape it on a flatfoot, and he'd end up looking like he'd been wrung out.

"We're looking for Dexter J. Theroux," the short florid one said. His big hands were working the hat he held so furiously that I worried it wouldn't survive the encounter.

"This is his office," I said, stating the obvious. But I didn't like the man's tone, or the shifty way both of them had looked around the room when they entered. Like they were disappointed not to see something that wasn't there.

Short-and-Florid smiled at me. An insolent grin that held a touch of lechery. I didn't like him. "I know that, sister," he said. "It's got his name on the door." He pointed at the black-edged gold letters on the frosted glass in our front door.

"So you can read," I said, matching his tone. "Am I supposed to be impressed?" I had my orders with regard to police officers too. Dex had told me long ago: never tell cops anything. Never offer and never volunteer. When it's time to tell a thing, you'll know it, he'd said. But in casual questioning, give them nothing at all.

The flatfoot didn't like my answer; I could see that on his ugly little mug. He looked at me evenly, as though deciding on the best way to proceed.

"All right then," he said, "we'll play it your way. Is he in?"

"He is," I said, rising. "I'll announce you."

"Don't bother." The tall cop spoke for the first time, then pushed past me into Dex's office. I peeked in behind them, partly to check on Dex's condition, partly to see if he wanted me to hang around.

"Sorry, Dex," I called in. "They wouldn't wait for me to see if you were free."

If Dex was upset, he wasn't showing it. "It's OK, Kitty," he said, opening his desk drawer and pulling out a couple more glasses. I was probably the only one who would have heard the steel beneath his affable tone. "I haven't seen O'Reilly and Houlahan for a while, have I, boys? They've just come for a visit, I guess."

"You guessed wrong, Theroux." The short cop didn't mince any words. "We've got a bit of a mystery down at the station."

"Yeah," said the tall one, his voice as coarse as tires on gravel. "Someone told us about a corpse you're supposed to have seen."

"Gentlemen, have a seat." Dex settled himself more deeply into his chair, while he pulled the stopper out of his current bottle of whiskey—Canadian Club today, I saw. He splashed some of the amber liquid into his own glass, then poured a couple of fingers into each of the clean glasses he'd taken from his desk.

"We're on duty," the tall one—O'Reilly—said, as he took a seat. Houlahan nodded his agreement, but pulled his glass closer while he sat down. Of this pair, I noted, Houlahan would be the easier to manage.

"If you don't need me, Boss . . ." I ventured, from the place by the door where I still stood.

"Oh, thanks, Kitty. Yeah, we're fine. Can you finish that typing before the day is through?"

I looked straight at Dex, but I couldn't speak my thoughts, and he didn't meet my eyes. I wondered why anyone would need to impress these mooks, then realized it was possible Dex wanted me to hang around, just in case.

I didn't say anything, just nodded. As I went back into the outer office, I left the door ajar slightly, hoping to catch snippets of the conversation while I performed my typing show.

"You were saying?" Dex's voice was calm, assured and unaffected by whatever he'd been drinking.

I rolled a clean sheet of paper into the typewriter and began hitting keys in a leisurely fashion, trying hard not to drown out the voices I could just make out from this distance.

"We got a report . . ." It was O'Reilly. I recognized his gravelly voice. "You told someone you saw a stiff . . . up close and personal like."

"Ah," said Dex. Silently I agreed. It was beginning to make sense.

"That's right," Houlahan chimed in. "At a house on Lafayette Square. But when we got there to check it out, guess what we found?" There was malice in the man's voice. At my desk, I braced myself for the worst, absently hitting a smattering of typewriter keys into the silence.

"A stiff?" was Dex's guess. From where I was sitting, it was a good one. It would have been my guess as well.

"Guess again." It was O'Reilly this time. From the sounds of him, he was chasing his words with a sip of his drink.

"I'm all outta guesses, fellas. That was my single one." I could imagine Dex leaned back at his desk, a studied look of bored patience on his face. But what would he be feeling inside?

I didn't get to find out because the shrill ring of the phone almost shot me out of my seat.

CHAPTER TEN

I PICKED UP THE TELEPHONE and choked out my standard greeting, hoping I didn't sound as flustered as I felt. "Good afternoon, Dexter J. Theroux, private investigator, how may I help you?"

"I'd like to make an appointment to see Mr. Theroux, please." The voice was feminine and self-assured. In our business that was a combo that paid the bills.

"Of course," I said easily, as though I made appointments for Dex every minute of the day. "When were you thinking? I'll see if I can adjust his schedule." I pulled the vast wasteland of Dex's empty appointment book toward me.

"I'd like to see him as soon as possible." It seemed to me that the self-assurance had slipped somewhat. "Would he have time for me tomorrow afternoon?"

"Well," I said, flipping through the empty pages noisily, "Mr. Theroux's schedule tomorrow *does* look very tight."

"Oh," she said, sounding disappointed.

"But I think I can squeeze you in at three p.m. You might have to wait until three fifteen. I'll try to avoid that if possible though." None of this was subterfuge for its own sake. I have discovered that clients are more willing to pay and pay well for a busy, in-demand detective than they are for a mook who spends most of his days looking at the world through the bottom of a glass and checking his eyelids for faulty weather stripping. I told myself it wasn't exactly a lie, more like a teensy misdirection. And Marjorie had told me the day before that the stove had been acting up. We were going to need a new one or at least a repair. I had to do everything I could do to make sure Dex had cash on hand.

"Three o'clock will be fine," she said, sounding grateful. "Thank you."

I pushed a smile into my voice when I replied, "Oh, you're welcome. Can I get your name, please?"

"Lila Dempsey," she said. "Mrs. Lila Dempsey."

Dempsey. The name hit home right away. I quickly weighed the possibility that this Lila was connected with the Dempsey we'd found in the tub on Lafayette Square. Then I weighed the possibility that she wasn't. But even with all that weighing, I came up with nothing flat. Sometimes thinking about a thing doesn't help at all. Sometimes you just have to wait and see.

"Very good, Mrs. Dempsey. We'll see you tomorrow." While I replaced the receiver, I pushed all that weighing out of my head. I could still hear the voices coming out of Dex's office. I hoped I hadn't missed too much. I retuned my ears to the conversation, clattering a smattering of letters on the typewriter for good measure while I did so.

"Listen, fellas," Dex was saying. "I don't know what you're gettin' at. You guys know me: I'm a law-abiding citizen. Believe me, if I'd seen a dead guy, your number is the first one I woulda called."

"I'm tellin' you, Theroux," said the gravelly voice, "the broad said you told her you went in the house and found Dempsey dead."

"I don't know what tune she's singing," Dex said, sounding sure of himself, "but I didn't hand her the sheet music."

"So let me get this straight." It was the gravelly voice again. "You were not in Harrison Dempsey's house on Lafayette Square last night?"

"That's right," Dex responded, sounding confident. "Not last night and not ever. But I will tell you this . . ."

The phone rang again. And I jumped again.

"Good afternoon, Dexter J. Theroux, private investigator," I chirped. "Can I help you?"

"Hey, kiddo, you sound chipper." It was Mustard.

"Do I? I don't mean to. I think I'm trying to sound like I'm not *not* chipper, if you follow."

"Not really," he said, sounding comfortable, "but I can live with it."

"OK," I said, deciding that *I* was OK with *that*. All I wanted to do now was get rid of Mustard so I could get back to my eavesdropping while there were still things left to hear. "Dex is in a meeting right now, Mustard. Can I get him to call you?"

"A meeting, huh?" Mustard sounded as though he might play with the euphemism—get to the bottom of it—but then decided he had more pressing concerns. "Actually, Kitty, I called to talk to you."

"To me? What for?" I tried to hide my surprise, but it wasn't easy. Mustard never had business with me.

"You have a rooming house, don't you?"

"Well, kinda. Not exactly. Let's just say I live in one. And the owners are good friends."

"Is there a room open?"

"I'm not sure. Why, Mustard? You suddenly need a place to live?"

"It's not for me," he said. "I've got a friend in a bit of a jam. It's . . . well, it's a long story. But she needs a place to stay. She can pay all right. But she needs a place in a hurry. You got something for her?"

"Well, like I said Mustard, it's not my place. I think we've got something open, but I can't give the yes or no, you understand."

"Can you call and find out?"

"No phone." Lots of people in the Southland were getting phones right then. But phones cost money, something we didn't have a lot of, so Marjorie had figured we could go without. It didn't bother me any. I had the phone at the office I could use anytime, and with cash as scarce as it was, there were plenty of other things on which we could spend the little money we had. "I can check tonight and let you know tomorrow though."

"Sure, sure," Mustard said, hiding his disappointment. I felt bad. Mustard had done a lot for me.

"Listen, I can give you the address, and you can take your friend up there and check it out. See if there's an opening. Maybe use my name if you think it'll help."

Mustard sounded brighter at the suggestion. "Thanks, Kitty. But like I said, this friend is in a bit of a jam, and I'm tied up for the rest of the day. Can I send her over to you there at Dex's? Then maybe the two of you can check things out, and I'll swing by your place tonight. If it's a no-go, I'll take her with me . . . figure out something else."

I hesitated only because I had the feeling there was something larger at work here. That this might even be Mustard in action, fixing something. I reminded myself again that I owed him a thing or two and relented. He'd said if things didn't work out, he'd come and get her later, so what could it hurt? "Sure," I said, "send her by."

"Great, Kitty. Thanks." The relief was plain in his voice, and I wondered anew. "Her name is Brucie Jergens. You'll like her; she's a sweet kid. Expect her there at the office within half an hour or so. I'll tell her you'll take care of everything."

Mustard hung up before I could ask him what he thought I'd be taking care of.

CHAPTER ELEVEN

I WASN'T ABLE TO THINK too much about Mustard and
what the fixer might be fixing, because as I hung up the phone,
the pair of flatfoots in Dex's office started making sounds like
they were getting ready to leave and I knew I'd missed the best
part.

O'Reilly and Houlahan moved through the office with a dis-
gruntled air, and neither of them spared me even a glance. I
noticed that Dex didn't escort them out.

As soon as the outer door had closed behind them, I made
my way into Dex's office, quick as you please.

Dex was still at his desk with a couple of fingers of whiskey
in front of him. The glasses the cops had used were still where
they'd left them. Both, I noted, quite drained.

"What'd I miss?" I asked, plunking myself down in one of
the vacated chairs. The seat was still warm.

Dex shook the bottle at me, a question in his face, but I
waved it away. He pulled yet another clean glass out of his
desk, dropped a couple of ice cubes into it, poured an inch or so
of rye over them, and pushed it in front of me. I looked at the
glass questioningly, but I didn't say anything and I didn't
drink.

"What did you miss?" he repeated absently. "Quite a bit.
Not much."

"Well, *that* covers it," I said dryly.

"It doesn't really, does it? Ah, well. Here's the thing: our
Rita—"

I interrupted. "Now she's *our* Rita?"

"Do you wanna hear this or not?"

I did. "Sorry. Go on."

"OK. *Our* Rita didn't waste any time when she left here. She went straight to the cops and told them I'd found Dempsey's body at his house."

"She did?" I couldn't imagine why she'd do a thing like that. Why she would even have wanted to.

Dex nodded. "She did. But wait, it gets better. She gave them the address on Lafayette Square, and these two flatfoots get the call and head down there. What do you figure they find?"

"No body?" I volunteered.

Dex looked surprised or impressed, I couldn't tell which. Maybe a bit of both. "How'd you know that?"

"I heard some of it," I admitted sheepishly. "It sounded like it was going that way."

Dex squelched whatever miffed feelings he had about his spoiled surprise and went on. "So, OK, no body. That's easy, right? Someone could have gone to the house after we were there, dumped Dempsey into the Los Angeles River, and he's halfway to China by now. Or maybe they throw him in the Tar Pits or bury him in the mountains or—"

"I get the idea," I said, interrupting him again.

"Yeah, well . . . my point is, absence of a body is not *that* big a deal. There are ways of explaining it, right?"

I nodded.

"But get this: the cops told me Dempsey's wife says he packed up and took the *Harvard* to San Francisco yesterday."

"Wait," I said. All of this was almost too much information. "There's a wife? How come no one mentioned a wife before?" I thought about Dex's three o'clock appointment for the following day: Lila Dempsey. Dempsey was a moniker that hadn't been far out of my head since I'd first heard it. Could Lila be Harrison's missus? I was going to ask Dex—and tell him about the appointment—but his mind was heading someplace and he took me with him.

"Hell," Dex replied, "there's a mistress, right? Stands to reason there's a wife someplace. You can't have one without the other."

I ignored him. "If Dempsey took a steamship to San Francisco yesterday, who was the stiff in the tub?"

"That's the big question, isn't it?"

I nodded. "It is."

"Too bad I don't have a big answer. But get this: the cops say they got an anonymous phone tip about the same stiff at that address this morning."

I tried to drop a neutral mask over my face when I realized what Dex was saying. I wasn't sure I succeeded. Drunk or no, Dex was a detective. I couldn't tell if Dex figured it was me who made the call. He didn't say so, just looked at me kind of probingly. I held my mask and hoped for the best. Dex didn't ask, so I didn't tell. He had taught me a couple of things after all.

"Say, I booked an appointment for you while you were busy." It was true that I was trying to change the subject a little bit. But it was also true that Dex needed to know.

"Well, *that's* good news. Let's hope this case doesn't resolve itself as quickly."

"The person you're seeing is one Lila Dempsey." I watched Dex's face while I told him, but nothing registered beyond what had probably been on mine when I heard her name: mild recognition followed by curiosity.

"Well, that *is* interesting," Dex said.

"Do you think it's Dempsey's missus?" I asked.

Dex shrugged. "Could be, I guess."

"Well, if it is," I insisted, "why would she wanna see you?"

Another shrug. "Here's where you might find patience a useful thing, kiddo." I checked Dex's face; he was definitely kidding me. "We'll just have to wait until tomorrow and see."

"So how'd you answer them?" I asked, changing direction completely.

"Who?" Dex asked, properly perplexed.

"Houlahan and O'Reilly. What did you tell them about the body?"

"I told them Rita made it up."

"*What?*"

"Yeah." He nodded, lit a cigarette, and tossed the match into the ashtray on his desk. "I told them if I'd seen a body, I would have called them straight off. But *of course* I didn't see any body. To see a body, I would have had to illegally enter that house, and they know I'd never do that."

"Hoo, boy," I said. "And they bought that?"

"Sure. What's to buy? There was no body."

"But, Dex—" I started.

"Yeah, yeah, I know. There *was* a body. But do you want the cops thinking I'm up to some monkey business with bodies they can't even find?"

He left the question open and I didn't reply. It wasn't the kind that needed one.

"So whaddaya think?" he asked me. While I considered my answer, I watched in fascination as he sent a whole platoon of smoke rings marching toward the ceiling.

I was flummoxed by the whole business—with Dempsey, that is, not the smoke rings. I knew what I'd seen. I'd felt the blood on my hands, seen the vacant eyes of the corpse in the tub. Seen, even, the driver's license Dex had pulled out of the wallet. Harrison Dempsey, it had said. There'd been no mistake.

"Dead is dead," I said finally. "I know what I saw. What *we* saw."

Dex nodded thoughtfully. "That's what I've been thinking. And that's why we're going to the Zebra Room tonight."

"Who are?"

"We are. You and me, kid. I want to have a look around, maybe talk to some people. I figured it might be fun for you to see the inside of a place like that. And it'll seem less fishy, a good-looking couple like us out on the town, instead of just me waltzing in there stag, asking questions no one wants to answer."

My hands flew to my dress. "I don't have anything to wear," I said.

Dex just grinned. "You'll think of something. I'll pick you up at your place at nine."

I started to get up, my mind already rummaging through my meager wardrobe, when another thought hit me.

"Why, Dex?" I asked him. "The guy you were supposed to be tailing is dead. You don't even have a case anymore."

"That's true," he agreed, without hesitation. "But Rita gave me eighty-three bucks. I offered her part of it back. She wouldn't take it. I feel like I oughta do more for the money. Besides, you said he's dead. His wife says he ain't. And the body we saw is gone. Doesn't it make you wonder?"

I shrugged and then I nodded. When I thought about it, it kind of did.

CHAPTER TWELVE

DEX LEFT FOR THE DAY as soon as our impromptu meeting was over, saying he had to get over to Mustard's to get a car for the night.

"And don't forget, I'll pick you up at your place at nine."

It was ironic that a day that had dragged by so slowly had ended in the kind of mad rush we only ever saw at rare busy times. People coming and going, the phone ringing. Thinking of it made me smile. It was one of the things I liked about working for Dex: you never knew what to expect.

I was making my final tidy of the office in preparation for packing things up and heading out for the evening, when I heard the outer door open again.

"What did you forget, Dex. . . ." The words died on my tongue. It wasn't Dex at all, but a girl—a young woman really—with tightly cropped dark hair. It hung around her eyes and down to her collar line so sleekly, it reminded me of the fur of a seal. She had big brown eyes rimmed with long dark lashes that made them look sooty.

"Miss Pangborn?" she said, with a confidence that belied her waifish appearance.

I looked at her curiously before I remembered. "Brucie Jergens," I exclaimed. "Mustard's friend! I'm sorry. What a day it's been. Forgive me. I'd forgotten all about you."

Her smile was wide and open and revealed even white teeth. "Nothing to forgive. I wasn't here to be hurt by your forgetting," she pointed out reasonably. "Now if I'd gotten here and you'd left without me, that would be a different story."

I gauged Brucie Jergens to be somewhere right around

thirty. I could tell she was somewhat older than me, but she was possessed of a merriness that made her seem a good deal younger.

"Let me just finish tidying up the office and then we'll go. Make yourself at home," I told her, indicating the waiting room chairs. "I won't be long."

"Thanks," she said, putting her handbag on my desk and taking a seat.

"How do you know Mustard?" I asked politely while I straightened up, making conversation but not quite knowing where to begin.

"He was friends with my husband, Ned."

"Your husband," I repeated, oddly surprised that she was married.

I saw a shadow pass over her face, and I almost knew what she'd say before she said it. "He died a few weeks ago. I'm a widow now." She said this last with such resolution that I knew it was something she was still trying on, like at Bullock's when you've found a sweater that's just the price and that you know will keep you warm, but you can't bring yourself to like it well enough to actually want it. This was like that.

"I'm sorry," I said mechanically. It was the right thing to say, but it's never enough. Still I wondered. Is saying something always better than saying nothing at all?

"It's OK," she said. Then she shrugged. "Well, as OK as can be. It was bound to happen though. We always knew there was danger. I just didn't . . . I just didn't . . . I just hoped the danger would miss him, is all."

I looked at her uncomprehendingly.

"Mustard didn't tell you?"

I shook my head.

"Well, then," she said thoughtfully, "maybe I've said too much."

"No," I said, "he probably would have said more, but we

were on the phone. He just said you needed a place to stay, and he figured I might know of something."

Brucie sighed, then smiled. "That'll do for now, if that's all right."

"Sure," I told her. "Sure, that's fine." I was curious, but I didn't ask. Brucie's life was none of my business. Hell, I didn't know her from Eve.

I grabbed my handbag and the coat I'd worn into the office that morning, and Brucie picked up her own handbag.

"Is that all you've got?" I asked her.

"With me, yeah. Mustard is going to bring my things by your place tonight."

We pushed out of the building onto the street into full and glorious sun. After spending most of the day indoors, I had to shield my eyes and blink while my body reevaluated its situation.

Brucie laughed when she saw the action. "You look like a mole coming out of her hole," she said brightly, as we walked north on Spring Street toward Angels Flight. "No offense though," she assured me quickly. "A *pretty* mole." Then she watched me closely to see if she'd hurt my feelings. She hadn't and I smiled to reassure her.

"Some days coming out, I *feel* like a mole," I told her. "You saw my desk; my boss has the only window in the place. When he's in there and the door is closed, I don't have any way of telling if it's light or dark out."

Brucie shuddered delicately. "That sounds horrible," she said. "I don't know if I could do that . . . work in an office. Especially one where I couldn't see outside whenever I liked."

I shrugged. "Actually, aside from the window thing, working in an office is more fun than you'd think. I never would have thought so before. But it's exciting sometimes. Being in the middle of so many things, but none of it really affects your own life." I stopped for a moment, considering. "I can't really explain it better than that. I guess you have to experience it."

"I can't imagine I ever would."

"I'm guessing you don't work in an office," I said. It was nice, this walking and chatting. Pleasant. I hadn't really had any girlfriends since I'd left school and started working. It made me realize how much my life had changed.

"Honestly, I've never worked at all. I met Ned when I was still in high school. We were so crazy in love; we didn't even wait for me to graduate."

"You went to high school together?"

Brucie laughed, as though that were the funniest question she could imagine. "Oh, no," she said. "He worked for Chummy McGee."

She said the name as though it were important, but it didn't mean anything to me.

"What did he do?" I asked.

"Ned? He was Chummy's right hand."

This too was said as though it had meaning, as though I should know what she was talking about. I didn't pursue it.

At the Angels Flight station house I hesitated. Normally, to save money, I scampered up the stairs adjacent to the funicular railway's tracks. On my way in to work in the morning, I'd ride the cars; down was always free. But I only ever paid for the ride home when I was feeling especially flush or especially tired. It may only have been the cost of a cup of coffee, but a whole week's worth of that added up to a loaf of bread. Plus I reasoned that none of it was going to be bad for my behind—especially after a day of sitting on it. I was in the embarrassing position of having to watch my nickels, but I couldn't very well ask Brucie to hike up the 150 to 200 steps to the top.

Brucie saw my hesitation and mistook its meaning. "Are you sure this is it?" she said. "I've ridden this thing before, but I would have sworn it looked quite different."

That made sense to me. "That's Court Flight," I said, pointing north. "It's a few blocks that way. That's farther from the office. That's the one people use when they drive into town because there's easy parking on the Bunker Hill side. This is Angels Flight." I pointed to the sign. "And my house is just a block from the station house at the top."

Brucie smiled. I thought she looked like a child anticipating a Sunday outing. "This is fun," she said. And I decided I could no more deny her a trip on Angels Flight than you would taking that child to the zoo.

At the ticket window, I prepared to pay for two adult tickets, but Brucie stopped me. "Here, let me," she said. I was going to insist, but she reached over me and handed the coins to the ticket taker.

"Thanks," I said, as we moved away from the window.

"It's my pleasure," she said candidly. "And please don't feel like you should have paid. I'm Ned Jergens's widow." There seemed to be sadness mixed into the mock bravado in her voice. "Money's nothin' to me."

I looked at her closely, but didn't say anything. There was more there that needed saying, I guessed, but it seemed as though Brucie didn't think it was quite time. I held my tongue while we waited for the train.

The ride up the steep hill in the tiny railcar seemed to restore Brucie's spirits. "This is wonderful," she said, as we chugged almost straight up, the downtown core getting smaller behind us.

I nodded my agreement. I did this trek—by foot or by train, the view was the same—every day, and I never tired of the experience. I knew that the reason was tied into memories of my childhood. Trips I'd taken downtown when I was a little girl, my tiny hand lost in my father's much larger one, but clinging on for all I was worth in the fear of becoming separated from him and lost forever. Or the occasional shopping day when my father would assign Marjorie to take me to Blackstone's department store to outfit me for another school year. Then home again, our arms laden with packages filled with new things for me. Sometimes Marjorie would have purchased a small package of fudge during the day, and she'd bring it to light as we sat on the train, letting the sweetness revive our tired limbs.

I didn't share any of this with Brucie, who chirped away happily about the view, the observation deck we passed under, and the other people in the tram. As much as I loved the short trip, it was pleasant viewing the familiar landscape through her fresh and enthusiastic eyes. When it was over and we were back on solid ground, Brucie went to the guardrail and looked wistfully back toward downtown. "That was a wonderful trip, Kitty," she said. "I forgot for a moment."

I didn't ask her what it was she had forgotten. I even had the feeling I wasn't quite ready to know.

CHAPTER THIRTEEN

WE TRUDGED up Olive to my house, which is a trek that has changed a lot in my recollection. Throughout my lifetime the neighborhood has been in constant flux. When I was very young, the beautiful Victorian mansions were already being torn down, and a more modern era has been encroaching ever since. My childhood home was flanked by nearly identical apartment buildings, the sunny garden I'd played in was now constantly in the shadow of the building next door. It didn't matter. No child had played in that garden for a long time.

When I brought Brucie into the foyer, I noticed she paused and admired her surroundings. The old house is an aging beauty certainly, but a beauty nonetheless. To me, it smelled like home, the scent of beeswax mingling with the flowers Marjorie coaxed from her shady garden, wafting together through the house to the large oak-paneled hall.

In many ways the big house hadn't changed since my father was alive. Marjorie and Marcus kept things just as spotless as they had when the house hadn't belonged to them. They hadn't even moved from the servants' quarters in the converted carriage house, preferring to rent the master suite and large guest bedrooms in the main house to the more affluent of their clientele. For all that, I couldn't help but think that the house was warmer now than it had been, and certainly brighter. The constant comings and goings of a large handful of paying guests keeping the Olegs busy, and the heart of the house quickened with life. My father's presence had been a dour one in many ways, but I hadn't realized until he was gone that his presence had been like deep shade; no matter how bright the sun, there'd been a cold there that nothing could ever really touch.

"Let's go find Marjorie," I said to Brucie, as I led her to the kitchen. At this time of the day, that's where she'd be, preparing the evening meal for her boarders.

When I introduced them, I could see Marjorie gently sizing Brucie up. "You're all alone, Mrs. Jergens?" Marjorie asked politely, though she didn't miss a beat in rolling out the biscuits for the evening meal.

"Yes, ma'am, I am," Brucie replied.

"And your husband . . . ?" Marjorie let her question trail off, but I could see she wanted an answer. There were certain types of people she'd not let stay in the house. There was, she insisted, a very thin line between a boarding house that could expect the very best people and one where those same people would not stay. She said it was all a matter of reputation. Many of our boarders were gentlemen of business, some of whom had fallen on difficult times. Paying a little bit extra to live in our house was worthwhile to them. They could stay there and imagine—or pretend, if that was their wont—that their circumstances had not been reduced, just altered slightly. Marjorie felt that letting the wrong people stay could alter this perception. So she screened carefully.

"I'm a widow, Mrs. Oleg," Brucie said, her eyes downcast, as though carefully examining the tile floor. "My husband died a few weeks ago."

"A widow, Mrs. Jergens? How sad to see that, a woman of your age. And you're all alone in the world?"

"Not in the world, no. I have no family in the city. But friends. I do have friends."

"She's one of Mustard's friends, Marjorie. That's how I came to know her."

Marjorie's face stayed neutral at the mention of Mustard's

name. I knew that didn't necessarily mean that Marjorie disapproved of him; it was more like the jury was still out.

Brucie wouldn't have seen Marjorie wrestling with her decision, but I, who knew the woman well, could see it as plain as anything. After all, for my entire life Marjorie had been like a mother to me. I saw her moving toward her decision, and I felt a little guilty. I didn't know much about Brucie, but I realized that if Marjorie knew even the little I knew, her decision would have been much easier. Then I chided myself for the thought. I really didn't know anything. I suspected that Brucie's Ned had been some sort of mob type who had come to an unpleasant end, but no one had actually told me as much. It was possible I had it all wrong. It was possible that Chummy McGee was actually an accountant or a lawyer and Ned had been his assistant. But I didn't think so.

I knew Marjorie had come to some kind of decision when, with the biscuits ready for the oven, she washed her hands, then smoothed them against her housedress. When she spoke again, I knew I was right. "We'll give her the big room across from yours, Miss Katherine." And then to Brucie: "It's got a nice view of downtown. Miss Elizabeth—Miss Katherine's mother—liked to sit there with her books and read when she was expecting." And so on, indoctrinating Brucie into the workings of the house almost without the girl's knowing.

"It's fifty dollars a month," Marjorie said quietly. "Can you manage that all right, dear?"

Brucie nodded. "I can, thank you. That will be fine."

"That's all settled then. Miss Katherine, I'm busy in the kitchen for the next little while. Will you show Mrs. Jergens to her room, please? Then both you girls come down for dinner in half an hour."

"She keeps calling you Miss Katherine," Brucie said, as we climbed the stairs. "It's like you still own the joint." I'd told

her a little about the history of the house on our walk from Angels Flight.

"Hard habit to break, I guess. We get along all right though.
Everything's changed," I said thoughtfully. "But in some ways
it's like nothing's changed at all."

"Is that hard though? You know, Ned and I had a little
house in Highland Park. I . . . well, I can't be there now. But
even if I could, I couldn't, if you know what I mean."

I didn't, but by then we'd come to her room. I unlocked
the door and threw it open with a flourish, letting her enter
before me.

"Wow," she said, spinning around in the center of the room,
the wood floor slippery against the smooth soles of her shoes.
"This pile may be old-fashioned, but the room is pretty swank."

I looked around, trying to see things through her eyes. And,
yes, viewed in that light, the room *was* old-fashioned. As was,
as she'd said, the whole pile. The cove ceilings, the clerestory
windows, and the bare wood floors. But the house had a sort of
genteel elegance, even with its aging bones. It had breeding in
a way. And blood, as my father used to say, will tell.

"Bathroom?" she asked.

I shook my head. "Down the hall on the left. But there's
one in my room. You can use that sometimes, if you like."

"What now?"

"Well, you're all set. Once Mustard gets here with your
trunk, you can settle in. And Marjorie said dinner is in a while.
Are you hungry?"

"I could eat," Brucie said.

"Well, that's fine then. By the time we're done with dinner,
Mustard will be here. Once you have your own things around
you, you'll feel more at home." Brucie's little face looked suddenly unguarded and terribly sad.

"It'll be all right," I said softly. "It doesn't seem like it now,
I know. But it all gets easier. I promise."

CHAPTER FOURTEEN

BY THE TIME we went down for dinner, Brucie's spirits had been miraculously restored, at least on the outside. She seemed to have that sort of personality. Resilient, I would have said on first meeting. Though there was something of the caged bird about her. Her wings might be clipped, and sometimes she might wish she were soaring, but you couldn't suppress her gaiety for long. As a result, our meal was a jovial affair. You got the feeling that Brucie was one of those girls that people say light up a room. By the end of the meal, Marjorie was clucking over Brucie maternally, Marcus seemed delighted just to be in her company, and the various elegant old codgers that currently shared our roof all looked ready to rush out and lay capes over puddles for her. Brucie had that effect on people, and most charmingly, she didn't even seem aware of it.

As I had predicted, just as we'd finished clearing the dishes from our evening meal, we heard the front door knocker.

"That'll be Mustard with your stuff," I said to Brucie, but she was already leaving the room.

"Is it all right if I answer the door?" she called back over her shoulder.

Marjorie and I nodded almost simultaneously. "Of course," I said.

I started to help with the washing-up, and after a while Brucie popped into the kitchen, Mustard in tow.

"Hey, kiddo," he greeted me. "Hello, Mrs. Oleg."

"Mustard has the most wonderful surprise," Brucie enthused. "You'll never guess."

"Ummm . . . probably not." The world was too vast. There were too many possible guesses. "Why don't you tell me?"

"We're going to the Zebra Room!"

"We are?" I said. I knew I'd be going. I didn't know yet how I felt about a whole group.

Marjorie looked only slightly disapproving. I realized it was because she probably had no idea what a Zebra Room might be.

"Dex came by to get a car," Mustard explained. "I told him I was coming up here to see Brucie, and he sez, why don't I just bring you two lovely ladies and we'll meet him there?"

I could feel the tiniest bit of glowering beginning from Marjorie, so I explained to her, "It's not a date. It's business. Dex is on a case, and he asked if I'd come along, kind of to help."

If Marjorie was mollified, she didn't show it. "It's not seemly, Miss Katherine."

I smiled at her reassuringly. "It's a different age, Marjorie. It'll be all right. I'm a big girl."

"Not that big," Mustard offered up gallantly. "But I'll be there to be sure she's all right."

"I'm not sure that makes me feel any better," Marjorie sniffed, as she left the room. But despite her words she did seem slightly reassured.

"I told Dex this afternoon that I really haven't anything to wear."

"Ha!" Brucie said unexpectedly. "Then you're lucky I'm here, because I have *lots*."

Mustard had not only brought a large trunk, but several boxes as well.

"Hats," Brucie said, explaining the boxes. "Well, some hats, some shoes."

We showed Mustard where to haul Brucie's stuff, then installed him in the drawing room with a glass of Marjorie's medicinal Irish whiskey before tripping back upstairs.

In her room, I discovered that Brucie hadn't been exaggerating. It seemed to me there was little in that trunk beyond what was appropriate to be worn to places like the Zebra Room.

We were not the same size. I was taller and more angular. Brucie was small, delicately made, and full-bodied. The basic differences in our shapes narrowed the possible clothing selection somewhat, but her wardrobe was so ample that several choices remained.

At her insistence, we settled on something I would normally never have worn, never mind had access to. It's not that it was particularly revealing; it wasn't. But the ivory fabric draped me so closely, I felt unusually exposed. The dress fell to a point just between knee and calf that Brucie pronounced acceptable though not perfect.

"Last year when I had the dress made," Brucie explained, "the hemline was the perfect length. But this year, hemlines are a few inches lower, so this would be too long for me. You're taller though, so it all sorta works out."

When I tried on the dress, she stood back and surveyed me critically. "You know, it's funny. It looks so different on you than it did on me. It looks like a different dress altogether. But it looks good. Oh, wait though; there's a hat."

Which set her back in motion, pulling open boxes within boxes, until she came across what she was looking for. It seemed so tiny to me, it could barely be called a hat; a wedge of shiny ivory fabric that she fixed on my head with a series of pins.

Once she was finished, she stood back and surveyed me again. Finally she nodded approvingly. "You still need a little lip rouge and maybe something for your cheeks, but other than that you'll do nicely."

She turned me so I faced the mirror on the back of the door. I gasped when I got a load of myself; the transformation was startling.

"I look . . . I look grown up," I said quietly.

Brucie laughed at my comment, though not unkindly. "But not *too* grown up. No one wants to look like that."

It was a silly thought—that grown-up thing—but not one without reason. I'd been a schoolgirl, and then overnight, it seemed, I was a grown woman with responsibilities. There'd been little time for transitions involving coming-outs and balls. And now . . . well, now I was going to the Zebra Room with my boss and his friend. Hardly a coming-out. Still it was an exciting night for me. I felt I was on the threshold of something.

"And this is what *I* need for the Zebra Room," Brucie said, bringing out a gown that had been wrapped in tissue and stored carefully in the trunk. "You'll see. The two of us will look like we were born for that place."

When she shook out the garment, I gasped. And I could understand her special care. The dress was gold lamé—not a fabric I'd seen before—and the bodice was affixed with beads so tiny, all you saw was the shine.

"It's Mainbocher." She breathed the name of a designer I'd never heard of before as though he were a religious icon. And then as though admitting something, she said, "OK, well it's *not* Mainbocher. But it's from a Mainbocher design. And I don't think anyone could tell that it wasn't, do you?"

I shook my head.

"Well, princess," she said, when she was dressed and had fussed appropriately over our hair and makeup, "we're set then. Let's have Mustard get our chariot ready."

And the funny thing was, in that moment I *did* feel like a princess. I felt like anything was possible. And I won't forget the night. Not ever. Though it ended so badly, in its infancy it was an evening that seemed made for magic.

CHAPTER FIFTEEN

THE ZEBRA ROOM astonished me. It was like nothing I could ever have imagined.

The Town House Hotel had opened just a year before. Bad timing, really. It had been designed and launched with a different era in mind. One of opulence and excess. One where affluence was inevitable and assured.

In the twenties the stock market had been unstoppable. People were even borrowing money in order to invest in the market. Everyone knew it would just keep going on like that—up, up, and ever up. I was very young, but you couldn't miss the optimism, even the arrogance. This is the way things would always be, the future an unbroken ribbon of glistening promise.

The only thing necessary in such a market had been venues of excess where people could go to unload some of their easily gained cash. With all of that in mind, the Town House Hotel on Wilshire had opened its doors. It boasted fourteen floors of elegant opulence and the first—the only—indoor Olympic-sized swimming pool anywhere in the Southland. It had restaurants and shops and services galore. And it had the Zebra Room, a club where Zelda and F. Scott would have felt right at home.

Based on the name alone, I'd expected a black-and-white decor. I was wrong but not disappointed. The club was done in browns and creams and whites with only accents of black. It managed to pull off elegance and whimsy all in one bite, and against this color scheme I could see why Brucie had thought we were perfectly dressed for the club. With me in ivory and Brucie in her gold lamé, we might have been created by the

Zebra Room's interior designers as a foil for the decor of the glamorous room.

Truly, though, I wasn't certain anyone would notice us. When we got there at ten o'clock, the club was filled to the rafters with people and noise and music and an air of such extreme frivolity, it seemed to me almost like a dream of what such a place would be. It was everything I'd imagined. More. The club seemed full of men in smart suits and beautiful women in dresses of every conceivable hue. The place looked full and rich and right. It made you think that maybe the *Times* was right; maybe there really was no Depression going on, not here. How could there be? Not in L.A.

When we entered the club, Mustard insisted Brucie and I each take an arm, though if this was for his sake or ours, I wasn't quite sure. He escorted us right into the center of the partying throng, where Brucie and I fell in behind him like small ships in the wake of a larger one. From there Mustard led us through the crowded room, ever more deeply into the club. I could tell he had a destination in mind.

I noticed that sometimes he gently elbowed members of the crowd aside. More often, people would notice him first and get out of his way as though he were Moses and they were the Red Sea. I wondered if it had to do with his reputation or the expression on his face. After a bit more observation I decided it was probably some of both.

"Is this a special night?" I said, moving close to Brucie's ear so she could hear me over the din.

"Whadja mean?" she asked.

"All these people. It looks like New Year's Eve or something."

"Or something," Brucie laughed. "At the Zebra Room, it's New Year's Eve every night."

I took this in but didn't say anything, intent on keeping Mustard's back in sight. He didn't slow his pace until he found what he'd been looking for: Dex had commandeered a banquette near the back of the room and was waiting for us.

"Get a load of you," he said, when he saw me. He had some dark cocktail on the table in front of him, though I wasn't surprised he'd gotten a head start.

"Yeah, our girl cleans up pretty good, don't she?" Mustard said, nodding approvingly.

He introduced Brucie, and I thought maybe Dex looked at her appraisingly when he heard her name, his eyes widening slightly, but I might have been imagining things.

The three of them chatted a bit over the din. We were close to the piano player, who was tinkling away madly while a canary in a bright pink evening gown belted out "Let's Do It, Let's Fall in Love" and other things by Cole Porter and the Gershwins. I tried to focus a bit on the conversation, but was overwhelmed by my surroundings. The sights, the sounds, the colors, the scores of people all bent on hilarity. All of it outside my experience and deeply interesting.

After a while, a waitress appeared at our table to take our order. Mustard asked for a manhattan, and though he already had a drink in front of him, Dex ordered one as well. Brucie asked for a silver fizz. When it came to be my turn, I had no idea what to ask for. Brucie saw this and came to my rescue.

"You don't drink much, do you, doll?" she said.

I shook my head. Really, I didn't drink at all.

"She'll have a Kir Royale," she told the waitress.

I looked a question at Brucie, and she said, "We'll start you with something light. It's almost like soda pop—just champagne mixed with crème de cassis." I kept looking at her. "Black-currant liqueur," she explained, smiling. "It would take a *lot* of those to get you looped."

"Is this a speakeasy?" I asked, when the waitress had moved away. I said it as quietly as I could while still being heard by my companions. I was unprepared for their laughter.

"No," Dex said. "It's just a nightclub."

"But what about Prohibition?" Every table in the place seemed to be covered with various drinks, many of them exotic-looking cocktails in interesting-looking glasses. And nobody seemed to be the least bit concerned about it.

"Well, it's a thing," Mustard said. "But no one in Los Angeles is paying much attention anymore."

"Really?"

"It's complicated," Dex said. "But the right people pay off the right people, and this"—he indicated the booze-laden tables—"this is what you get."

After a while of watching and listening, what had appeared at first to be an unrestrained horde of people began in my mind to sort themselves into little groups. The tables—perhaps sixty of them counting the banquettes that followed both walls—were mostly taken by parties like ours, small groups made up of good-looking couples intent on having a good time. There was another group near the piano player and the singer, enjoying the show the duo provided. Still another group lounged around the long polished wood bar near the entrance. This group was mostly masculine and purposeful-looking. They looked as though they weren't just there for fun and frivolity, but like they had business to conduct. Or like they never stopped conducting it.

I noticed Dex's attention settle on the men at the bar, and after a while he got up and sauntered over there, greeting a well fed–looking man in a bespoke suit like an old friend.

"That's Lucid Wilson," Mustard said, noticing my interest. I shrugged. The name meant nothing to me. It registered with Brucie though. She seemed to shrink into herself slightly. I looked at her curiously, but she didn't meet my eye.

After a while Lucid led Dex through a door at the side of the club that I hadn't noticed before. A few minutes later a tall girl with wavy black hair under a narrow black hat came out and headed toward the ladies' room.

"Dance with me, Mustard," Brucie said brightly, making me think I'd been mistaken about the air of quiet she'd owned a few minutes before.

"No one's dancing," Mustard pointed out.

"Aw, c'mon." She stood, grabbed his hand, and played at pulling him up. "Be a sport. They'll dance if we dance."

Mustard laughed and relented. "You're a pretty pushy broad," he said through a smile.

"How the hell do you think a girl gets what she wants?" Brucie said gaily, winking at me over Mustard's shoulder as she led him away.

Watching Mustard and Brucie dance, the caged bird analogy I'd thought of at the house came back to mind. Only now she'd been released from that cage and was determined to fly. She looked set to have some fun. For his part, when Mustard looked at Brucie, the lines that normally creased his face seemed to fall away. Was he sweet on Brucie? I wondered. Had he always been, or was I watching the birth of something new?

While I sat alone at the table and watched the dancers, the waitress came back with a huge raft of drinks on a tray. I wondered that she could carry that many, let alone sort out whose drinks were whose.

She placed the Kir Royale in front of me—a dark purple drink in a champagne glass. I sipped at it tentatively. Brucie had been right; it tasted good. Like some fizzy, vaguely naughty juice.

A couple of times, I looked over at the door Dex had disappeared through, but there was no sign of him. I quelled the fingers of worry I started to feel. He was a big boy, used to such things. He knew how to take care of himself.

I went to the powder room as much to waste time until everyone came back as to do any serious business. Plus I was tired of sitting there all alone feeling as conspicuous as a bump on a log.

Like the rest of the club, the powder room was unlike anything I'd ever seen. A long row of stalls mirrored by a long row of elegant sinks. A smiling attendant kept her position somewhere near the middle, an array of perfumes, sewing materials, and other niceties ready should I need to fix my dress, my hair, or anything else.

At the far end of this gallery was a small but well-appointed lounge area. The walls were painted dark chocolate, setting off the two zebra-striped sofas and a chair. The dark-haired girl I'd seen enter a while ago sat in the armchair, her shoes pushed off and her legs over one of the arms of the chair in a most unladylike fashion.

A girl with dyed yellow hair and a bright green dress sat on one sofa. Her shoes were off as well, but she had her legs curled under her. The two were chatting earnestly. When I came in, both raised their heads and looked at me, as though checking to see if I was anyone they knew. When they didn't recognize me, they went back to their conversation. I dropped myself onto the other sofa, pushed off my shoes, and tried to look bored and tired. The tired part wasn't hard.

They chatted about inconsequential things. At least they seemed inconsequential to me, being filled with names and places that held no meaning.

"Do we know you?" It took a moment to realize that the black-haired girl was addressing me.

I shook my head and tried to smile. "No." I indicated my bare feet. "I just need a moment of quiet."

"Still," the girl demanded, "you look familiar. Have I seen you in here before?"

I started to reply in the negative, then had a thought. "Maybe a few times. A while ago. With Harrison Dempsey." I watched their faces as I said his name. The blonde's lit with a sort of dull recognition, while the black-haired girl laughed outright.

"Ha!" she said. "There's someone I *know* isn't here tonight."

"How do you figure?" I asked.

"Are you saying he's here?" The girl looked incredulous.

"No, no. I'm here with some other friends. And . . . and I haven't seen him for a while, but I don't figure there's any reason he wouldn't be here."

"Are you kidding?" the girl said scornfully. "There's about thirty thousand reasons for him *not* to be here."

I must have done a good job looking confused—it was easy, I *was* confused—because she went on. "He's into a couple of people here for a *lot* of spondulix."

I looked at the girl uncomprehendingly.

"Spondulix?"

"You know. Cabbage, spinach, dough."

"Money?" I tried.

"Right." The girl nodded, as though she were thinking I might be not much brighter than a pile of spondulix myself.

"What's a lot?" I asked.

"I'm not sure," the girl admitted. "But I get the feeling it's the kind of dough that floats businesses and big houses, you know? Not the kind you need to play the ponies."

"So thousands?"

"More like thousands and thousands. He had a *very* bad run at the tables. An' last week? Him and Lucid got into a big scene right here at the club. Did you hear about it?" I shook my head, and she went on, as though relishing having someone to unload this bit of gossip onto. "Lucid told Harry that he'd run out of good time—that's what he said—and that he'd better come across with the spondulix or there'd be hell to pay."

"So . . . gambling?" I said.

The girl nodded. Then she shrugged, as though she considered it lightly. As though she really didn't care. "Sure, gambling. *Everyone*'s into Lucid for gambling."

"Not me," the blonde piped up.

The dark-haired girl ignored her. "So yeah, gambling, sure. But I think it's more than that. Don't ask what though, 'cause I don't know. It's not like *he* ever tells me anything." She said the last reproachfully, and I was tempted to ask who the he in question might be. The only thing that stopped me was the fear that she'd clam up. And there were still things I wanted to know.

"No kiddin'?" I said instead. "What about Rita?"

I couldn't be sure, but I thought I saw a look of loathing flit over the dark-haired girl's face. "What *about* Rita?"

"Was she here with him?"

"Sure," the girl said, looking at me speculatively. "She always was. Say, how do you figure in?"

I aimed for a look that said embarrassed, or maybe humiliated. "I don't like to say," I said, hoping they'd fill in something unimaginably lurid and not ask me about it.

They did. The blonde girl colored slightly and hid her mouth with her hand. "Oh," she said, with a concerned sound. I realized I'd built a picture so bad, it wasn't even one I had the tools to look at myself.

"You friends with Rita?" I asked. The blonde girl shook her head vehemently, but the dark-haired girl just laughed.

"Friends? C'mon. She's not the type to have friends. You probably figured that."

I shrugged. "So Harrison . . ." I said, trying to bring the conversation back around, but the black-haired girl cut me off.

"Oh, that. You forget that bum, honey. Focus on whatever you got now. Lucid is mad as hell at Harry. And he's not the only one. Harrison Dempsey is a dead man, if you know what I'm saying. Even if he's still alive, he's a dead man walking."

CHAPTER SIXTEEN

WHEN I GOT BACK to the table, I was relieved to see everyone had returned to their seats. And everyone was relieved to
see me.

Dex didn't mince any words. "Where the hell did you get to?"

Mustard looked as though he'd been concerned as well.
Brucie, on the other hand, did not.

"I *told* you guys she was all right. Didn't I say she was all
right?" And then to me: "Where'd you go, doll?"

"The powder room," I said. There were things I needed to
tell Dex, but they would have to keep. I didn't think he'd want
me blabbing about business stuff in front of Mustard and
Brucie.

"That was an awful long powder," Dex huffed. I looked
at him closely, touched to see he really *had* been worried
about me.

"Next time I'll leave an itinerary," I said, maybe only half
in jest. "Or a trail of bread crumbs. Where did *you* go?"

"There are private rooms back there." He indicated the
spot where he'd disappeared behind a door perhaps half an
hour before. "I know some guys, but no one knows anything
about our boy." Brucie looked curious, but Dex didn't fill her
in. "One of Lucid Wilson's boys figures maybe Dempsey blew
town, but I'm not buying it. It seems like he had too much to
lose to run out."

"Now what?" I asked.

"Now nuthin'," Dex replied. "We did what we came to do. I
say we have another drink and then blow this joint."

Brucie looked disappointed, but the plan sat all right with

me. I'd come and seen and experienced, and it was enough. It had been a long day and I was tired. Plus I had information I wanted to give Dex in private, though I didn't know if I'd be able to do that tonight or if it would have to wait for the office the following day.

Brucie wouldn't budge until she had one more dance. My boss surprised me by not only agreeing but obliging. Then he surprised me again, executing the moves of the Balboa lightly and expertly. Dex's and Brucie's torsos touched, but their feet flew so quickly, my eyes could barely follow.

While Dex and Brucie scuffed up the linoleum, Mustard and I sat at the table finishing our drinks.

"You wanna?" Mustard said, tipping his lowball glass toward the dance floor.

I just shrugged. I did but I didn't. And the part of me that really, really did was almost overshadowed by the part who was putting up a show of nonchalance.

When Mustard got to his feet, drained his almost empty glass, and extended a hand and a grin in my direction, I wasn't entirely surprised.

"C'mon, kid," he said, pulling me in the direction of the dancers. "A dress that nice shouldn't oughta be wasted sitting on it."

The canary's voice was belting out something dark and smoky as we approached the dance floor. My feet and my heart took no time at all to find the rhythm.

Like Dex, Mustard was a surprisingly competent dancer, and it wasn't until we were dancing—the dance floor soft on my shoes, the lights and other dancers blurring into a single color—that I realized how much I'd really wanted this moment. To have come to this beautiful new nightclub, sipped a pretty drink while wearing a pretty dress, and put my shoes and the dance floor to good use. It seemed almost like a dream.

I don't know when I felt the transition. They did it so

smoothly that I figured it wasn't the first time they'd changed partners on a dance floor. But suddenly it was Dex who was leading me in a slowed-down version of a varsity drag, and when I looked around, Mustard and Brucie were almost clear across the floor.

"That was quite the magic trick," I laughed up into Dex's face. I had to raise my voice slightly to be heard over the music and the din of the crowd. "What a handoff. You guys have done this a time or two before."

I noticed that the smile he sent back to me reached his eyes. That didn't always happen with Dex. He nodded, agreeing. "Maybe a time or two," he said. "But I'll tell you a secret." He inclined his head over mine, and I leaned up to hear him better as we danced. "With as much history as me and Mustard have, it's good to know how to swap girls on a dance floor without them getting any the wiser."

I laughed outright at that. Both at the idea of the two of them with enough time on their hands to actually perfect that skill, and at me being one of the girls in such a swap.

It had to be asked, though I wasn't sure I wanted to know. "So why'd you swap now?"

"Ah, lookit those two," Dex said, indicating Mustard and Brucie. "Sure it's too soon for her to even think about it, but don't you think the two of them just seem to fit somehow?"

Dex danced us past them, and they didn't even notice. Brucie was laughing at something Mustard had said. For his part, though he danced gracefully enough, Mustard looked slightly red and slightly awkward in the reflection of all that gold lamé.

"Why, Dexter J. Theroux," I said, as we danced away, something in the magic of the night and being on the dance floor in the arms of a handsome man making me feel kittenish, a coquette-in-waiting. "I never figured you for a matchmaker."

Dex laughed at that. "And don't start figuring me for one now. I wouldn't wanna have to change my business cards."

We laughed at that as well. But it put work back into my head. The song had ended, and another started on its heels. Still we danced on. This looked like it might be the only quiet moment I'd get with Dex.

"Dex, I've been wanting to tell you . . . when I was in the powder room earlier . . ."

Dex looked at me askance, as though afraid of what I might tell him. "What goes on in there is between a lady and her compact."

I reclaimed my right hand and whacked him in the shoulder with it. He obliged me by saying, "Ow," though he didn't look particularly hurt. "I was *talking* to someone in there. You wanna hear this or not?"

"If not hearing it involves more violence, then yes, I do."

"It's about Dempsey."

"Dempsey was in the ladies room?"

"Oh, pipe down, mister," I said, half laughing, half exasperated. I'd never seen Dex in a mood so closely approaching jovial. "I was talking to these two young women in there. I didn't get the idea either of them knew Dempsey very well personally, but they certainly knew who he was."

"You were asking people about him in the powder room?"

"I wasn't asking, exactly. It just . . . it just sorta came up."

Dex looked skeptical, but he wanted to hear me out. "Go on," he prompted.

"Well, I was sitting there, and these two girls started talking to me. They thought they knew who I was."

"They were talking to you in the powder room?" Dex didn't sound any less skeptical.

"There are couches and stuff in the ladies', Dex. Like a little lounge. Women go in and sit there. Sometimes we chat."

"Gotcha," he said. "Go on."

"Like I told you, these two thought they knew who I was. Like I looked familiar, you know? That they'd seen me there before. So I let them think that—let them think I'd been in the club before with Harrison Dempsey."

"Continue," Dex said. I could tell he was at least slightly impressed with my fast footwork, and I don't mean on the dance floor.

"They said Harrison and Lucid got into a big to-do at the club last week. This one girl said she didn't feel it was a gambling debt. Or maybe not *just* a gambling debt. But something really significant."

"A gambling debt can be significant," Dex said, with the air of someone who knew.

"Well, either way, they seemed to think it was enough to get him killed. 'Thousands and thousands.' And one of them said she heard Lucid tell Dempsey he'd run out of good time and that he'd better come across with the money or there'd be hell to pay. They didn't say *too* much, Dex. It didn't sound like bragging or anything. In fact, it sounded like they were being careful what they said and who they said it to. But they also said they figured Dempsey would be killed."

"They said that?"

"Not exactly. They said he was a dead man walking."

Dex didn't look skeptical now. At my words, I saw his eyes widen slightly and understanding flood in. "Well, that's it then, isn't it? That's what happened to our boy. Dead man walking. That's close enough for the kind of jazz we play around here."

CHAPTER SEVENTEEN

KNOWING THAT MUSTARD would be bringing me to the club in his car, Dex hadn't bothered to get a ride of his own. He'd taken a taxicab to the hotel. I was feeling happy enough that, for once, I quelled any remark I might have made about him taking the streetcar instead of the more expensive hack.

Mustard had parked on Wilshire across from the hotel and down the block a piece. Brucie and I were both in heels, and Mustard offered to go on ahead and bring the car back, but we argued that the heels weren't that high and the evening was lovely. It was a nice night for a short stroll after the dense smoke and thick noise of the club.

There was a sweetness to the air that night. I'll never forget it. The clarity of the night was heightened by my own sense of well-being. For the first time since my father had died, I felt careless. That is to say, I felt without cares.

Here I was, out on the town. I was wearing a beautiful dress, and my hair had never looked prettier; Brucie had seen to that. I was in the company of two handsome men who cared about me, and a sweet woman who I thought would become a friend. I had just come from the swankest hotel in the city and not been made to feel as though I didn't belong, not even for a second. All of this made me feel on the verge of something fine and good and right. And as I laughed at a joke Mustard had made and as I let Dex take my elbow as I stepped off the curb, I thought, Here, finally, is adulthood. Not so scary as I'd feared.

There was a small park across from the hotel. Nothing

more, really, than a handful of palm trees and some benches. As we moved into it, Dex stopped to clip a cigar, and the rest of us paused to wait for him. Just as our little group hesitated, we heard the sound of a car coming around the side of the hotel too fast, which was not in itself unusual, but the sound of squealing tires brought our heads up.

The next thing I was aware of was Dex on top of me. "Get *down*," he ordered. And then came the sound of a car backfiring, not once but several times. I didn't see sky again until after I'd heard the car squeal away; then Dex was helping me up.

"You OK?" he asked.

"*I'm* OK. But I'm not sure about this dress Brucie let me wear," I said, smoothing down the shimmery ivory while looking around for Brucie.

We all became aware of Brucie's injury in the same instant. Even Brucie herself.

"My god," she said, more wonder in her voice than pain. "I'm bleeding." A bullet had pierced her shoulder and the gold lamé, which she had just a moment to bemoan before the pain started in earnest.

"I'll go get an ambulance," Dex said, but Mustard stopped him.

"Whoever did the shooting was probably gunning for you, Dex." Mustard in action was a soothing presence. There was a sort of unhurried speed about him. The hint of an efficiency I'd yet to see in full force. "Whatever questions you were asking back there must have caused some concern. You three stay here; stay low if you can. I'll run ahead and get the car and bring it back. It's a shoulder wound; we'll be OK. And I'll be faster than an ambulance anyway."

He didn't wait for an answer, but sprinted away, moving his blocky form more quickly than I would have credited.

While we waited, Dex and I did what we could to stanch the blood that leaked from Brucie's shoulder. Dex ripped a sleeve off his white shirt, and we pushed the cloth into the wound. I knelt on the ground beside Brucie, stroking her head with my hand. I didn't know what else to do. I could smell the grass crushed under my knees. It smelled like spring and renewal and promise. It smelled like a lie. It could only have been a few minutes before Mustard screeched up with the car, but it felt like so much longer.

I jumped in the back, and Mustard and Dex carefully placed the injured girl across the seat with her head in my lap. Then we beat it up Wilshire toward the Good Samaritan Hospital, only a short distance away.

Once there, it's possible we might have gotten the usual hospital runaround about paperwork and next of kin, but Mustard and Dex weren't having it. And the admitting nurse seemed to know better than to delay the admittance of a well-dressed girl with a gunshot wound brought in by a couple of mooks who looked as though they may well have a roscoe or two between them. I don't think I've ever seen a hospital staff move more quickly, and I know I'd never seen Dex and Mustard acting mookier.

After the doctors had gotten Brucie sorted out, they decided to keep her in for a day or two. They told us that she'd lost a lot of blood and, in the early stages, would need constant monitoring.

Probably sensing she'd have a fight on her hands if she didn't comply, the nurse let us in to see her. By that time, it was two in the morning. Brucie looked so tiny and vulnerable in the hospital bed, her skin almost paler than the crisp white sheets.

I shot a glance at Mustard and then looked quickly away. There was thunder in his face, and something else. Something so personal it just didn't seem right to look straight at it.

The nurse didn't let us stay long. "All right, you three, out of here now," she said, once we'd seen Brucie. "She needs to rest and that's all she needs. You can come back tomorrow during normal visiting hours. But now let her sleep."

We left reluctantly, but we left. The nurse wasn't taking no for an answer, and in any case, we could see she was right. Brucie needed to rest and recover, and she looked to be in very good hands.

"You take care of her," Mustard admonished the nurse, once we were out of Brucie's room. There was something stern in his face, something that didn't invite conversation. I saw it, but if the nurse did, she gave no sign. She'd probably dealt with tougher nuts in her time.

"Like I said, come back tomorrow. We'll look after her."

There was nothing else we could do, so reluctantly we took our leave, though I, for one, felt confident that Brucie was getting the best care possible. After all, I told myself, I'd come by the hospital the following day and see with my own eyes that she was fine.

As things turned out, I was wrong.

CHAPTER EIGHTEEN

ON THE WAY HOME in the car, Dex was unusually hard on himself. I'd never seen him take himself to task for anything. Not really. But he did so now and it was frightening.

"What was I thinkin'?" he said very seriously. "I'm investigating something and I make a party of it? I know better than that."

Mustard and Dex were in the front seat. I sat in the back alone, for the moment forgotten. I was staring out the window hard and trying not to think about poor Brucie, something that was made all the more difficult by the bloody spot on the backseat I avoided looking at.

The heat had burned off the day, and all that was left was the warm sweetness I'd noticed earlier. Only now the promise I'd felt had fled. The sweetness felt cloying, and sour on my tongue. Funny how a shooting could change your whole perspective.

"Hell, Dex, you don't even know that's what it was about," Mustard said. "You don't know anything."

"Yeah, well, I got an idea, don't I? I go into the club asking questions, and we get shot up on the way out. That doesn't happen every day."

"Is that what you were doing?" Mustard said. "Asking questions? Of Lucid Wilson?"

Dex stared straight ahead and grunted.

"Ker-riste," Mustard said with some heat. "Well, I guess you must have asked the right questions."

"Or the wrong ones," Dex said quietly.

Mustard took his eyes off the road for a moment and looked at Dex closely. It was a while before he spoke again.

"That too," he said finally.

By the time they dropped me off on Bunker Hill, it was almost three o'clock in the morning, and I knew it was possible that Marjorie would already be up. Wednesday was her baking day. She had to get up practically in the middle of the night so that the bread we'd enjoy over the coming week would be ready for table by breakfast.

As much as I loved Marjorie, I hoped not to run into her now. And never mind the fact that I didn't feel like giving explanations. I needed to be in the office in a few hours. I needed to sleep.

I had barely gotten into my room, thankful that I'd managed to come home without alerting anyone, when I heard a soft knock on my door.

"Come in," I called quietly, not surprised when Marjorie popped her head in. She looked half embarrassed to be checking on me and half just plain relieved. And maybe there was another half—though that would be too many—that looked disappointed or angry or some other parental emotion I didn't have a name for.

"Good to see you," she said, the fear and relief in her eyes contradicting her calm tone. The worn cotton housedress told me that my fear had been correct: Marjorie was dressed for baking day. No matter what I would have done, those sharp ears would have heard me if she was already awake.

I didn't stop her as I usually do when she started straightening things here and there in my room. I knew it was a hard habit for her to break. Maybe too hard. And I could see it was a way of working off the excess energy she'd built up worrying about me.

"It's good to be home."

"Mrs. Jergens?"

"In the hospital."

"Oh, dear." Marjorie looked genuinely concerned. "Nothing serious, I hope?"

"Not as serious as it could have been, I guess," I sighed. Then I gave in. I knew she'd get it out of me eventually. Besides, who else would I have to tell? "A gunshot wound."

"A gunshot wound," she repeated. As always, most of Marjorie's thoughts remained unstated, but I could see her eyes run over me, checking my apparent safety as carefully as a mother's hands would have done. "Oh, dear," she said again. "How awful. Was there . . . was there an awful lot of blood?" I followed her glance and saw there was some blood on the dress I was wearing, the lovely ivory dress.

"There was, yes. But we took her to the hospital, and they fixed her all up. I imagine she'll be back here in a day or two."

"Do you think . . ." Marjorie ventured. "Do you think that's a good idea, Miss Katherine? Perhaps she's a dangerous sort."

I smiled through my tiredness. "She might be at that, Marjorie. This situation tonight though wasn't her fault. She wasn't being at all dangerous either. And she *does* seem very nice."

"I'll give you that, miss," Marjorie sniffed. "But I say she'll bear watching." By now my room was fully tidied, and Marjorie stood before me, rubbing her hands together gently. A nervous gesture, I knew. There was more she wanted to say. More she *could* have said, but I knew she wouldn't. Nor was there anything *I* could say to make things entirely right. The fact was, there had been a few minutes there when I was actually in danger. And there was no sense trying to hide that from Marjorie. The blood on my dress told its own story. As much, I knew, as the fear in Marjorie's eyes.

Before she let me get to bed, Marjorie insisted I give her the dress so she could try to soak the bloodstains out of it. "It's a lovely garment," Marjorie sniffed primly. "It'd be a shame to see it ruined." I knew that for Marjorie there was more at stake than the future of a single dress. Washing the blood away—saving the dress—was something she could actually do to make things right. Something, in a way, she could do to save me.

I was too tired to argue, and she was right in any case. Doing the work now would probably save the garment. But with uncharacteristic darkness, I thought if all that had been ruined this evening was a single dress, we would be lucky indeed.

CHAPTER NINETEEN

IN THE MORNING, I was especially glad that Angels Flight is always free on the way down. I wouldn't have liked to spend the nickel, but forced to go down all those stairs on foot, I would have been a danger to myself and others.

There was no sign of Dex at the office. It wasn't a surprise but it was a question. Dex was always late. It made me wonder what he did in the morning when he didn't come in. Did he wander in the park? Do some secret charity work? Or was it possible that every morning he found the idea of another sunny day too difficult to face?

I was having a hard time facing the day myself. I told myself that the single Kir Royale I'd consumed had not gotten me drunk and was not now causing a hangover. Still, I'd felt better, though it likely had more to do with the total four hours of sleep I'd managed to get than any champagne concoction I'd sipped at.

When Dex breezed into the office at around eleven, he looked a lot better than I felt. His shirt was crisp and clean, he had on a new collar, he was shaved within an inch of his life, and his shoes were shined.

"What's with you?" I asked.

"Whadjamean?" he asked, all innocent-like as he perched himself on the corner of my desk in his usual fashion.

"You look . . ." I'd started to tell him he looked normal, then realized this might not be the most politic thing to say. "You look rested, I guess. Or something."

He laughed, a self-conscious sound. "I feel . . . I dunno . . . clearer today than I have for a while, Kitty. It's awful that

Mrs. Jergens was shot; don't get me wrong. But I can't help but think that bullet was intended for me. Not for my shoulder either. When I got home last night I got to thinking about . . . well, about a lot of things. About life and death and how very short it all can be. This morning when I woke up, it just felt good to be alive."

I didn't say anything for a moment. What was there really to say? My usually morose and sodden boss seemed oddly renewed. And I knew I should have been happy, but it was like the earth had shifted beneath my feet. There are certain things—and certain people—that are just meant to be the way they are. You *count* on them being thus. And I hadn't counted on this new development. Rather than pursuing this line, I opted to retreat onto safer ground: the business at hand.

"I've been thinking about those girls, Dex. The ones at the Zebra Room I told you about last night."

"When we were dancing?" he said, his eyes laughing. I looked away. A lighthearted Dex would take some getting used to.

"Right. When we were dancing."

"It all sort of fits, doesn't it? If what those girls said is right, Harrison Dempsey was a marked man," Dex said. "And it doesn't sound like much of a stretch that whoever he owed money to might have wanted to bump him off."

"It's not good business though," I said.

"How so?"

"Well, you don't get paid if you go around icing everyone who owes you money. I mean, do that enough and you end up with no one at all to pay you back."

Dex stroked his chin and stretched out his legs in a way that told me he was thinking. Then he said, "OK, point taken. Still someone chilled him off—"

"*Maybe* chilled him off," I pointed out. "The police didn't find a body, and his wife says he's not missing."

"Well, someone was dead, that much we know. We saw that for ourselves." He thought some more. "So what have we got? A body that may or may not have been Dempsey. A possible attempt on my life that got a friend of Mustard's clipped. A client that doesn't want her money back. What do you figure that adds up to, kiddo? What do you figure our next move should be?"

I looked at him searchingly for a moment, trying to determine where he was going with all of this, because I knew he was drawing me to a path that led someplace.

"We leave it alone?"

He nodded slowly, his pale blue eyes bright.

"Right. We leave it alone."

CHAPTER TWENTY

IN THE EARLY AFTERNOON I ditched out to see Brucie. Dex said it was OK. It was another slow day and we even had a bit of cash, plus he felt kind of responsible for what had happened to her, so he said he didn't mind if I went.

"In fact," he said, before I left, "take these four bits, and buy her a nice mittful of posies from me."

I took a Red Car to the hospital, which was about a forty-five-minute trip. It made me realize at least one of the reasons Dex was so resistant to taking streetcars: with all those stops, it could be slow. Another reason was that you couldn't control who you shared the ride with. At various times between downtown and the hospital, I had to sit next to or near a couple of squalling babies, an old man with the smell of a three-day drunk and seven days unwashed on him, and a woman who coughed so hard, I feared she'd dislodge something vital.

I spent the time trying to read the paper, trying to drown out the coughing and the squalling and the smell of the drunk, and looking for some mention of either gunplay outside a Wilshire hotel or the discovery of an unidentified body with mysterious holes in it the night before. There was nothing about either one.

I arrived at the hospital with an armload of floral material, only to be told that Mrs. Jergens had left the hospital just half an hour before. I was glad, because that meant Brucie had pulled through just fine. But I would have been gladder still if I didn't have another forty-five minutes of streetcar to look forward to before I got back to the office. I thought about going straight home and seeing Brucie for myself, but decided against it. It had been nice of Dex to let me have part of the afternoon off, but, I reasoned, he might have need of me back at the office.

I was right.

It was after three when I got back. I saw that the door to Dex's office was closed, and I heard the mumble of voices—one male, one female. Lila Dempsey. I'd hoped to make it back before she got there, but the streetcar had made that impossible. And I hoped like hell that she'd found Dex in good condition— which seemed like a good bet, all things considered.

I found a dusty water pitcher in the back of one of the filing cabinets—it must have been used by the office's previous occupant, we didn't have a lot of use for water pitchers in our operation—and filled it in the bathroom, plunking the flowers into it unceremoniously and setting it on the edge of my desk. I poked at them a bit, trying to remember the floral arranging I'd learned at school. That felt like a lifetime ago though, and the faint skills I'd gained seemed to have fled. No matter what order I put them in, the flowers came out looking tired and wrong. I kept at it, knowing there was some formula that I'd seen others use. Some secret combination that would bring the whole thing to extravagant life. It eluded me.

I knew that all these flower shenanigans were really in aid of one thing: forcing time to go by more quickly until I found out what Lila Dempsey wanted with Dex.

I thought about rapping on the door and letting Dex know I was back, but once I was done with my flower arranging, I opted instead to "catch up on my typing." Dex might appreciate the gesture.

I was only through about half a sheet of *rat-tat-tat* when Dex came out of his office, pulling the door closed behind him. My typing had alerted him to my presence.

He just looked at me for a moment. I looked back at him.

"So *is* it the wife?" I asked.

"It is."

"What does she want?"

He shot a look over his shoulder at the closed door before answering. "Wants me to find someone." He dropped his voice still lower. "Says he's missing." Dex added this with a dramatic roll of his eyebrows. "And she wants some water."

Of course. The one day the water pitcher was stuffed with flowers, I needed it to serve actual water. "I'll get her some," then, "if I guessed who she wants found, would I be right?"

Dex pointed at me and winked. "You would," he said. "Nice flowers," he added as he headed back into his office.

CHAPTER TWENTY-ONE

I'D EXPECTED some slightly older but no less dramatic version of Rita Heppelwaite, all sizzle, some steak, and lots of makeup and jewelry to go with it. Lila Dempsey couldn't have been more different. If anything, she was slightly younger than Rita—somewhere between twenty-five and a well-preserved thirty—with golden hair and skin so pale you got the feeling that if the sun were illuminating her from behind, you'd see right through her.

She was wearing a crisply cut gray suit of light wool with a cream-colored blouse beneath. The skirt stopped an inch or so below her knees. Below that, her calves were trim and her ankles slender. On another woman, the suit might have looked severe, even masculine. On Lila Dempsey though, it just seemed to enhance a delicate femininity. She looked like a blue blood; there were just no two ways about it.

As I brought the water into Dex's office, I could see that she also looked anxious. There were small bags under her slate gray eyes, and it looked as though she'd been crying. She had Dex's handkerchief in her hand. I was glad to see that it looked like a clean one. She'd threaded the hanky through her fingers nervously, plucking at it occasionally, as though reassuring herself it was still there.

She stopped talking the moment I came in, so I dropped off her water as quickly as I could, then skedaddled under her "thank you" and got back to my desk.

There was no question of eavesdropping this time. Unlike the brace of flatfoots the day before, Lila Dempsey was potentially a paying customer. We got few enough of those that both Dex and I took special care not to mess up when one was around.

When Lila Dempsey left the office, it felt like déjà vu all over again. Only this time, it wasn't Harrison Dempsey's curvaceous mistress who Dex escorted to the door, but his coldly beautiful wife. And like that other time, as soon as the door had closed behind her and we heard her footsteps retreating toward the elevator, Dex came over to my desk and made like he would have plunked himself down on the edge of it, but for the makeshift vase stuffed with flowers that had taken the spot where he usually perched his behind.

"What's with the posies?" he asked.

"You bought 'em," I replied. "Brucie had been released from the hospital by the time I got there."

"Well, that's good," he said. "And high time I bought you flowers anyway. A man oughta do that for his secretary every once in a while."

"Cut the chitchat," I said pointedly. "You know I'm dying to find out what she was doing here. So spill already."

Dex grinned, but didn't keep me in suspense any longer.

"You're gonna like this, kiddo," he began. "She said she heard I was doing work for Dempsey, so she figured she'd bring me some more business."

"Working *for* Dempsey?"

"Right. I could have corrected her, told her I was actually working for her husband's mistress. . . ."

"But I take it you did not?"

"You take it right. But strictly speaking, I did not tell a lie."

"But strictly speaking, you didn't tell the truth either. You ever think about going into politics?"

Dex added a shrug to his smirk.

"So why did she want to bring you more business?"

"She says her husband is missing."

I felt my eyebrows arch.

"That's what *I* thought," Dex said. "But she said he usually checks in every few days when he's out of town."

"I take it he didn't check in?" Dex shook his head, and I went on. "OK, what else?"

"Well, there's not much more, really. She wants me to find her husband."

"Man, this Dempsey is one popular egg."

"Another twenty-five bucks a day. Plus expenses. So listen, get Mustard on the line. I'm gonna need a car for a couple of days. She wants me to go to San Francisco, since that's where Dempsey is supposed to have gone."

"A car?" I asked. "For what?"

"San Francisco," Dex replied, as though I hadn't been paying attention.

"Can't you steam up there? It's a lot quicker to go by sea, for one thing."

"I know that. I told you: she's paying expenses. That's a car, for one. And I'll need to get around once I'm there and . . . never mind, Kitty. I'm not having this conversation again. Just get me a car, OK?"

I sighed but gave in. He's my boss after all. "OK. But do you think you'll find anything there?"

He shook his head. "Absolutely not. But that's what she's hired me to do, and I'm doin' it. I gotta earn my twenty-five a day, right?"

"Plus expenses," I added.

"Plus expenses," he agreed.

CHAPTER TWENTY-TWO

MUSTARD SOUNDED PREOCCUPIED when I got him on the phone. Not like his usual jovial self at all. He didn't even joke with me when I told him I needed to arrange a car for Dex's San Francisco trip. He just made the arrangements and told me he'd have it brought around. He was going to be busy, he told me, and there'd be no one in his office for the rest of the day.

As I hung up, I realized I'd forgotten to ask about Brucie. I was going to call Mustard back, then decided it could wait. I'd see her myself when I got home.

There was something about Brucie that didn't feel right to me. Not about the woman herself—she seemed sweet and lovely—but about her situation. I had the feeling that Mustard and Brucie hadn't been entirely forthcoming about the details of why she needed a place to stay.

I thought back to Mustard's first call about her. Mustard had said he had a friend who was in a jam. But the nature of the jam had never come up, nor had anything beyond her recent widowhood. There was a story there; I was sure of it. I just didn't know if I'd ever hear the details.

Rain was threatening when I hit Spring Street. It was gray, and a wind was kicking up the branches of the big trees that lined the street and the bits of detritus on the roadway. It felt like the world was holding its breath; like this was the beginning of something that would only get bigger.

I hurried toward Angels Flight before the sky opened up. The hat I'd popped onto my head when I'd dressed in the morning had nothing to do with keeping off rain. The big bouquet of flowers I carried wouldn't suffer from getting wet, but it probably wouldn't help them after a hard day of getting dragged around either.

At the station house, I coughed up the five cents for the ride up. What with my trip out to the hospital on top of staying up so late the night before, I was pooped. Plus, I reasoned, Dex had scored another job today; no matter that we both thought it slightly pointless, I'd be getting paid for sure.

Marjorie was in the foyer polishing the dark wood of the hall table as I came through the door. I love the smell of the polish—have loved it since girlhood. There are moments in my upbringing I can't think about without pain, but the smell of Marjorie's beeswax furniture polish brought back everything that had been right about my childhood. When I thought about it, most of the good memories were tied in to Marjorie and the house; very few of them centered on my father, who'd spent those years preoccupied with making money and mourning his dead wife, my mother.

Viewed in a certain way, you could make my father's life a warning sign for your own: be careful what you worry about; life is brief, and fate has a short temper and no sense of humor at all. Boiled down, my father's life had been without purpose, perhaps without use. All those years building something that had failed in the end. All those years mourning someone who mourning could not bring back.

If I were very honest, I would identify the resentment built into those feelings, because during all those years, there I'd been. Starving not for silks or steaks, but for a loving hand on my head, a reassuring word. Until his death, I'd never lacked for the things that money could buy, but in other departments, I was forced to go without.

"Why, those are lovely flowers, Miss Katherine." Marjorie looked up from her polishing as I entered. "Who gave them to you, if I may ask?"

"That'd be something," I said, taking a whiff of the big bouquet and imagining the beau who would give them to me. "But no, they're for Brucie. Is she in her room?"

"You said she was in hospital, miss." Marjorie looked honestly confused.

"She was. Last night. But I went up there today, and they told me she'd been released. I just figured she'd come back here."

Marjorie shook her head.

"I guess . . . I guess I'll just put these in her room then. OK if I grab a vase?"

Brucie's room was unchanged from the day before. The bed unslept in, her trunk and boxes in disarray after our preparations for going to the Zebra Room. That all seemed much longer ago than it actually was.

I left the flowers in a vase on the bureau and, as an afterthought, added a note. "Let me know when you get in," I scratched, "even if it's really late."

I was oddly disappointed at not seeing Brucie. The little bit of contact we'd had made me realize how much I missed having women of my own age in my life. Women to share laughter and secrets. I hadn't had that at all since I'd left school so abruptly two years before.

This thought made me realize something else: seeing my old friends was within my reach. And I had a sudden yearning to see them. Dex was going to San Francisco in the morning. He didn't know it yet, but when he left he'd have a passenger.

CHAPTER TWENTY-THREE

I GOT TO THE OFFICE an hour earlier than usual, a small valise in one hand. It was the sort of case I would have used to spend the weekend at the house of a friend when I was at school. I hadn't used the case for a while.

I'd gotten in early because I wanted to be sure to catch Dex before he left. I just managed it. He looked as though he'd only stopped in at the office to pick up the car and get everything he needed for his trip. When I came in the door, his hat was on his head, and he was doing something with his jacket. It was hard to tell if he was coming or going, but I was betting on the latter.

"Where are you off to?" he asked, a light lift to his eyebrows.

I nodded, extending the valise slightly. "I'm coming with you."

"Coming with me?" he repeated. "Look Kitty, I don't need a driver or a babysitter."

"I know, Dex, but I'm not babysitting this time. And I won't be any trouble at all. But I have oodles of friends in the city, and I haven't seen them for a long time." Dex seemed to hem a bit. And then he hawed, so I pressed on. "It's not like you'll need me in the office while you're gone. And when we get there, you can just drop me off and then pick me up when you're ready to come back to Los Angeles. . . ."

I might have continued in this vein, but Dex held up a warding hand. "All right already," he said. "I get the message. Sure, you can come. Why not? And you're right; it's not like there'll be anything to do at the office. Anyway it's a long drive. A bit of company couldn't hurt anything."

And so we drove. The rain that had threatened the day before had come and gone unseen in the night, and the air felt clean, the usual city dust subdued for the moment by the big street cleaner in the sky. Mustard had secured an almost-new Packard for Dex's trip, and the big car seemed anxious to cover miles, to get us quickly to our destination.

When I attended school in San Francisco, a trip like this by car wouldn't have been possible. You could have done it, but the trip would have taken a long time, winding your way through the variously finished roads that made up California's El Camino Real. It would have been barely thinkable to do the whole drive in less than a couple of days, and all of my trips to and from school had been done either by train or steamship. Now the new highway ran up the coast all the way from the Mexican border almost to Canada. We weren't going that far, so we didn't need all of it, but the parts we *did* need were impressive. If I hadn't already known this was the grandest highway in the country, signs along the way let me know. I believed them too. I'd never seen anything like it.

I started the trip with the best of intentions to keep Dex company, but the Packard just purred up the highway, the whitewalls humming over the pavement, while Lorenz Hart crooned gently about ten-cent dances on the radio. All of these things worked against me, and before very long, I was snoozing away on my side of the deeply upholstered front seat. I didn't wake up until that peaceful rhythm came to an abrupt halt.

"Where are we?" I asked Dex groggily, noting the ocean in front of the angled parking spot and not a lot else in sight.

"The last sign said Bradley," Dex said, "but there doesn't seem to be a whole lot here. C'mon, kiddo. Let's see if we can find some lunch."

I looked around again, and sure enough, a diner sat neatly across the road from the ocean. Incongruous when we entered: orange vinyl banquettes, a jukebox, black-and-white linoleum floor, and a view that would stop a millionaire's heart. It was easy to imagine you could see clear to Japan.

We grabbed a booth with a view of the ocean, though truly most of them had one. We weren't sitting there long before a waitress approached us with tired-looking menus that had each seen more than their share of grease. She was wearing a faded yellow uniform with a skirt just short enough to show us legs so heavily veined that it was easy to imagine that there were no shoes that would provide relief from endless days spent on her pins.

"Travlin' through?" she asked, her eyes never leaving Dex's.

"Does anyone ever say no?" he replied.

She nibbled the end of her pencil as though thinking. "Not so much," she said finally. "At least, not if I don't know their face." She didn't add that she'd like to get to know Dex's face better. She didn't need to. I'd seen him have that effect on women before.

"You have menus there for us darlin'?" he asked amicably. She passed them over, and he asked for coffee, looking at me while he did so.

"Sure. Coffee sounds perfect," I said, and the waitress looked at me as though slightly surprised, as though she were noticing me for the first time.

When the coffee came it was good and black. I tried not to notice the slight chip on the rim of my cup. It wasn't the kind of place where noticing would make any difference.

Dex ordered a Denver omelet, and I opted for a slice of cherry pie. After sitting in the car for hours on end, I wasn't feeling very hungry.

When our food came, Dex hit his omelet solidly, while I picked at my pie. It's not that it wasn't good. It was just fine, in fact. But the events of the last few days were catching up with me, and my brain was tired of thinking about it all. But while Dex cleaned his plate with the last of his toast, I brought it up anyway.

"Brucie never came home," I said, moving a bit of pie from the extreme left of my plate to the extreme right, then using the tines of my fork to squeeze a big chunk of cherry left in the middle.

Dex looked up from his plate tidying. "Whadjamean?"

"You know she paid for a room at my house, right?" Dex nodded. "And Mustard had dropped off all her stuff. But yesterday I went to the hospital to see her, and like I told you, no Brucie. So I figured I'd see her when I got home, but no Brucie there either. And I checked her room before I left this morning—she hadn't been back."

Dex looked concerned while I spoke, but when I'd finished, he said, "Why are you telling me this?"

Why? It was a good and reasonable question. One I didn't have an answer for. "Well, for one, she's injured. But it's more than that. She's something to Mustard. I can see that. You noticed it at the club too, when they were dancing. But Mustard hasn't said what."

"Well, he wouldn't, would he?"

I nodded agreement. He would not. For one thing, Brucie had been a widow for less than a month. For another . . . well, he was Mustard. That seemed reason enough on its own.

"And . . . I don't know. I just . . . I just have a funny feeling about the whole thing. Like there's something the two of them aren't telling me. About Brucie's past, I mean."

Dex looked thoughtful while the waitress refilled our cups with coffee. He didn't speak until after she was gone.

"She was Ned Jergens's wife, right?"

I nodded. "I thought it looked like you recognized her name when Mustard introduced you. Who was Ned Jergens?"

"He was Chummy McGee's right-hand man."

"I keep hearing that," I said. "But it still doesn't mean anything to me."

Dex kinda stretched, as though he were weighing his words before he spoke. "Do you know who Chummy McGee is?" he asked. I shook my head, and Dex continued. "Well, Chummy pretty much has the L.A. waterfront sewn up."

"What does that even mean?"

"Well, the gambling ships off Santa Monica, for starters. You know the ones? Chummy's outfit is responsible for those."

"You mean he owns them?"

"More like he owns the action on them—the gambling action. At least he owns a piece of it. The piece that counts. Then the booze that gets brought in by sea—"

"I guess that would be most of the booze in L.A."

Dex nodded. "Chummy again. The club in Santa Monica—you know the one—on Front Street on the Boardwalk?"

"Sure I do. Club Casa Del Mar?"

"Yeah, that's it. Chummy's turf entirely. A lot of gambling, and whispers of white slaving too."

I could feel my eyes get wide. "Really? I thought it was a private club."

"Well, there's that. But there's more there too. But it's whispers, you know. No one really talks about stuff like that. Not out loud anyway."

"This Chummy sounds like a pretty powerful guy. I guess that means his right-hand man would have been pretty important too."

Dex winked at me. "Now you're getting the picture."

"So I guess what you're *really* telling me is that Brucie Jergens's husband probably didn't die of natural causes."

"I always said you were a quick study, kiddo. But yeah, I'd guess he didn't die of a heart attack."

I stopped and thought for a minute. Something was beginning to make sense. What had she said? *I'm Ned Jergens's widow. Money's nothin' to me.* It wouldn't be, either. From what Dex was saying, it was a fairly safe bet that Ned had died while on the job. If Chummy McGee was half the mobster Dex was describing, he'd make sure Ned's widow was taken care of.

On the other hand, Mustard had indicated that Brucie was in some sort of trouble. What could that have meant? And then it occurred to me. "She needed a place to hide out," I said aloud. "That's what Mustard meant. He was trying to hide her from something. From *someone*. That's why he wanted her at my place; he figured she'd be safe there."

"I dunno, Kitty. That sounds a bit farfetched to me. I mean, if he was trying to stash her, why would he take her to the Zebra Room the other night?"

"I'm not sure," I admitted. Dex had a point. "Maybe he figured she'd be safe in plain sight?"

"Or maybe he was so bamboozled by her, he let what he wanted get in the way of what he knew was right. Though that doesn't sound like Mustard."

I agreed. It did not.

"But what about Mustard?" I asked. "How does he fit into all this?"

"What do you mean?"

"Well, how does he even know Brucie? Or Chummy for that matter?"

"You'd have to ask him that," Dex replied.

"But still," I insisted, "they must have some sort of connection, right? Does Mustard work for Chummy?"

"You get that out of your head, Kitty," Dex said, with more force than I felt my comment had demanded. "Mustard is *not* a gangster, so don't even think that. And certainly . . ." He shot a look over his shoulder as though checking to see who was there. There was no one. It was after the lunch rush, if there even was such a thing in this place. The only other patron was an old man in a threadbare suit eating a piece of apple pie à la mode with obvious enjoyment. Dex dropped his voice and started again. "Certainly never, ever say it."

I ran my finger absently around the lip of my empty coffee cup, contemplating my boss. This was a side of him I hadn't seen before. I didn't think I liked it. Even if he was quite often morose, he was usually confident. The two balanced each other out—Dex's personal yin and yang. This was different. I wondered if it was possible that with the receding of his own darkness, he was also losing the edge that was the only advantage he'd had in a tough game.

The other possibility was that I was overreacting. That Dex's alarm had come from a genuine concern for his old friend. Or maybe even that there was more to Mustard and his underworld ties than I'd ever suspected. Maybe it was a bit of both.

"I didn't say he was a gangster, Dex." He indicated I should lower my voice, and despite the nearly empty restaurant, I did. "I was just thinking, what is it Mustard does, exactly? And how does he always have these connections to everything?"

Dex seemed to think a while before answering. "Like I said before, Kitty, those are questions you'll have to ask Mustard yourself. And not just 'cause I don't want to answer you, but 'cause I think the man himself could best explain it. Let me tell you one thing though: no matter what you may think or even what you may sometimes hear, Mustard is not a gangster. Whatever he does, he does on his own."

"Sometimes with you," I pointed out.

"Sometimes with me," Dex nodded. "But that's different. He helps me out sometimes, but it's nothing to him. Mustard and me . . ." He hesitated. I thought he was searching for words. "We share some things, Kitty. We've been through a lot together."

I nodded. "You've told me a bit."

"Have I?" And then smiling, he said, "I guess I have. You know I don't remember any of what I told you, don't you?"

I thought about mentioning what he'd told me about his wife, Zoë, and asking what had happened to her and to their son. But when I looked into Dex's clear eyes and noted again the new lightness about him, I decided that this was not the time. "I guess I do know that," I said instead, not entirely certain I was telling the truth.

"So if I've told you some of this in the past and you don't want to hear it again, you'll hafta stop me. But like I said, we've been through some stuff together, Mustard and me. Stuff that tests a man. I know that in a tight spot Mustard will cover my back. I reckon he has reason to know the same thing about me. The other things? I'm not sure they're as important. But the part where I know I can count on him, no matter what . . . well, it means a lot."

Dex was being oblique enough that I figured he'd never get around to answering what I'd asked. What he *was* telling me was maybe more significant: that sometimes knowing the inside of a man was as important as—maybe more important than—knowing the outside. Important enough that it even made the other stuff not matter so much.

At least that's what I thought he was telling me. I'd have to think about it for a while, and as things turned out, I had several hours of sitting in a car in front of me without a lot scheduled *besides* thinking.

Dex called for the check and we got back in the car. As we drove, I didn't see the vine-dotted hills of Salinas or the majestic coast off Big Sur. I saw a mud-filled trench, smelled cordite, and heard men dying. And I saw Mustard and Dex back-to-back, bayonets extended, confused and afraid, but knowing the only true thing in the world.

CHAPTER TWENTY-FOUR

WHEN WE GOT TO SAN FRANCISCO, it was raining. Which is no big surprise in itself; it rains there a lot, or so it seems when you're from Los Angeles where rain is more the exception than the rule. And while the rain in my home city may be less frequent, when it *does* happen, it's much more dramatic.

The rain in San Francisco is part of the landscape; it falls upon the steep and pretty streets casually. When it rains in San Francisco, it's easy to feel it will always rain, has always rained. It feels like it's meant to be.

This difference in the rain sums up the difference in the two cities. Los Angeles rain is wild, rugged, and determined. It is infrequent, but when it comes, it beats upon the city like a living thing, as though it intends to stay alive. San Francisco rain is confident. It understands that it has a proper place in the world, in the natural order of the city. It is a part of the fabric of the place, of the life. It lacks the wild edge of Los Angeles rain. It lacks a certain desperation.

So we arrived in San Francisco in early evening, at what appeared to be the height of a cleansing downpour. I gave Dex an address in the 2000 block of Broadway in Pacific Heights. We found it without any trouble, though Dex whistled when he pulled up to the curb. "That's quite the pile," he said as he dropped me off. He was being dramatic, but if anything, it was an understatement. Cleverly Manor was quite the pile indeed. It commanded all of that part of Broadway, and it had a view of the downtown core and the bay from every window at the front of the house.

"That's quite the heap too," he said, pointing at a low-slung two-seater sports car parked at the curb. It was the color of rich cream. "An Auburn Speedster, if I don't miss my guess. I don't think much of the color though . . . makes it look like a woman's car."

"It probably *is* a woman's car, Dex. It's probably Morgana's."

"Nice," he said. He stayed in the Packard with the engine idling, while I walked up the steps and knocked on the door. When the maid who opened the door told me Miss Morgana was at home, I turned around and waved, slightly touched that Dex had insisted on making sure I was all right before he zoomed off into the city.

Morgana Cleverly was delighted to see me, though somewhat surprised. We had been friends since childhood, with much in common including fathers deeply involved in the business of finance. From the looks of things at Morgana's house, however, her father had invested more wisely than had mine. I knew that, in any case, San Francisco investors had overall fared better than those in Los Angeles. For one thing, none of the San Francisco–based banks had gone under, which was more than you could say about those in my home city.

Morgana herself looked polished, well groomed, and expensively turned out. At twenty-three, she looked slightly older than she had when I'd seen her last, but the two extra years suited her. The things that had been kittenish in the girl I'd known had matured, and she stood before me now a sleek and happy cat.

"I would have called," I told her, when she found me, valise in hand, where the maid had left me in the vast foyer. "But so much has changed, Morgana. I . . . I couldn't bring myself to discover what might not be the same here as well."

Morgana's startled expression changed into one more familiar, and she moved to give me a hug. "Come here, you goose," she said, embracing me. "Of course nothing has changed," she said, "and everything has. We're grown-ups now, aren't we?"

I nodded. But I felt as though I'd been a grown-up for a long time.

"I was afraid you'd be away at school."

"Vassar?" she said. "I decided to put that whole thing off for a time. I've been having so much fun here, I couldn't bear to pull myself away. But what would you have done if I wasn't here?" She poked one elegant finger at my valise. "It looks as though you've come to stay."

I smiled at her, embarrassed, but only slightly. "Only one night. Perhaps two. I had the chance to come to the city, and I decided to take it. I hoped to find you at home," I told her, "and I had the feeling I would. Call it intuition. But there were others I could have visited if you weren't here. You were my first choice though."

"I'm so glad, darling. But come, let's not stand here. We'll have tea brought 'round. We've got so much to catch up on."

And we really did. Though we'd once been best friends, circumstances had forced . . . not a rift but a very definite separation. I'd not wanted her to see me as a possible charity case. For her part, she now told me she hadn't known what to say to me when she'd heard what had become of my father. Her family had been fortunate, mine had been destroyed, and she'd felt guilty and unsure. After a while, she said, time had passed, and our lives had become what they were.

A servant had opened the door, but Morgana herself led me down elegant dove-colored hallways to her own beautifully appointed sitting room. You could see at a glance that nothing here had changed in a significant way. The soft-slippered servants remained at their posts. A swimming pool the color of the Mediterranean in summer still dominated the garden, and even on a rainy autumn day, I knew the staff would be keeping it heated and ready, should it please us to use our afternoon in this way.

As inviting as that sounded, on this day we did not swim. Instead we sat in Morgana's private suite, the air cool enough that we could see mist rise off the pool where the warm water met with the cool air. Beyond the pool dropped the city and, beyond that, the bay. This might not have been the most choice spot in San Francisco, but I had a hard time imagining what would be better. I said so aloud, so Morgana set me straight.

"Daddy is building a house at Belvedere. He says that the noise of the city is growing irksome to him."

"Belvedere," I repeated. "Where's that?"

Morgana pointed out into the bay toward an island I'd never noticed before. "You'll think I'm fabricating, Katherine, but it's out there, for heaven's sake. He's acquired thirty acres and the best architect in the city—someone stuffy and British, though I can't think of his name—and they're concocting the most monstrous estate that can be conceived."

"But why, Morgana? Cleverly Manor is perfect." And it was. There was room there for ten families. Perhaps twenty, if they were Irish. And the house was beautiful and modern, having only been completed in the mid-1920s.

"Oh, he has all these wonderful *reasons*, Katherine. And when he tells them to me, they all make perfect sense. But to be perfectly honest, I think he's doing it to keep an eye on me. An *island*. Think of it. I'd be trapped! I'm sure that's what he's thinking."

"You're being silly," I said.

"I'm not! Wait until you see. Belvedere is like the *moon*, Katherine. No restaurants, no stores. Just all these stately *homes*. Tea on Sundays, dinners on Saturdays. Reading, embroidery, piano."

I laughed, and after a heartbeat or two, she laughed along.

"You're being silly, Morgana. You know you are. If, as you

say, he's only just acquired the land and hired an architect, it will be years before he's finished the house. Years and years and *years*. Probably way beyond the time you'll still be living at home. You'll be off and married and have your hands full with your own small Morganas by the time he's done with it. Darling, he's not planning to trap you; he can't be. He's planning for when you're *gone.*"

I felt the most loving twinge of envy then; I can't think how else to explain it. Everything in Morgana's world seemed to have gone on unaltered. Oh, time had continued to pass; she was older and had the concerns of a young woman instead of a girl. But her home was intact, her parents stood over her shoulder and watched out for her, and the dove grey walls continued to shelter her, just as they had when we were children.

My life was very different, as were my concerns. I would not have wished less for Morgana, and I certainly wouldn't have wished her ill or evil, but I wouldn't have been human had I not wondered why her life should have continued as planned, while mine . . . well, mine seemed to career on unexpected course after course. I had uncertainty and she had safety. I wondered what that felt like.

Over tea, she told me about a half year spent in Europe with two of our mutual friends, along with a couple of aunts to chaperone. I found that I'd gotten used to tableware that was more rough and ready. It was strange to use elegant china again. I sat in a slipper chair near the window, where I could see the last of the rain and a newly rising fog while carefully balancing my cup in my hands. The porcelain was almost translucent and as delicate as the wing of a baby bird.

Morgana had started the telling cautiously. I was aware of her intelligent eyes on mine when she began talking about her trip to Europe. I suppose she was afraid that I might be

hurt by tales of her time abroad, since in my reduced circumstances trips to Europe were completely out of the question.
I was glad when she relaxed after a while. After all, my mis-
fortune had nothing to do with her. I was glad to see that not
everyone was in the same boat. It would have been a very full
vessel.

"Europe is somehow less jolly now, Katherine," she said, as
she finished her story. "Maybe it's the Depression touching
things there as well? I don't know. But there's a shadow now; I
can't describe it. I didn't enjoy this trip as much as our last."

That had been the summer of our eighteenth year. Morgana's parents had called it our proper and modern coming-
out. My father had just grunted and signed the necessary
checks.

"But listen to me," Morgana said, after a while. "I've been
going on about everything here. Tell me what you've been doing with yourself. Tell me about your life."

Hesitatingly at first, I did as she asked. I told her about Dex
and Mustard and my job. Almost from the beginning of the
telling, I could see Morgana was fascinated. I knew that, from
where she sat, I was describing an inconceivable life, more foreign to her than any she'd seen in Italy or France.

And not just foreign. As I spoke, I saw a growing admiration light her face. I didn't understand at first. And then I did.
The things Morgana had were wonderful, but she'd not done
anything to cause them to be. My life was uncertain. There
were elements of it I could never hope to control. But it was
mine. I didn't usually think of it this way, but I realized then
that, for better or worse, I had a hand in shaping my life, creating my future.

I thought about the boarding house my home had become.
I thought about the office. About not always having enough
money to take Angels Flight home when, in another time, I
would have had a car and driver or perhaps, as Morgana did,

my own little car. I thought about Dex and Mustard, and oddly enough, I thought about Brucie.

So much had changed. In a way I was surprised when I realized I wasn't jealous of Morgana and her life. And I realized that somewhere along the way I'd begun to make my own.

CHAPTER TWENTY-FIVE

AFTER WE'D SPENT A FEW HOURS catching up, Morgana insisted on ringing up a bunch of our old friends and organizing a night on the town. It wasn't as easy as it would have been a couple of years before, Morgana explained between calls, because several of the girls had gotten married.

"And that's all right," Morgana said, "that's going to happen. But Cecily Watson? Well, Cecily Marksham now. She won't be coming." Morgana pantomimed a protrusion from her own slender tummy. "She's due in December."

"Cecily a mother?" The thought shook me slightly. "Who did she marry?"

"No one you'd know," Morgana said. "Albert Marksham, of the Humboldt Markshams? See, I didn't think you'd have reason to know him. He's nice enough, I suppose. He seems to be, at any rate. But he's a bit dour for someone so young. Old before his time. He'd not have been my choice."

I laughed at that. "Oh, Morgana! If you and Cecily were now making the same choices, I *would* be concerned."

And so it went throughout the remainder of the early evening. Morgana on the phone, seeing who among our old friends she could round up in my honor and, between calls, gossiping with cheerful abandon about how all of our lives had turned out.

I'd not brought any evening wear with me. Honestly, I had no evening wear beyond what Brucie had given me, but it didn't feel necessary to point this out. Morgana, of course, had a closet groaning with things. She was slightly more filled out than I was, but that wasn't a problem. As I'd done with Brucie's dress on the night of my visit to the Zebra Room, I just wore something Morgana hadn't worn for two years. It fit me perfectly.

Morgana drove us to the Embarcadero in the cream-colored Auburn Speedster that Dex had admired so much. We walked arm in arm and enjoyed losing ourselves in the bustling throng. Street vendors plied their wares, but mostly the foot traffic looked busy, like they all had places to go, the terminus being the Ferry Building that loomed over the waterfront and the watercraft that would take them to various destinations within sight of its piercing tower.

"See," Morgana said, as we crossed the footbridge from Market Street, "this is what Father would have me become: a tourist in my own city, bound by ferries and schedules."

She sounded so put upon that I laughed again. "You've nothing to fear, my angel," I told her. "I tell you, he schemes for himself, not for you."

Afterward we clambered back into Morgana's little car and drove farther on Market Street. She stopped in front of a club and let a valet take her car. The club appeared far more sophisticated than I would have expected from her. I chided myself on this; it was time for me to upgrade my expectations of her. I was thinking of Morgana as I'd known her in our girlhood. She was a woman now.

If I didn't know that before we walked into the club, I did moments after, when every male head in the place swiveled to look at us, and by us I'm quite sure I mean her. I forced myself to look at Morgana again, without the shadings of childhood. What I saw surprised me. Once through the sleek glass and metal doors, she moved like a fish who'd been dropped back into her tank—with confidence and assurance and as though she belonged there.

For my part, I felt a bit like a fish too—one that was out of water. Given the choice, I probably would have picked some place that served tea to meet up with our old girlfriends. Or maybe fancy coffee if we were feeling daring. Clearly, Morgana had other ideas.

"There's a blind pig on Fifth Street that I go to sometimes," she told me. "But this place is one of my favorites. And with the girls coming and it all being in honor of you, I thought something a little more upscale was called for."

She was right. I was not so prudish that I would have totally discounted the idea of a blind pig, but I'd never been to an illegal drinking parlor of that stripe and nature, and I didn't think tonight would be a good time for me to start.

"There are roulette tables in the back room." She indicated an unmarked door deep across the club's chromium and black vinyl interior. The club looked modern, expensive, and entirely vulgar. I was guessing that was the point.

"I like to play sometimes," she told me, as though admitting a secret. "Not tonight though. Tonight we'll all just catch up."

"Miss Cleverly!" the maitre d' gushed, when he caught sight of Morgana. He was so pleased to see her that his mustache quivered faintly. Something about those quivering whiskers put me in mind of a squirrel looking at an acorn. "So delighted to see you again. Your usual table?"

I raised an eyebrow. If Morgana came here often enough to have a table that was usual, she came here a lot.

"Not tonight, Zack. I've got some friends coming. Old friends from school." She indicated me, and Zack inclined his head at me politely. "So maybe somewhere quiet where we can chat. Not *too* quiet though, Zack. You know I like to see what's going on."

"Very well, Miss Morgana," Zack said. "I have just the thing."

He led us to a raised banquette, not far from the door that led to the gaming room. I had the feeling that giving us this table was as much for his benefit as it was for ours: it probably wouldn't hurt an establishment like this to fill a very visible table with young women.

"It's perfect," Morgana said, taking her seat in a rustle of silk. "And bring me a sling, wouldja Zack?"

I was pleased that from my vast experience with night-clubs—having been to the Zebra Room a total of one time—I was able to order a grown-up drink with confidence.

"Kir Royale, please."

Our friends began arriving in short order. Oddly, I found them all vastly changed and completely the same. This one grown more stout, that one more plain. This one was a duck-ling who had become a swan. All had genteel backgrounds, but our surroundings and the times we lived in had made us seem common, at least in this venue. We spoke that way. We drank that way. We laughed without covering our mouths, and we ate whatever we liked with abandon. Mrs. Beeson would have been mortified. We had a wonderful time.

Deep in the evening—and all of us filled with drink and food and fun—a harried woman entered the club, her general air of distress catching my eye right in the middle of one of Gladys Carmichael's most engaging stories.

The harried woman was so out of context for me that at first I couldn't place her. And then I did: Rita Heppelwaite. What had thrown me off was not only that she was in San Francisco, but also her mien. I had not before seen her when she didn't look voluptuous and ready for something warm and exciting. Tonight she didn't appear to be either of those things. In fact, she looked off-kilter and distraught.

I nodded at appropriate moments as Gladys continued her story—something about the first time her beau had met her grandmother. It hadn't gone well. Beyond that, I couldn't have said—I was watching Rita Heppelwaite make her way across the crowded club. It looked to me like she was searching for someone. Fruitlessly, because she just kept on searching. When finally she came to the door at the back of the club that

Morgana had pointed out to me earlier, Rita took one last furtive look around, then disappeared through it.

"Excuse me," I said, rising. I didn't realize I'd interrupted poor Gladys until I noticed everyone looking at me oddly. "I'm sorry, darling," I said, patting her hand, remembering as I did so that none of us had ever listened very deeply to Gladys's droning stories. "I need . . . that is . . . I'll be right back," I said, and I rose and left the table without giving anyone a chance to reply.

The room was crowded and it took me some time to make my way to the door. Before I did though, I noticed Morgana behind me.

"What are you up to?" she asked.

I smiled, feeling suddenly seventeen again and on some silly adventure that would land both of us in dutch with Mrs. Beeson.

"I'm not sure," I replied. "That is, I saw a woman come through the club and go into the gaming room. A woman I know from Los Angeles. She's one of my boss's clients—or she was—and I don't know, Morgana. It just seemed odd, and I wanted to see where she was going."

"You're funny," Morgana said without rancor, even while she got us moving again. "You've turned into quite the little detective yourself, haven't you? Well, you're not going without me. You'd not get into the gaming room without me anyhow. They don't let just anyone in, you know. It's a secret. Come on." With that she pulled me behind her until we reached the door.

Once inside I could see that she was right. I'd never have gotten in by myself. A man slouched near the door, never taking his eyes from it. He was in his mid-thirties, with sparse hair and a good suit. I would have been more likely to take him for a doctor or a lawyer with bad posture than a house peeper.

When he saw Morgana, he nodded to her respectfully. "Evening, Miss Cleverly." Judging from this, I gathered she was a good customer back here. I found myself only slightly shocked at the realization.

"Evening, Silk. This is my friend, Miss Katherine Pangborn. I was just showing her around."

Another polite nod, this one in my direction. "Go ahead, Miss Cleverly. Just let me know if you need anything." Silk might have looked like a doctor, but he didn't sound like one. He sounded like he was in the right job.

"Thanks," she said, as she moved me more deeply into the room. "I'll do that."

I was so agog at my surroundings that at first I forgot all about Rita Heppelwaite. Where the front of the club had been deeply modern, back here was a sea of green baize and smoke. The patrons were predominantly male; the women that were there were mostly scantily clad, showing plenty of cleavage and carrying drinks or hawking cigarettes. When I remembered to look for her, I realized Rita should be easy to spot. But she wasn't there.

I turned to Morgana, shaking my head. "I'm sure I saw her come in here."

Morgana spread her hands in a universal—if dramatic— gesture. "We'll ask Silk," she said, leading me back to the entrance.

"Miss Pangborn thought she saw someone come in here. Someone she thinks she knows." I was glad Morgana hadn't said it was a friend. Clearly, for Rita to get in, Silk must have known her. And she wasn't any kind of friend of mine.

"Uh-huh," Silk said.

"But we can't see her now. Is there another way out?"

"Sure," he said, pointing to a door in the back wall neither of us had noticed before. A potted palm stood between the door and the room, not hiding it exactly, but blending it into the decor. He grinned. "Place like this has to have a back way out."

"Where does it lead?" Morgana asked.

"Back alley. Dead end one way. Boynton Court the other. Couple of buildings with fire escapes either way offer other options. But listen, you said 'her.' It was a dame?"

"That's right," I said. "Quite a beautiful one. Dark red hair. Lovely figure . . ."

"Sure. I know her, all right. That's Rita Mayhew. And I know that's the twist you were lookin' for, 'cause she was in here for just a few minutes. Then I saw her take the air." He pointed again at the door. "It didn't look like she was coming back here either. Where you know her from, miss? She's not in your league at all."

"Los Angeles," I said. "And what league is she in?"

"Well, she's not the roulette player you are, Miss Cleverly. But then she's missing something you got. Something she won't ever have."

"What's that?" Morgana asked.

"Well, don't take this the wrong way," Silk said, looking abashed. "But you can afford to lose. It gives you an edge. Her type—" he hooked a thumb at the door "—her type never can. Fact, she's in to Hopscotch for five large."

"Five large," I repeated. Five thousand dollars seemed an impossible amount of money to me. A lifetime's worth of trips on Angels Flight. A trip to Europe. A car. A new stove. More.

Morgana didn't bat an eye. "That's a lot of change," she said.

"You're not just whistling 'Dixie,'" Silk nodded. "That's why I let her in here tonight. Figured she musta come through with Hopscotch's dough. Else why would she even be in town? She knows she's gonna get zotzed if she doesn't pay up." He described a gun with his left hand, indicated pulling a trigger. *Zotzed*. I shuddered.

"Would that really happen?" I asked. "Would she really get . . . zotzed?"

Another shrug from Silk. "You didn't hear it from me."

Somehow this apathetic denial was more frightening than anything he'd said before.

Heading back to our table, I saw the back of a man's head. It looked familiar. All of my old friends were looking at him, and each face held a look of sheer horror.

CHAPTER TWENTY-SIX

"ONCE A WEEK, like clockwork, this guy went to his barber for a haircut and a shave. One day he goes in to get his ears lowered and his chin scraped and notices there's a different barber. Doesn't think anything of it. Sits down in the chair, starts talking baseball, the weather, the price of biscuits, who knows? Next thing you know, *fffft*." Dex sliced his index finger across his own throat. "Straight razor. They left him in the chair in front of the big picture window as a sign."

"What kind of sign?" Gladys asked shakily. Our other friends were just as mesmerized, their faces never leaving Dex's. And he does so love an audience.

"The kind of sign that says: This man messed with the wrong people." Dex shrugged his shoulders, as though acknowledging another element of the universe's great inevitable. "There you are, kid," he said, noticing me. "I was startin' to get worried."

Though he'd been putting on a show for my friends, I could see something was different about him tonight. Something that had been absent when he'd dropped me off earlier in the day. And then I realized that the brightness he'd worn since his near escape the night of Brucie's shooting was gone. He looked like the old Dex again. I'd barely gotten to know sunny Dex, and I missed him already.

"Dex, what are you doing here?"

"Your boss has been regaling us with tales from the underbelly of Los Angeles," Susan Hammond said with a delicate shudder. "I didn't realize your life had taken such a dangerous turn."

"How did you find me?" I said to Dex.

"I'm a detective, remember?" he said, smiling.

Morgana snorted. "I'll bet Smith told him, is what. Or he flattered one of the house girls."

"You were right the first time," he said, extending his hand to Morgana. "Your houseman told me. How do you do? I'm Dexter J. Theroux."

"I figured that much," Morgana fairly purred. "And I'm—"

"I know who you are," Dex interrupted, keeping her hand in his just a beat too long. "The girls here told me who Kitty was with."

"Kitty!" Edwina Bryson twittered. "That's funny. I never would have thought of you as a Kitty, Katherine."

I didn't like the way this was going. Not any of it. "What are you doing here?" I asked again.

Dex was suddenly more serious. "We've gotta go" was all he said.

"What? Now?" I asked. "But it's almost midnight. Where are we going?"

The other girls had fallen silent, watching the exchange between Dex and me with rapt expressions. "You're on a case," Morgana breathed. "You didn't tell me you were on a case, *Kitty*."

"I'm not. It's almost midnight," I said again. "And don't call me Kitty."

"Why?" Morgana pouted prettily. "*He* does."

"I can't make him stop," I said.

"We gotta go," Dex said again.

"Oh, for heaven's *sake*," I said, exasperated now. "All right. But will you at least tell me where we're going?"

Dex shook his head. "Not here."

The girls were all watching this exchange closely. I could see that they'd suddenly cast me in a role from a detective novel, something shoddy and forbidden, where there's a woman on the cover doing a lot of heavy breathing. If I'd been in a lighter mood, I would have laughed, seeing my exchange with Dex through their eyes. Here I was—Katherine Pangborn from school—in a nightclub in San Francisco sought out by a darkly handsome man with a dangerous demeanor. A man who told stories threaded with violence and who was now urging me into the night with him. I saw admiration in their faces. And unexpectedly, I saw some envy there as well. I could have told them about how I often didn't have the nickel I needed to take Angels Flight, but I did not. I didn't mind them thinking I was in the middle of an adventure. And anyway I presently had my hands full with Dex.

"Fine," I said to him, "we'll go, if it's so all-fired important. But when will we be back?"

I was dismayed when he shook his head. "We're not coming back. We're heading straight back to L.A."

"But my things . . ." I started to tell him that I had to get my valise from Morgana's house, but he intercepted me.

"Already in the car."

"And my dress . . ." I indicated the evening dress I wore.

"You can keep it, Katherine." I started to protest, but Morgana's eyes beat me down. It wasn't charity, the look said. It *was* too small, though she wouldn't have liked to say that in public.

Defeated, I slumped back in my seat, taking a final sip of my Kir Royale before saying good-bye to my friends. Short as the visit had been, it had been wonderful to see them. We all made promises to keep in touch, which none of us probably meant even while we said the words. Envy or no, our lives had gone in very different directions.

Dex and I had a few minutes to wait for the attendant to bring the car. "I was having a really good time, Dex," I said, as we stood at the curb. And even while I said it, I hated how plaintive my voice sounded.

"I know you were, kid. I could see that. They're nice girls

too. They care about you. You'll come back sometime. See
them."

"Will I?" I asked.

"Sure you will, kid. Sure you will. You'll do whatever you
like, you'll see."

It wasn't until we were under power that I asked Dex what
had been so all-fired important that he needed to roust me out
of my perfectly fun evening.

He looked over at me with a smirk, though the smirk held
a shadow of something more. "We're going to see a dead
guy, Kitty."

CHAPTER TWENTY-SEVEN

WHILE WE DROVE, Dex told me that he'd followed Dempsey's trail around the city. It had grown cold after a while, but then one of his police sources told him that Dempsey's body had been found in the bay that very afternoon, fished up by a workboat. There hadn't been a lot of detective work in *that*, Dex explained: the man's wallet was still in the breast pocket of his suit jacket, making it easy enough to identify him, as long as you could read.

"The stiff still had his driver's license on him," Dex explained as he drove. "Presumably the same one I looked at the other night."

"OK, wait," I said, holding up a hand. "A couple of things here aren't sitting well with me."

"Only a couple?" This time Dex's grin was unimpeded by anything besides good humor.

"Well . . . in the first place, it's after midnight. Just where do you think you're going to see a dead guy at this time of night?"

"An old army buddy of mine works in the morgue here. He said if I wanted to see the body, he'd only be able to get me in after midnight."

"So you're not supposed to be there?"

"Not really," he said, parking the car on what seemed to be a completely deserted street.

"What do you need me for?"

"Well, you were there, kiddo. You found him. I figured two sets of eyes were better than one." Dex had started to get out of the car. I followed him.

"But then what's the hurry to get back to Los Angeles, Dex?" I said, while I scurried to keep up with him. "Couldn't we just stay in town and then travel back tomorrow?"

"We could," he said, not slowing his pace while he nodded. "But we're not. If this is the stiff we saw in the house on Lafayette Square—if this is Dempsey—then our business here is done. I'd just as soon get home."

I fumed a little while I continued to struggle to match Dex's long strides. Sure, I'd been having fun and had been looking forward to spending the night at Morgana's and catching up some more, but this wasn't my junket, after all. I'd bummed the ride from Dex. That meant he got to call the shots. He didn't tell me I could like it or lump it, but I got the general idea.

I was so engrossed in these and other faintly mutinous thoughts that at first I scarcely noticed our surroundings. What brought me out of it was a smell, antiseptic yet slightly sweet, as though the sweet part were an additive used to cover something deeper.

The building was long and low; the corridor we tracked down, dimly lit. Badly lit, really. It made me think the lights had been added long after the building's construction; the morgue had probably been here since before the city got electricity.

The sounds of our footfalls echoed slightly off the concrete floors, polished by a million feet, a hundred thousand gurneys, the brushstrokes of thousands of sweepers.

Dex ignored several doors with vaguely medical-sounding names until we came to one marked Josiah Elway, M.D., Assistant Medical Examiner. Dex rapped on the door, once and sharply, before letting himself in.

The face of the man who sat behind the desk moved quickly from surprise to genuine pleasure. He seemed to me to be painfully thin, made to appear even more so by the faintest whisper of the mustache that marched under his nose.

"Dex, old dog," he said, clapping him on the back. "You *are* a sight for sore eyes." I was surprised at the clipped sound of his voice. He had a way of speaking that was similar to Dex's. Judging by the way he pronounced certain words, he and Dex might have come from the same small Ontario town.

"*Doctor* Elway," Dex said carefully. "Huh! They'll give anyone that title these days, won't they?"

"Just about," Elway said, indicating we should sit. "Can I buy you a drink?" he asked, sliding open a desk drawer and pulling out a bottle of something amber—bourbon or scotch or Irish or rye—I could never tell the difference if I didn't see a label, and this bottle didn't have one.

"I wouldn't say no, but Kitty here will likely pass. She doesn't much care for the stuff." Dex introduced me then, if slightly belatedly, and the two of them settled in for a chin-wag that made me seethe all the more at having to leave *my* friends so I could come here and listen to Dex with *his*.

I let them reminisce and tiffle for about fifteen minutes. To hear their stories, you would have thought that the war had been a jolly undertaking indeed. They had apparently had *peerless* fun in the trenches and almost had a party avoiding mustard gas. And too many of their sentences started with things like "Remember that Cagey Watson from Swift Current? What a guy! Poor kid had never been off the Prairies. France wasn't ready for him."

Thinking back to what Dex had told me about what he'd seen in France, it was likely that this banter masked deeper feelings about the experiences the two men had shared. Shared and survived. Under different circumstances, I would have had more patience for it all. As it was, in that quarter hour I could feel the temperature of my blood slip ever upward until I knew I had to either say something or risk bursting something vital inside my head. Should that happen, I thought darkly, at least I was in the right place.

"Dex," I said, more tentatively than I felt, "it's getting late. . . ."

"Late?" he boomed. "Hell, it's early. It's first thing in the morning." Both men guffawed heartily at this small joke, but I wasn't having any of it. Not when I could already hear the slight thickening of Dex's voice.

"Please, Dex. You said you wanted to drive back to Los Angeles tonight. If we don't get going soon . . ."

"All right, all right," he said, putting up his hands as though to ward off my words. "We'll get going. But Josiah's just poured us fresh drinks, so . . . we'll finish those and then . . ."

Another fifteen minutes and what seemed to me to be innumerable war stories later, Dr. Elway led us to the crypt. Outside the double doors I hesitated.

"What's wrong, kiddo?" Dex asked, when he saw me stop. "Your first time, huh?"

I just looked at him. He knew the answer.

"Well, I won't soft-soap it. It may not be pretty." He shot a glance at the doctor, who shook his head no. It wasn't going to be pretty at all. "But it'll be over soon, and then we'll head back to L.A. No bad dreams, 'cause we've got a lot of miles to cover before we sleep. OK?"

I nodded and bit my lip. Oddly, as we moved into the crypt, the thing that pushed into my head was the face of Mrs. Beeson. All of the work she'd done, preparing her charges for the "journey of life" she was always going on about. And none of her preparation had been about this or anything like it.

Either side of the long room was lined with highly polished metal drawer units that reminded me of giant filing cabinets. The far wall looked as though it might have held windows, but these were blocked over with dark curtains, and I couldn't tell if the windows were blocked to keep out the eyes of gawkers or the light.

Dr. Elway led us to a shrouded form on a gurney.

"I knew you were coming," he said, "so I left him out."

Elway moved as though to pull back the sheet, but Dex stopped him. "Wait a second, Jos." And then to me: "You ready, kiddo?"

I bit my lip and nodded my head. I was as ready as I was going to be.

But when Dr. Elway pulled the sheet away, I discovered I was wrong.

The body we'd seen in the bathtub had looked decidedly human. As though, but for the mortal wound, Harrison Dempsey could have just gotten up and walked away. He'd looked lifelike. Rather, he'd looked close to life, if not in it.

What was left of the body we'd seen at Lafayette Square was not like that. For one thing, the face and most of the extremities were gone. For another, what *was* there was the dark purple of a bad bruise. All of it. And the smell . . . the smell was beyond description. I'd recognize it if I encountered it again though. It was the odor of death.

"How'd that happen?" Dex asked gruffly.

"Well, they found him in the bay. So it was most probably sharks."

Sharks! I looked at the body again, and I could see it: it looked as though some creature—maybe several—had nibbled on him and found that he wasn't as tasty as had been hoped.

This thought brought the nausea that had been lurking just below the surface. Mortified, I turned away from the table, spied a bucket nearby, and barely made it there in time to heave what was left of my two Kir Royales into it.

"You all right, kid?" Dex was there with a hand on my back, pushing a clean handkerchief at me while politely averting his eyes.

"Thanks," I mumbled, taking it. Then I added, "Sorry."

"It's OK. It's always rough the first time, eh, Jos?"

"Rough. Yes. It's true," he said encouragingly, from across the room. "One forgets, doesn't one?"

"That's probably why that bucket was right there," Dex pointed out, with a forced cheerfulness.

"I'm OK now," I said, forcing myself back toward the body. "Just ignore . . . never mind. Where were we?" I pushed the soiled handkerchief in my purse so I could return it to Dex in its original condition. "Yes . . . sharks . . ."

The corpse had no face. His right hand was gone, as were parts of his left arm, though the hand itself was still there. But even though the body had spent some time in the drink, I recognized the rich, shiny finish of the man's suit and the pattern of his tie. There was no doubt that this was the guy we'd seen in the bathroom of the house on Lafayette Square.

"It's the same guy, isn't it, Dex?" I said quietly.

"Sure looks that way, kid."

"But that doesn't make any sense," I said. Dex's look stopped me from saying anything more. The doctor may be an old friend, but it was clear Dex didn't want me going over the case in front of him.

"You have a time of death, Jos?" Dex asked the other man.

The doctor looked thoughtful. "It's hard to say exactly, Dex. The cold water slows decomposition on the one hand, and as you can see, sea creatures can speed things up on the other. But educated guess? I'd say two days. Maybe three."

"Cause of death?"

"Well, that's easy, isn't it? Even with the corpse in this condition." He indicated the place in the fabric of the suit where the bullet had ripped through. Then he pushed aside the unbuttoned shirt and gave us a look at the spot in the corpse's chest where the bullet had gone in. Then to my horror, he said, "Give me a hand here, would you, Dex?" The two of them flipped the corpse face-down. "See," he said, pulling the shirt aside and pointing to a spot on the dead man's back. "Exit wound. Clean as anything. Fairly large caliber, I'd say."

"The bullet went right through him?" I asked, surprised.

"Sure," the doctor said. "It's not uncommon. You see it with big bullets, especially at close range."

"So this was close range?"

"Again, the time he spent in the water and the damage the sharks did make it more difficult than it would be if someone had brought him in here fresh." I cringed at his choice of words. "But, yeah, based on what we've got here, I'd say no more than ten feet. Maybe less, like eight or even six."

There wasn't a lot more that this particular corpse could tell us. Before we left though, I asked if we could take fingerprints from the hand he had left.

"Why, Kitty?" Dex asked. "We know who he is. It's not like he had a police record or anything. There won't be anything to find."

"I dunno, Dex. It feels like the right thing."

"Women's intuition?" Dex smirked.

"Sure," I said, humoring him. "Call it that. But can we do it?"

Dex looked at Josiah, who shrugged. "Why not?" he said.

I left them to it. I couldn't even watch. A girl has to have limits, has to know where they are. I didn't have any of my lunch left to lose.

CHAPTER TWENTY-EIGHT

"I'M CONFUSED," I said to Dex as we blazed southward into the night. I was driving, for the moment. I'd seen how much of the amber liquid Dex had consumed while he was wagging chins with his pal. I insisted, and Dex finally gave in, but he told me he'd take over if I got tired.

"What are you confused about?"

I thought for a moment before answering. "Well, everything really. We find a dead body. Fine." It hadn't been fine, but there were degrees of everything. "Then witnesses said he was alive. And now he's dead again."

"And there's no question about the man's identity," Dex said. "His wallet was still in his pocket. His I.D. said who he was, plain as day."

"Right," I agreed. "So what happened?"

Dex shrugged. "Beats me. But ours is not to reason why—"

"Don't quote Tennyson on me, Dex. It's too damn early in the morning."

Dex grinned at me sleepily. "It's funny when you curse."

"Another thing I was wondering," I said, ignoring him. "Your pal, the doctor, back in Frisco?"

"What of him?"

"Well, you seemed a little cagey around him."

"I did?" Dex sounded genuinely surprised.

"You did," I said, nodding. "Back in the . . . in the crypt. I got the distinct impression you didn't want me to say anything in front of him."

"Oh, that," he said. "Sure. That was because I didn't want you to say anything in front of him."

I looked at Dex to see if he was teasing me. And he was, but only just.

"See, it wasn't about my friend, kiddo. Just anyone. You and I know things no one else knows. When you think about it, a lot of things. Like only you and I seem to have seen the dead man in the tub. Next thing you know, everyone says he's right as rain and visiting in San Francisco."

"And now he's dead again," I supplied.

"Right. And that he owed money to some pretty serious muscle in Los Angeles. People knew *that*."

"And that someone shot at you outside the Town House the other night. That's probably related. Because you were asking questions, right?"

"Right. But it's not just knowing one thing, Kitty. It's knowing all the individual things, then putting them together. So now Dempsey is dead, and it looks like our case is closed again. But you still hold on to the pieces. In case knowing them later is a good thing."

I wasn't quite sure I followed exactly, but it did remind me of something else.

"I've got another piece, Dex. Last night, at the club with the girls, I'm pretty sure I saw Rita Heppelwaite."

Dex suddenly looked interested.

"Why didn't you tell me before?"

"I forgot, more or less. What with you coming in and rousting me out of there." I told him about going into the back room with Morgana, about what we'd seen then, and—more importantly—what we hadn't seen.

"The gunsel at the door knew her. But he knew her as Rita Mayhew, which kinda got me. Why would she have a different name?"

Dex looked thoughtful. In the dim light of the car's interior, I could see the lines on his face deepen while he considered my words.

"Lots of reasons," he said finally. "Most of them to do with not wanting to leave too strong a trail. But which is the real name? That might be an important thing to know. Which is the trail she's trying to cover up? Ah, well, it doesn't matter now, does it? Not to us anyway."

It was my turn to contemplate quietly. While I did so, I focused tightly on the road in front of us. The way the car's headlights seemed to swallow the white lines between lanes, like it was hungry for the miles we were covering.

I struggled for some type of answer, but then a sound in the car made me realize I didn't need to worry about answers for the moment. A sort of light snore echoed out of my boss, and when I looked at him, I realized he was fast asleep.

I thought about waking him, but decided he needed to sleep as much as he needed to sleep it off. I pushed on for another hour or so, but not far south of Santa Cruz, the urge to sleep caught up with me as well. I thought about waking Dex to take over the driving, but I knew it hadn't been long enough for the alcohol to have worked its way out of his body. When I saw a small road leading down to the ocean, I pulled the big car off the main highway, pulled over to the side of the road, killed the engine, and gave in to the demands of my body. The day had been too long. I told myself I needed ten minutes of rest. Maybe fifteen. I think I fought sleep for about a minute. But when the urge became too strong, I gave up the fight.

CHAPTER TWENTY-NINE

"WAKE UP, sleepyhead." It wasn't the voice that woke me, but a gentle poke in the ribs.

I looked around groggily. It was not full day, but it would be soon. Light was exploding across the ocean in front of us. Somehow, in the full dark and in my sleepy state, I'd managed to park the car facing the ocean full on. The gold and red lights of dawn were chasing away the remnants of night across an endless sea. It was beautiful. Before I said anything at all to Dex, I just sat there for a moment and drank it in.

The day was going to be hot; you could feel it in the way the sun belted off the car. But for the moment, it was cool enough to be comfortable, and the scent of the ocean chased the stale smell of Dex's booze out of the car.

Dex got out and stretched his legs, then walked around to the driver's side and opened the door. "Here," he said, "skootch over. We've gotta get a move on. And if I don't get some coffee soon . . . well, I don't know what I'll do, but neither of us wants to find out."

"Santa Cruz isn't far back," I said, while I did as he asked. "Maybe ten or fifteen minutes."

He started the engine. "Naw, I'd rather not go in that direction. I'd rather not go back. We'll find something along the way."

And we did. Another roadside diner, this one looked like it was a haven for the trucks that increasingly plied the three-year-old highway, offering food and gas twenty-four hours each day.

We cleaned up, ate up, and gassed up all in under half an

hour. We were back on the road by seven. I didn't ask what the big hurry was simply because I was still too tired to formulate the question. And I don't think we'd been on the road ten minutes before I was fully asleep.

Once again it was the cessation of movement that woke me.

"We're here," Dex said, as he saw my head come up.

"Where's here?" It felt like a replay of the previous day's stop at the diner on our way to San Francisco. Though, if possible, this time I was even more disoriented than I had been then. We weren't at my house. And we weren't at the office. It took me a moment, and then I recognized our surroundings. "We're at Lafayette Square?" I groaned.

Dex nodded. "I told you, I wanted to tell Mrs. Dempsey straightaway."

"You told me?" I thought for a moment. "No. No, you didn't. I'd have remembered that."

"Maybe you were asleep," Dex admitted, as he got out of the car. "Anyway, I stopped at Port Harford and called her. She's expecting us."

Before I followed, I pulled the rearview mirror toward the passenger seat and peered cautiously at myself. My pale and tired face peered back. Just as I'd feared, I was completely beyond hope. My hair looked as though . . . well, as though I'd slept in a car. And the cosmetics Morgana had applied so carefully the night before were doing nothing to help the situation. Dex stood outside the car impatiently, but I wouldn't budge until I'd at least pulled a comb through my hair and taken a couple of swipes at the bruised makeup.

"You could have dropped me off at home before we came over here," I groused, while we waited for the door to open. When it did, all thoughts of grousing were swept away. Though it was not yet six o'clock at night, Lila Dempsey was wearing a peignoir with a fur-trimmed collar and little else. Her getup didn't leave much to the imagination. The pale lilac material clung to her like a shimmery skin.

"Mr. Theroux," she said, ignoring me completely. "It's very good of you to see me at home. Please come in."

She led the way from the huge foyer into an even larger sitting room. The entrance was through one of the hallways on the right that I hadn't chosen on the night Dex and I had been there. It was a dramatic room done in shades of ivory and rose. A woman's room, I thought, wondering if *Mr.* Dempsey's sitting room was somewhere else in the big house. Or maybe he'd have a smoking room or a den or a trophy room or some other such room marked with an appropriately masculine name.

"Please," she said, standing in front of a rose damask davenport with a couple of armchairs in the same pale fabric. A coffee table stood in front of it; a crystal ashtray and some matching glasses and a decanter holding amber liquid sat upon it. "Have a seat."

We did as she asked, Dex and I each taking an armchair, while Lila Dempsey half reclined on the davenport. "Can I offer either of you a drink?" she asked, indicating the decanter. I think she asked us both, but her eyes never left Dex's while she spoke. It was an offer, but to my ears it sounded like an invitation as well.

Dex accepted, then shot me a look that said I should do the same. Perhaps he thought that accepting her offer of good bootleg whiskey was the least we could do, considering the news we brought. I shrugged and asked for a small one. After all, I didn't have to actually drink it.

Lila Dempsey poured an inch or so of whiskey into each of the crystal glasses. She handed one glass carefully to Dex, pushed one unceremoniously across the coffee table at me, then took a sip of her own drink.

"So Mr. Theroux," she said, reaching for a cigarette from a

dispenser on a side table. "The fact that you're here makes me think you have news for me."

She sat on the sofa expectantly, the unlit cigarette poised in her hand. Dex obligingly plucked a crystal lighter from the coffee table and lit it for her, then helped himself to one of the cigarettes. Since Lila Dempsey hadn't acknowledged my presence at all, besides the moment when she slid my drink over to me, I felt invisible. That was fine. Considering the news we'd brought, invisible was probably a good place to be. I settled into the big chair and watched the scene unfold.

"Mrs. Dempsey, I take it you haven't been notified yet?"

"Who?" she said. "Who hasn't notified me of what?"

Dex took a deep breath and plunged ahead. "I'm sorry," he said. "I don't know quite how to say this. I suppose you might already have surmised from this personal visit that our news is not good."

"What?" She looked genuinely surprised. She took a long drag from her nearly new cigarette. Then, like a proper lady, she dropped it whole and still smoking into the ashtray. Dex looked thoughtful while he picked it up carefully and extinguished it for her. I could tell he was thinking about just what to say.

"Your husband . . . your husband appears to have gone to San Francisco, just as you supposed he had."

Lila Dempsey nodded. Leaned forward slightly. "Yes . . . and?"

"I was not able to ascertain the entire extent of his business there." Dex spoke so carefully I wondered if *I* even knew everything that he did. "But . . . well, Mrs. Dempsey, there's just no sweet way to say this. I'm afraid your husband is dead, ma'am."

I was watching Lila Dempsey closely while Dex broke the news. I was looking, I guess, for signs of either guilt or lack of surprise. I saw neither. The woman's face registered genuine shock and distress, which I thought was rather at odds with the fact that she'd seemed disappointed that Dex hadn't come alone.

Now, with word of her husband's death new and raw, she finally acknowledged my presence. Her eyes sought mine out; something plaintive in them. "Is this true?" she asked, as though hoping I'd refute it.

"I'm afraid so, Mrs. Dempsey," I said. "I saw him with my own eyes."

"I'm surprised the coroner's office up there hasn't called you already."

"I've been out a lot the last few days," Lila said. "I might have missed the call."

"Expect a call from them then," Dex said, not unkindly. "And I would imagine they'll want you to come and identify the body," Dex added, "but at this point I don't think there's really any doubt."

I don't know how I expected Lila Dempsey to act when we told her the news of her husband's death—I hadn't expected her to fall to pieces or anything—but her reaction was different than I thought it would be. It was the quiet devastation that impressed me most deeply. And in that moment I realized that, for whatever reason, the flirtatiousness with Dex had been an act.

After Dex told her that her husband was dead, Lila Dempsey didn't scream at an unforgiving god; she didn't rend her clothes or pull her hair. Nor did she say, "What shall I do now?" But I heard it, just the same. I heard it in the helpless movements of her hands, like the useless flight attempts of small, damaged birds. And I heard it in the pulse I could see jump at the base of her pale throat. I heard it in every movement, every motion, every breath she took. It was as though her center had been pulled away. One thing was clear to me from this quiet, drama-less display: whatever else she was or had been, Lila Dempsey hadn't known about her husband's death.

While Mrs. Dempsey flailed with these new emotions and

Dex did his best to comfort her, I excused myself. Lila didn't look up when I told her I was going to use the powder room, and as it was, I didn't need directions.

In the champagne-and-rose-colored bathroom I locked the door, and then, steeling myself against images of the dead man, I stepped right into the tub. I'd seen the corpse myself. And what had Dex's friend said? The bullet had gone right through him. That meant that if he'd died in this room, there would be some evidence.

I found what I was looking for about halfway up the wall. I found a place where the perfect tiles were even more perfect. One was a little more rose, another slightly less champagne, and unmistakably, the grout between them was brighter, newer. I wouldn't have bet my life on it, but it looked to me as though those tiles had been recently replaced.

I used the bathroom uneasily, uncomfortable even drying my hands on the towel. I ran my brush through my hair and rubbed my finger on my teeth, but I knew that the balance of my own repairs would have to wait until I got home.

Back in the sitting room, Dex looked up gratefully when I came into the room. I didn't want to stay any longer, and I could see he didn't want to either. There wasn't any reason. The cat-and-mouse game Lila Dempsey had enjoyed with Dex was over now. It was clear the fun had gone out of it for her. We could see that she needed and wanted to be alone, perhaps to lick her wounds and figure out what came next.

She let us out herself, but at the door she put a hand on Dex's arm to stop him.

"I can't face it alone, Mr. Theroux," she said. I could see that her nails were buffed to a dull shine, but they were without color.

"What's that, Mrs. Dempsey?" he said, his hat still in his hands.

"San Francisco, Mr. Theroux. Identifying the body, as you

said. I can't . . . I couldn't bear it. And I'll need to make arrangements for . . . for the body to come . . . to come back home. Will you come with me? Please. I'd pay you, of course. Your usual rates."

Dex agreed, of course. It wasn't like he had a million other things to do, and what the hell, he was probably thinking, he already had a car.

They arranged that he'd pick her up the following day.

I didn't try to get included in the trip. Genuine grief or no, I figured I'd had enough of Lila Dempsey to last me a lifetime.

CHAPTER THIRTY

BY THE TIME I GOT HOME, I was so tired I could barely see straight, despite the extended nap I'd had in the car. There's sleep, I guess, and then there's sleep. The kind you get in a car can't compare to the good quality stuff you get in your own bed.

But before I got anywhere near that peace and quiet, there was Marjorie to deal with. Nor had I gotten very far either. She accosted me on the first-floor landing, the day's dying light moving playfully through the stained-glass window, casting odd shadows on both our faces and our hands. She had a broom in hand, and it looked as though she'd been carefully sweeping the polished wood stairs and the carpet that covered them. She wasn't fooling me any, though. I had a hunch she'd been doing busywork at the front of the house all day, in order to be certain not to miss me on my return. I chided myself for being paranoid, but her first words made me realize I hadn't been.

Marjorie told me in no uncertain terms that she'd been having kittens about my absence. Those were the words she used.

"But, dear Marjorie, I *told* you I was going. I'm sure I did."

"Hmph!" she sniffed, sweeping a perfectly clean riser absently, as though a lack of activity at this moment was unthinkable. "Is that supposed to make me feel better? You off in that city of vice with that employer of yours?"

I hid my smile as well as I could behind my hand. I should have spared myself the effort. Marjorie saw it, of course.

"And don't you smile that way, miss! I know what youngsters get up to in these crazy times."

"Well, Marjorie, city of vice? You'll have to admit that's somewhat melodramatic. It's just a city like any other."

"Don't you read the newspaper?"

I gave up that angle. I knew what a losing battle looked like when I saw it.

"I told you before I left that Dex was going anyway. I thought tagging along would give me an opportunity to catch up with my friends."

"And did it?" she demanded.

"It did. Though not as much as I might have liked because here I am, back already. And all in one piece too." I was dog tired, but I gave her the most winning smile I could muster.

"And Mr. Theroux. He was . . . that is, was he . . ." I waited for it. I didn't know where she was going, so I couldn't offer any help. "Was he a gentleman?" she said finally.

"Dex? Of course, Marjorie. He doesn't think of me that way at all." The words earned me another grunt, but I could see she was somewhat mollified. As she could see for herself, I was back safe and sound, even if I was almost asleep on my feet. "I'm just that tired," I said, taking a step up. "And I have to go to the office tomorrow. Maybe we can talk in the morning over breakfast."

Marjorie seemed instantly contrite. "Of course, Miss Katherine. I'm sorry. I forgot myself this time. I was just so worried."

We said good-night and I started to head up the stairs, but just as I got to my room, she caught up with me again. "One thing, Miss Katherine. It's about your friend, Mrs. Jergens."

"Brucie?" I asked somewhat guiltily. I hadn't given her a thought in what felt like days. "How is she?"

"Well, that's just it, miss. She's not been back at all."

The words so caught me by surprise, I took a moment to filter them. "She's not here?"

"No, miss. In fact, I've not seen her since that first evening, when you all went out."

I checked Brucie's room. It wasn't that I didn't believe Marjorie, but I wanted to see for myself.

Sure enough, everything was just as it had been when I'd last seen it. The disarray we'd left when we prepared to go out. The note I'd written for Brucie before I left for San Francisco. The flowers in a vase on the bureau, not dead but certainly beginning to look rather tired.

Marjorie had followed me up the stairs and was framed in the doorway. "You see?" she said. "She's not been back at all."

"I *do* see, Marjorie. And it's very worrisome. I'll call Mustard from the office tomorrow. It's possible he knows where she is."

I said it lightly. I meant it that way too. Probably, I told myself, she was holed up someplace comfortable, recovering from her injuries, while some besotted someone—and it wasn't hard to paint Mustard into that picture—peeled grapes for her.

I told myself these things, and I tried to sound convincing. But I couldn't convince myself, and even to me the words felt quite hollow. At some level I feared the very worst.

CHAPTER THIRTY-ONE

THE NEXT DAY I was happy to take Angels Flight down Bunker Hill and then walk the few blocks to the office in bright sunshine. The funny thing about a routine is you don't miss it until it's gone. Parts of the trip to San Francisco had been really enjoyable, but it was good to be back and doing the things that made up my everyday life.

Stopping for Dex's ice before I remembered he'd be in San Francisco and wouldn't need it. Nodding hello to the shoeshine boy who always hung about the front doors of our building during business hours. Greeting the elevator operator and inquiring about his wife, because I knew she'd been ill.

I got a sense that something wasn't quite right even before I tried the office door. Call it a sixth sense or even intuition, but I *knew* the door would be unlocked when I tried it. And I knew it had no reason to be. Dex had planned to leave in the morning without stopping by the office. No one else had a key. I looked at the lock. It was clear a key hadn't been used, in any case. The lock was broken.

I poked my head inside, heart pounding, trying to decide what to do. Times were hard. If someone was inside trying to find valuables, they wouldn't have much luck. But I didn't want to surprise them either. Better to leave and go and get help. Even the elevator operator or the shoeshine boy could provide some sort of backup. And by the time I returned, maybe whoever had been in the office would have cleared out with whatever pitiful plunder Dex's office was likely to turn up.

I started to back up the way I'd come, but a voice stopped me. A young man emerged from behind the door, a gun clutched tightly in his fist. Though he looked like he might know how to use it, his simple country clothes put a lie to possible expertise with a handgun. He aimed the gun squarely at my chest and motioned for me to enter the office and close the door behind me. I didn't feel like I had a lot of choice.

"You're Kitty Pangborn," he said. It wasn't a question, so I didn't say anything. I wasn't even sure I *could* have said anything at that point; my voice seemed trapped somewhere in my chest. But the fact that he knew my name—and that he knew me as Kitty—gave me pause. He wasn't just here for the typewriter then. Or Dex's Chicago World's Fair highball glass. He knew who I was.

He waved the gun around some, indicating I should take a seat in one of the waiting room chairs. "And no funny stuff," he warned. He needn't have worried on that account. All of my funny bones were suppressed at that moment. I didn't feel humorous at all.

I took a seat gingerly, careful not to do anything he might construe as funny. The man wasn't dressed like a killer, but since he was armed with a handgun and he didn't seem shy with it, I judged him to be very dangerous indeed.

I sat primly on the hard-backed chair—my hands on my purse, my purse on my lap—and looked up at him expectantly. I didn't say a word.

With his free hand, he lit a cigarette, dropping the spent match on the floor. I looked at it with distaste but didn't say anything.

"I'm looking for my sister," he said.

"Well, you've come to the right place," I said, mustering all of the confidence I could into my voice. Instinctively trying not to show my fear. "But generally in this business, clients come with money to get us to find someone, not guns."

"Listen to me, twist," he said. I was surprised to find myself faintly hurt by the term. I'd heard it before, of course, but never applied to me. A twist was generally the kind of girl I'd never been. "I didn't come here to hire a shamus. I told you, I'm looking for my sister, and I know you know where she is." He waved the gun in a menacing way.

"She sent me a letter a few days ago telling me a friend of hers had made arrangements for her to stay with you," he continued. "So I come down from Bakersfield yesterday, just like she told me, and go to the place where she said we should meet—and nothing."

"Brucie?" I asked, the light suddenly dawning as I made the Bakersfield connection. "You're Brucie's brother?" I searched his face for a familiar stamp, but didn't see anything. He was a lot taller than Brucie, for one thing, which I knew meant nothing because men generally are. But the coloring was different as well. Though his hair was pale, he had an olive complexion, just about the opposite of Brucie's dark hair and pale skin. His features weren't at all like hers either. Where Brucie's face was delicate, gamine, there was a coarseness to the cut of this man's chin and nose. I realized that if he weren't scowling at me and waving a gun in my direction, he would probably have been handsome. It was difficult for me to see it at that moment, though. It's funny how handsome isn't the first thing you notice when someone is brandishing a gun in a menacing way.

But handsome or not, I didn't see a lot of physical similarity between Brucie and this young man. I knew that didn't necessarily mean anything. It happens that way in families sometimes. Sometimes siblings can be like peas in a pod. Other times there's little physical to connect them. In any case, he was worked up enough that I figured he was telling the truth.

He nodded. "Who'd you think I meant?"

"Oh, for heaven's sake." I felt as though I'd suddenly had enough. "A gun? Brucie is my friend. You're not really planning on shooting me?"

"In her letter, Brucie told me she was in awful trouble. She said if she didn't show up at the market on Olvera that I was to know something terrible had happened and to be prepared for the worst. That's what she said: the worst. So I found a guy there in the market, and he sold me this gun."

"And then you came here to shoot me."

"No, ma'am." That rankled. Ma'am. We were probably about the same age, and no one had ever called me ma'am before. "I went out to her house—her and Ned's—in Highland Park. She weren't there but the house was in an awful state."

"What do you mean?" I said, fully alert now, the gun forgotten for the moment.

"A window was broke, in the back. So I went inside, and the place had been messed up bad."

"Messed up," I repeated. "Like what?"

"Ransacked, I guess you'd say. Drawers pulled out and dumped on the floor, pillows with the stuffing on the outside, blankets ripped up. It seemed to me someone was looking for something."

It seemed that way to me too. "Then what did you do?"

"I tried to find her friend, Mustard. She sent me his address. But I couldn't find no sign of him. And *then* I came here."

"Why here?"

"It was in the letter she sent. Brucie said you'd know where to find her."

"Did she also tell you to wave a gun at me?" He just looked at me, the gun steady in his hand. But I was no longer afraid. "Never mind. So you came here this morning to try and scare me into helping you find Brucie?"

"No, ma'am." There it was again. "Last night."

"You spent the night here?" He just nodded. "But you were standing there when I came in. Like you were waiting."

He looked sheepish now. "I rested in the big chair in that

office over there." He pointed at Dex's domain. "I don't think I slept much. When it got to be eight o'clock, I got myself up and ready. I knew someone would come in before long."

"Brucie was shot a few days ago, outside a nightclub. I thought . . . I thought they were shooting at our friend. The man whose office you slept in. But now . . . well, if what you're saying is so, maybe it was Brucie they were aiming at all along."

"Brucie was shot?" I could see the knuckles on the hand that held the gun whiten.

"Oh, for heaven's sake, put that gun away." I was now confident he wouldn't use it. "Brucie was injured, she wasn't killed. We took her to the hospital and it was serious, but she was in no danger of dying from her injury."

"So she's fine?"

I shrugged. "I think so. I *hope* so. I have no reason to think she's not," I said, as reassuringly as possible. "It's just that . . . well, no one's seen her since the day after the shooting. So, yes . . . Brucie's missing. But I want to find her. You can help me. But I won't be able to try to find her if you kill me. Besides, you look like you could use some coffee."

He reddened slightly and lowered the gun and tucked the weapon into the back of his pants. "Sorry," he said, even more sheepishly. "I guess I'm not thinking quite straight."

Once the gun was out of sight, I took a deep breath. As cool as I'd been when he was waving it around, a part of me had been deeply frightened. I don't care much for guns at the best of times, and this wasn't one of those.

"OK then, you need coffee," I said, getting up to make it. "Come to think of it, I need some too. Then we'll try and figure out where to look for Brucie. What's your name, anyway?" I asked, while I fiddled with the percolator and the hot plate.

"Calvin, ma'am."

"Calvin what?"

"Calvin Carlisle, ma'am."

"Calvin Carlisle. All right then. You already know my name: Katherine Pangborn."

"I thought it was Kitty."

"It's not," I said darkly. "You can call me Katherine or Miss Pangborn, take your pick. But stop calling me ma'am."

CHAPTER THIRTY-TWO

DESPITE OUR RAGGED INTRODUCTION, Calvin seemed to be a nice kid. He was rougher around the edges than his big sister. I decided that a few years of living in the city had polished Bakersfield right out of Brucie. But once the gun was safely tucked away and he had some coffee in him, Calvin relaxed somewhat and proved himself to be bright and engaging and deeply concerned about his sister. More: he was determined to find her. I didn't even know where to begin, but Calvin had some ideas.

"In her letter, she didn't tell me exactly what she saw, but she let me know it was bad. The letter was funny though. Like she'd been afraid of someone else reading it. It was written in a sort of code. One only she and I would understand."

She'd used the patois of their family, he told me, the inner language it seems every family but mine always has. It also made some references to things that only Brucie and Calvin would have known about. An incident when they were young, for instance, something that had happened with some of the town kids that had frightened both of them as children. Something that had seemed so awful to them at the time that Calvin wouldn't fully explain it to me even now.

"In the letter she told me that the day Ned was killed she saw something she shouldn't oughta. Something she wished she hadn't seen. And now she's gotta lay low; that's what she said. She even told me she was thinking of coming back to Bakersfield for a while."

"What do you think she saw, Calvin? Did she give you any hints?" We were sitting at my desk—I behind it in my usual seat, Calvin across from me with one of the waiting room chairs pulled up. I'd brought thick slices of buttered bread for my lunch that day, with a slab of Marjorie's good banana loaf as a sweet. We had these between us with the coffee on the desk. It was nowhere near lunchtime, but Calvin looked as though he could use a meal and I didn't mind sharing.

"I've been thinking about that a lot, Miss Pangborn." He broke off another bit of bread, chewed it thoughtfully, and then washed it down with a mouthful of coffee before he spoke again. "I reckon it must have had something to do with that husband of hers."

I looked at Cal sharply. I'd heard Ned Jergens spoken of with love—by Brucie—and with respect—by Mustard and Dex—but here I heard something a little different.

"I gather you didn't like him very much," I prompted.

"Well, I know it ain't right to speak ill of the dead—" he paused, but I could tell he was contemplating doing exactly that "—and he was good enough to Brucie and all. Didn't hit her none or nuthin' so far as I could see. But he was . . . well, he was flash. Show-offy, you know? And he acted like he was better 'n everyone."

"What did he say he did for a living?"

"Oh, we knew what he was, all right. We knew what he did. He might have hid it from us, but Brucie liked to brag about it. That her husband was a torpedo."

I stopped him at that. "But he wasn't, was he? I thought Ned was Chummy McGee's right-hand man, not a gunsel."

Calvin looked at me like I was a child. "How far is one of those from the other?" he asked. "Sure, Ned might have had some kind of *seniority*." Calvin spat the word out like it tasted bad. Like he couldn't get it out of his mouth fast enough. "But that don't change what he was. And, yeah, it meant he could give my sister a nice house and pretty things, but what's the balance? Look at her now—her husband's dead, and she's either hiding somewhere or . . ." His voice trailed off pathetically, but even though he left the words unsaid, they hung in the air between us. Considering everything, we both knew there was a good chance that Brucie was dead.

CHAPTER THIRTY-THREE

WHEN I TRIED Mustard's line and still didn't get an answer, I started to get even more worried. Mustard had business concerns, mysterious as they might sometimes be to me. When he didn't answer the phone, he always left someone in place to answer for him. But not today. Today the phone just rang and rang.

With Mustard and Brucie both missing in action, it seemed to spell an even darker vision of doom. I wished Dex wasn't out of town. Even hanging around with private detectives for a while, I didn't actually know how to *detect* anything on my own. Not really. I could have used a dose of Dex's confidence and knowledge right then. But it wasn't an option.

Even with a couple of cups of my good strong coffee inside him, Calvin was asleep on his feet. I told him he could curl up in Dex's office chair for a while and get some shut-eye. I knew he'd feel clearer with a bit of sleep, and I felt as though I needed a half hour of quiet in order to think things through. Someone somewhere knew something about Brucie. And I had no idea of where to start looking.

While Calvin slept, I took the envelope with Harrison Dempsey's fingerprints out of my handbag and locked them in the safe in Dex's office. That done, I called a locksmith. His shop was just a few blocks away, and on the phone he sounded just as hungry as a lot of businesses had gotten to be. He said he'd be around to fix the lock in a quarter hour.

After I hung up the phone, I sat at my desk, finally taking the half hour alone I'd promised myself to think things through. When that didn't produce any big results, I got lucky: I got a break.

That break came in the form of the mailman, who entered just as the locksmith was leaving. Our postman was a polite little man called Murphy—I wasn't sure if it was his front or last name, he'd never explained—who dropped off the mail every day at eleven o'clock sharp. On this day, he came in with his usual cheerful greeting and dropped the normal stack of mail on my desk. "You got a postcard from Italy," he informed me. "Sounds like your friends are having a great time."

Murphy went on his way, and I tried to think who might be sending us a postcard from Italy even while I rifled through the short stack of mail. And then there it was: a gondola on the Grand Canal. I turned the card over hungrily. I recognized Mustard's handwriting at once: the extreme left slope to the letters, the ink so dark a blue it was almost purple. Indigo, you would have said. And applied firmly, as by the hand of someone who didn't mess around much.

Dear Dex and Kitty,
The Grand Canal is wonderful, just as we remembered it
when we were here last. The water is inviting, but we've
resisted the urge so far. Linnie and I wish you were here so
very much. If you came, you'd have to be careful. It's a long
journey and some of it is perilous, but we think it's worth
the trip.
  Miss you and wish you were here,

M & B

M & B. Who could that be but Mustard and Brucie? The Linnie part I didn't get at all. And I was sure that, like the message Brucie had sent to her brother, in this postcard they were addressing us in some kind of code. *From Italy?* That seemed improbable. They hadn't even had time to get there, much less enjoy the Grand Canal. They'd only been missing for a couple of days. To get to Italy from Los Angeles would take a couple of weeks by ocean liner, if they got lucky and made all the right connections.

I turned the card over and studied the image, looking for a further clue, but there was none. A very typical Venice shot. A hand-painted photograph of a gondolier on the Grand Canal looking utterly content moving his boat through the water, as though he had been born to the job. Behind him, the unmistakable architecture of the most famous of Italian cities.

Flipping the card back over, I looked at the stamp, then furrowed my brow in concentration. An American stamp. From Italy. That made no sense. Then I looked at the postmark and a light dawned.

I knew where they were.

CHAPTER THIRTY-FOUR

IT WAS FOURTEEN MILES from Dex's office downtown to our destination. In a car we'd have managed the trip in an hour. The Red Car went there, but it took over two. I chafed at the delay. This was one day that, if I could have gotten my mitts on a car, I'd have done it. But with Dex out of town and Mustard out of sight, that wasn't an option. So I tried to curb my impatience. The whole experience gave me a better insight into how Dex must sometimes feel. I couldn't decide if that was a good thing. Or not.

We got off the Red Car at what had once been the Grand Lagoon. It was still marked as such, but the lagoon itself had long ago been filled in. Still, it remained the center of the amusement park and it seemed a good place to start.

I'd probably been barely into my teens the last time I'd been to Venice—perhaps 1922 or 1923, certainly no later than 1925. I was a little dismayed by the changes I found. When I had been there last, Venice had been a declining dowager. A shadow of the grand vision its creator, Abbot Kinney, had around the turn of the century, but still an enjoyable place to spend an afternoon. To ride the roller coasters, get frightened in the fun house, indulge in the indoor saltwater plunge, or even meander along the boardwalk.

The vestiges of all these things were still in place, but to everything there was an air of neglect and decay. The Race Thru the Clouds roller coaster was as I remembered, but it looked ill-kept, and it would have taken a braver thrill seeker than I've ever been to try it. The short lines waiting to ride made me think I wasn't alone in this. The Rapids, which I remembered as an exciting ride up a light-studded, manmade mountain before plummeting down in a tiny car, wasn't running at all. Worst of all was the smell. It wasn't overpowering, but it permeated the entire area. It was difficult to place. Then I realized it wasn't one thing, but a mélange of several—the ever-present oil smell combined with human waste and perhaps worse.

"Why are we here?" Calvin asked, for perhaps the sixth time.

"I told you. I'm following a hunch. Please. Indulge me. It's not like you've got anything else to do."

I'd thought about leaving him back at the office, but it had seemed a good idea to bring him along. I really didn't know what we were going to find, and at least he had a gun.

I took the postcard out of my handbag, confirming what I'd read. *Linnie*. That's what it said. And if I wasn't mistaken . . .

I led Calvin to the faded visitor's map that still stood at the far end of the filled-in Grand Lagoon. The map was beautifully done but old-fashioned, rendered with the artistry and whimsy typical of the early 1900s. One of the corners had rotted away, and the paint was flaking off in places, but near the center, not far from the place where we stood, I saw it: Linnie Canal. In the illustration it looked as though it fed right into the Grand Lagoon. It wouldn't do so now, of course—not with the lagoon filled in—but it meant we weren't far from our destination. I smiled, suddenly sure I'd read things right, and led Calvin off to find it.

Closest to the Grand Lagoon, the Linnie Canal was part of the amusement park, though some of the amusements were now abandoned. As we followed along the banks of the canal, the amusements gave way to the vacation bungalows that had been built when Venice of America was a new and shiny dream. Now most of them were derelict. The stench and decay all around us wouldn't have been anyone's idea of a grand vacation.

"It would help if you told me what we were looking for,"

Calvin groused, as we trudged along the bank. I didn't reply. After all, I didn't know myself, so I really didn't have anything to tell him.

Aside from a few pathetic ducks that paddled in the water of the canal, we didn't see any signs of life. I felt certain there would be rats scurrying everywhere. I didn't see any, but the lack of visual evidence didn't make me feel any better. You just knew that they were there somewhere, probably waiting for dark.

After a while an old woman came out of one of the small houses on the other side of the canal and trundled along the bank. And though I kept a sharp eye out, we didn't spy anything else of note.

We followed the canal until we couldn't anymore; then carefully crossed a rickety bridge to the other bank and started to head back toward the Grand Lagoon.

As we passed the house where I'd spotted the old woman, I heard my name.

"Kitty." It was more of a hiss than a word. It was quiet, that hiss, and sounded as though it had come from a bit of a distance.

I turned quickly—we both did—but there was nothing there besides an abandoned bungalow. But suddenly, with an eerie confidence, I knew.

Checking both ways, up and down the canal, we could still see the lonesome ducks, but there were no human forms in sight. I grabbed Calvin by the arm and wordlessly pulled him into a small unkempt yard in front of one of the derelict bungalows. Then, with an assurance I didn't entirely feel, I led him up the front steps and right into the house. Calvin looked confused, but he followed me without protest and with the air of someone who had resigned himself.

As soon as I closed the front door behind us, we heard a voice. "Who's the pup?" It sounded just like Mustard, but it looked like the old woman we'd seen walking next to the canal. She wasn't bent over now, or walking painfully as she had been when we'd first seen her. At close range I could see that Mustard's disguise hadn't been very thorough—a head scarf, an old coat, a woman's old-fashioned lace-up shoes. I gathered that the view from a distance had been all that mattered.

"That's quite the getup," I said, my mirth at the sight of him almost overpowering my nervousness. "Are you going for the prize of world's ugliest woman?"

"Cal!" My head shot up at the female voice, and my heart brightened as Brucie flew into the room and into her brother's arms. Her shoulder was bandaged, but other than that she looked right as rain.

"So are you going to tell me why you're playing dress-up," I said to Mustard, "or is this what you do on your days off? Come down to Venice and don an old woman's clothes?"

"You're right," Mustard said, straight-faced. "This is what I do for fun." He was shedding his ridiculous costume as he spoke. I was relieved to see everyday Mustard emerge within a few seconds. "And Venice is just the place for it . . . no one around to see. I'll ask it again though: Who's the pup?" His expression was neutral, but I could tell he wasn't excited about seeing Calvin, who was now in a corner, speaking urgently and quietly with Brucie.

"It's her brother," I said, noting the small look of relief I saw wash over Mustard's face as he digested what I'd said. "He showed up at the office this morning."

"Where's Dex?"

"Back in Frisco. It's a long story and I don't feel like telling it right now. You got anything like tea around here?"

"There's a kitchen," he replied, leading the way. "Come on."

Mustard put a kettle on a stove so ancient, I was surprised to see it still worked. The little house was tidy, however, and well stocked. The only place the cottage looked derelict was from the outside. I wanted to ask about it, but I had so many questions I didn't even know where to start. Mustard saved me the trouble.

"I don't really dress up in old women's clothes for fun, you know."

"I guessed that," I said with a smile.

"I mailed the card yesterday, so I figured you'd show up today—though I thought it would be you and Dex. Or even just Dex. So I put on this getup and kept an eye out for you."

"But we saw you a while ago. Well, we saw you being *her*. You didn't say anything. Or wave."

"I wanted to be sure you weren't followed."

"And we weren't?"

"Didn't look that way. Did you see anyone?"

"Just some ducks," I said. "Since we left the Grand Lagoon. You two been holed up here the whole time?"

Mustard nodded. "Yeah. Turns out it wasn't Dex those torpedoes were gunning for. It was Brucie."

"I figured that out by myself."

"Yeah? I figured it at the hospital. I went to see Brucie the day after the shooting. When I got there a couple of gunsels were hanging around outside her room. I figured they were waiting for a quiet moment." He made a slashing movement across his throat with the tips of his fingers.

I gulped. "You figured they were there to kill her?"

"I'm sure of it. So I just bundled her up and got her out of there. The doctors kicked up a bit of a fuss. Said she wasn't ready to go home. And they were probably right, but I figured if I left her there she'd be leaving feet first."

"You didn't just up and walk her out." It wasn't a question.

He grinned, a little rakishly, I thought. "No, you're right. I didn't just waltz her out. But we fooled those torpedoes pretty good, me and Brucie. They're probably still wondering what happened to her."

I digested this. Clearly, Mustard wasn't going to illuminate the details, but I'd caught the gist of the thing and that was important: Brucie had been in danger and now she was not.

"She looks fine now," I said after a while.

"She does, doesn't she?"

"She does what?" Brucie said, entering the kitchen with her brother in tow.

"I was just saying you look well. Mustard said he hustled you out of the hospital before the doctors said you were ready."

"Oh, silly," she said, smiling at Mustard fondly. "He was jumping at shadows. I came with him just to shut him up."

"Huh," Mustard said, pouring boiling water into a teapot. "Some shadows. You'd have been pushing up daisies by now, sister."

"But, Mustard," I said, "why here? I would have thought you'd head for the country or something."

"That's easy. This is my place. I don't get here very often, but it's here for me when I need it. Hidden in plain sight."

"Dex knows about it," I said, suddenly understanding the postcard. The little code was probably something they'd worked out.

"Sure he does. But just him and no one else. Well, now the three of you."

Calvin piped up. "Four," he said.

"And the disguise . . . ?" I asked.

Mustard nodded. "I've used it before."

"You really think all this was necessary?" I asked, with a gesture that indicated Brucie, the little house, the discarded scarf.

"It was the only way," Mustard said. "At first I thought stashing her at your place was enough."

"Maybe it would have been," I said, perhaps more sternly than I'd intended, "if you hadn't paraded her around the Town House Hotel in a gold lamé dress."

"Now, Kitty," Brucie said, "don't take that tone. Mustard didn't really know."

"She don't like to be called Kitty," Calvin interjected.

"What didn't Mustard know?" I asked.

I saw the two of them exchange glances, but I didn't think to wonder about it in that moment.

"I saw . . . I saw Ned killed," Brucie said haltingly.

"I'm not sure," I said, "but I think I knew that."

"I saw him die," Brucie replied. "But I didn't tell you I saw who killed him."

CHAPTER THIRTY-FIVE

BRUCIE TOLD HER STORY without passion. The words came slowly, carefully, as though she'd removed herself from the scenario. I could understand that. The husband she'd loved had died violently. The way to get through it was to make it be someone else's story as much as you could. To distance yourself from the place where your heart connected with all of it. I thought I could hear this in her voice.

She told us about a Saturday afternoon in Westlake Park, at Wilshire and Alvarado. Just her and Ned, who'd stolen a few hours to be with his wife.

They'd rented a punt in the morning and spent a relaxing hour or so on the lake. You can imagine them, weaving their shared dreams, their heads close together, co-conspirators of their future, or thrown back in laughter, so pleased with this stolen sliver of time.

He wears a boater hat; it's old-fashioned, but it makes them both laugh. That and the awkward way he handles the paddles. He's strong enough, but no country boy. He's inexpert with the mechanics of pulling a boat through the water. More laughter.

It's a cloudless day. The sun is a benign disc on the horizon. It's warm on the water but pleasantly so. Everything is perfect.

There are other boats on the small lake, but neither of them notice. *Lost in love*, as they say, and not paying attention to anyone, anything.

When the big yellow punt approaches, they pay no attention. There are other boats on the water, other lovers. It's their world but they're willing to share it. Their hearts are made large by the love held within. When the other boat bumps theirs lightly, they look up, the laughter dying on their faces. Ned reaches beneath his light jacket for his gun; he's never without it. It's too late though. He dies as his hand touches the metal.

The impact of the bullets causes the little punt to list dangerously. Brucie follows the motion, slides into the water just ahead of the burst of bullets intended to take her.

She's an accomplished swimmer and has instinctively taken a deep breath before submersion. Underwater, she wiggles her feet out of her shoes as she dives, finding Ned deep in the reeds at the bottom of the lake. There is no need to check his vital signs or even hang on to the slightest ray of hope: she can see that her husband is dead.

Their punt is above her, upside down in the water. She pushes herself toward it, emerging into the protection of its inverted hull with the last of her held breath. Though her instinct is to raggedly inhale as much oxygen as possible, greedily filling her lungs, she knows she must be quiet. She can still hear their voices; they are not far away. They think they have killed her too. And she can tell that they hope that they have. She understands why they think she should join her husband in his watery death. There is one man in particular. And she has seen his face.

CHAPTER THIRTY-SIX

WHAT I DIDN'T UNDERSTAND—and I told them so now—was why on earth they would have gone dancing—*dancing,* of all things—in what was not only one of the most popular nightspots in the city, but was also clearly in the middle of Lucid Wilson's turf.

"She hadn't told me then," Mustard said, a slightly defensive note in his voice. "Not that she'd seen who it was and certainly not that it was Lucid Wilson himself. I mean, what are the chances?"

"What do you mean?" I asked.

"Well, Lucid doing the killing himself." Mustard looked speculatively at Brucie, like he still expected her to fill something in. She didn't take the bait. "I mean, a guy at that level? Sounds pretty personal."

I nodded. I could see what Mustard meant.

"And you didn't know why Lucid Wilson would have wanted to kill your husband . . . personally?" I asked.

"I wasn't even sure it *was* Lucid himself until I saw him that night at the Zebra Room," Brucie said.

"I'm guessin' that's where he saw you too," Mustard said.

"But how could you not know it was him?" I asked. Something wasn't sitting right with me. "You obviously would have seen him before; it sounds like you and Ned went to nightclubs enough. You would have crossed paths."

"C'mon, Kitty," Mustard said, "take it easy on the kid."

"I knew he looked familiar," Brucie said. "But I couldn't quite place him. You know, out there on the lake in daylight—and it all happened so fast—I just wasn't sure."

"See? That makes sense," Mustard said. I didn't like how puttylike he'd become in the few days I hadn't seen him. He seemed quite willing to believe anything, as long as it was Brucie doing the telling.

"So then you saw him at the club," I pressed Brucie. "And *then* you knew."

"That's right."

"And so your first reaction is to drag Mustard and Dex up on the floor for *dancing*." It still wasn't making sense to me.

Brucie studied her shoes. They were dark puce in color, each one decorated with a wide fabric bow. "I figured . . . I figured if Lucid saw me enjoying myself and not being bothered, he'd maybe think I hadn't seen him that day."

This actually made some sense to me and I relented slightly. I'm not sure that in her puce shoes I would have done the same, but I could see where she was coming from.

"So *now* what do we do?" I said, letting things go for the moment. "I mean, your little house here is cozy, Mustard. But she can't stay here forever."

"No, not forever," Mustard agreed. "But for the time being. Me, I've got to get back to my office. That's gonna be easier now, since Brucie's brother is here. He can stay with her until I . . . until I take care of a few things."

I looked at Mustard and thought about what he meant. I even considered asking him, then thought better of it.

"Can you handle a gun, pup?"

"Calvin," I said, knowing Mustard had forgotten the youth's name.

"Calvin, you know your way around a gun?"

"Sure," Calvin said. "I even got one."

"That's all right then," Mustard said. "You shouldn't need it, but it's best to be prepared. I'll be back to get you guys in a day. Two at the most. There's plenty of food and stuff here."

"I'm not stayin' here another two days!" Brucie complained.

"Oh, but you are," Mustard said. "We'll not have you gettin' shot up again. But two days is all it should take."

"What you gonna do?" Brucie asked.

We all looked at Mustard, but he didn't say anything. I thought his determined face spoke volumes.

"I think I know what he's going to do," I said finally.

"Do you now?" Mustard said.

"I do. You're going to fix it."

CHAPTER THIRTY-SEVEN

THOUGH THE GRAND LAGOON was no longer either
grand or a lagoon, we made our way back there carefully. Mustard didn't say anything, but I could tell he had one sharp eye
out for any kind of monkey business. I was relieved not to see
any.

"Where'd you park?" Mustard asked, when we got close to
the Grand Canal Restaurant.

"Park?" I said with a slight smirk. "How did you even figure I could get my hands on a car?"

"Well, Dex has the Packard, for one . . . oh, right. You said
he's in Frisco."

"Right. And even if I had wanted a car—which I wouldn't
have just to come down here—how could I have called to get
one? You weren't there."

"Good point," he said. "But I don't like the way this is going."

"That's all right. I kinda like the idea of seeing you on a
streetcar."

It was a joke, of course, but in the end I was right. Mustard
on a streetcar was a humorous sight. And he didn't go without
putting up a fight. "Look, we'll find a phone. Call a taxicab. It
won't be that hard."

"Aw, don't be a baby, Mustard. Here it comes now; we don't
even have to wait. And don't worry. I won't tell any of your
friends you rode the Red Car."

He harrumphed at that, as though he didn't care what his
friends thought. Maybe he even believed it. But I knew better.

It was around three o'clock by the time I got back to Spring
Street. I found myself looking forward to an hour or so of just

sitting at my desk and relaxing. It had been an exhausting few days, and I felt as though I could use an hour or so alone just to recharge.

As the elevator approached the fifth floor, I thought about making myself a cup of tea, flavoring it with some of the honey Mustard had surprised me with a few weeks before, when he'd come back from a trip to the San Gabriel Valley; then I thought about just sitting in the office and lazing around until it was time to close up shop for the day. It was a good plan, but I didn't get to put it into action.

As I had that morning, I sensed something was wrong before I even got to the office door. Unlike the morning, however, there was nothing in this assessment that was due to my sixth sense. The frosted glass in the office door, where the words "Dexter J. Theroux, Private Investigator" were painted in black-edged gold letters, had been smashed.

Peering through the hole, I could see that glass covered the office's scuffed hardwood floor. The door was unlocked. Whoever had done this had simply smashed the glass, then reached through and opened the lock from the inside. When they were done, they hadn't bothered locking up. Thinking about this though, I found myself ridiculously glad the glass was broken and not the lock. It would have seemed a real shame to replace a lock twice in a single day. As it was, the glass had been there longer than I had.

I took care not to step on the glass as I entered. I didn't want to grind it down further; I knew who'd be cleaning this mess up. Unlike the morning when I'd entered cautiously, fearing someone was there, I wasn't concerned that anyone would be in the office. The breaking glass would have been heard in the other offices on our floor. I was guessing that whoever did it had broken the window, gone about their business, and then skedaddled.

Determining what that business might have been took me a

while. We didn't have much that was valuable in the office. Even my typewriter would have fetched only a buck or so at a pawnshop. But these days it was hard to tell. With breadlines getting longer, jobs getting harder to find, and the Okies adding their presence to the city's increasingly unemployed throng, small crimes like this had been on the rise. When a man couldn't find honest work in order to buy milk for his babies, sometimes dishonest things started looking like an option. At a time like that, even the dollar you'd get for a used typewriter might start to look better than going hungry.

As I entered the office, however, I could see this wasn't the case. When I saw my typewriter sitting in its usual place on my desk, I was almost disappointed. After all, if the thief wasn't after the typewriter, then what *was* he looking for? Dex's green ashtray? The heel of a bottle of bourbon Dex might have stashed somewhere? His heavily doodled desk blotter? I'd almost feel sorry for the thief who wasted time on our operation. Item by item, there wasn't anything in the office of Dexter J. Theroux worth stealing.

It took me a few moments of inventory before I noticed. It just wasn't the first place you looked. Once I saw it though, I couldn't look away. The office safe was standing open. On inspection, the only thing missing was the set of fingerprints that had been taken from Harrison Dempsey's corpse.

CHAPTER THIRTY-EIGHT

THERE WASN'T MUCH I COULD DO. I called a glazier, of course. Like the locksmith earlier in the day, he sounded hungry and was happy enough to promise to hustle right over to fix the broken pane. Getting Dex's name painted back on the door would take a little longer. The manager of our building insisted that all the doors be done by the same person. Since this same person was his brother-in-law, we'd have to wait a few days. Apparently brothers-in-law were not as hungry as everyone else in town.

I thought about calling the police, of course. But only for a minute. I could just imagine the faces of the two flatfoots that had been in the office a few days before. "You had *what* stolen? And *whose* fingerprints did you say they were?" Considering the events that had led to their coming to the office, I didn't think that was the best idea. Besides, you called the cops when you had the remotest hope of getting a thing back. But if someone had broken into our office with nothing in mind but getting Harrison Dempsey's fingerprints, there was no chance at all that the cops would be able to recover them. Less than no chance.

Which led me to another thought. As far as I could see, only three people in the world knew we had those prints: me, Dex, and his coroner pal, Josiah Elway, in Frisco. Yet the proof was in the pudding. I got up and peered into the safe again, reshuffled the few semi-important papers and the cash float of five dollars and fifty cents that we kept in there for little more reason than justifying the presence of the safe. That stuff was all there—even the fin and the change. But Dempsey's finger-prints? Those were quite gone.

I checked the rest of the office again. As far as I could see, nothing had been touched and nothing was missing. Dex's top left office drawer was locked, so I couldn't tell if anything had been taken from there, but the fact that it was still locked and the lock hadn't been broken led me to believe that whatever had been in there was still in place.

The glazier got there and replaced the glass in the door quickly and efficiently, his stubby fingers nimbly removing the broken bits, then fitting a new precut sheet of pebbled glass where it belonged.

"I like these office windows just fine," he said with some satisfaction while he worked. "Keeps my kids in socks."

"You replace a lot of them?"

He looked up from his work with a grin. "You have no idea."

Which I took to indicate that those glass panels weren't the best for security.

Once I was alone again, I sat at my desk in the quiet and newly resecured office and just thought of all the things that had led me to that spot. After a while I figured that what I was thinking, Dex probably wouldn't like.

Harrison Dempsey's fingerprints had been stolen from the safe. It was just another odd piece of the case that had begun the day Rita Heppelwaite first visited the office. The case that had been over almost before it started, yet now wouldn't seem to go away.

I thought about it. First Rita showed up and hired Dex to follow her beau. Then the beau was killed almost under our very noses. That was too much coincidence. Almost as though— and here I got excited and my thoughts seemed to begin to line up—almost as though someone had *wanted* Dex to see the mur-derer enter the house. *Wanted* there to be a witness. What no one could have anticipated though was the designated witness falling asleep. If what I was thinking was correct, Dex falling asleep might have thrown a monkey wrench into the works.

I suddenly felt very confident that, whatever we'd seen or thought we'd seen, we didn't have the whole story. Maybe not even a fragment of it. It was even possible that we had only the piece that someone had wanted to give us, and perhaps not even a whole piece at that. It was an odd feeling, this new confidence. Marred only by the things I *didn't* know, and there were many. But I had the feeling that if I looked at it all clearly enough, and if I just added one more piece, everything would begin to make sense.

And quite suddenly, I knew where I might find that extra piece.

I was in motion almost before I knew I was going anywhere. The feeling was a little disconcerting. Grabbing my handbag and my coat, even though I didn't think I'd need it. Locking the office door behind me. Taking the elevator back down to street level. Letting my feet guide me in the opposite direction of the funicular trains that would take me home to Bunker Hill. I made myself aware of this in case I was trying to fool myself into thinking I was going home. I wasn't. At that end of Spring Street, I finally had to admit to myself that there was only one place I could be going.

I kept my eyes off the fortress-like facade of the Los Angeles Stock and Oil Exchange. Though the building hadn't been completed at the time of the crash, what it represented had meaning to me. My father had died because of what that facade represented.

It was hard *not* to look at the E. F. Hutton Building across the street from it. Even though it was a beautiful art deco tower, there was something about the building that jolted. An edifice to a time that was over before the structure could even be completed. It was also a reminder. As difficult as things were for so many people, as long as soup lines kept forming and even though thousands of good men found it difficult to put bread on their family's tables, the swells were still here. Paying for private schools and big cars and summers abroad and going on just as they always had, only now they had to step more carefully to avoid the poverty that was blooming everywhere they looked.

The Banks-Huntley Building was next to the Stock Exchange and kitty-corner from Hutton's ode to bad taste. Like so many on that part of Spring Street, the building was almost new, though it lacked the empty grandeur of either of the others.

I didn't check the building directory but waltzed into the elevator as bold as you please. I told the elevator operator I wanted the floor where Harrison Dempsey's offices were, and the kid put the elevator in motion without batting an eye. As we moved upward, it was obvious to me that—based on the address and the fact that he was known in the building—Harrison Dempsey had a pretty significant operation.

It was easy to find the office. The Dempsey Corporation took up more than half of the twelfth floor of the Banks-Huntley Building. The fixtures in the office gave nothing away to me. Based on what I saw, the Dempsey Corporation could have been an architectural firm or in real estate or oil. Maybe all of the above and more besides. But everyone there looked very busy, which suited me just fine.

The first hurdle was easy. Almost too easy by half. A severe-looking woman with a hard helmet of hair and the slightest hint of a mustache gave me the once-over and said, "You're here to temp for Slacum."

It wasn't a question, so I gave her a smile and half a nod.

"We've been waiting for you all day," she bit out. "Well, go and have a look around and settle in a bit for tomorrow. You'll find him down that corridor. Second to last door on the right."

With that she went back to her typing, leaving me to flounder for a moment, not quite sure what to do next. She settled the matter herself.

"Did you not hear me?" she asked, steely voiced. "Second. To. Last. Door. On the right. Get a move on. He's waiting."

I didn't really have much choice. I set off down the corridor. But when I saw the door she'd sent me to—clearly marked Everett Slacum—I veered off down another corridor, deeper into the office.

"You look lost." The man's voice surprised me. I hadn't seen him approach. He looked and sounded friendly enough though.

"I guess I am, just a bit."

"What are you looking for?"

"Harrison Dempsey's office," I said, with as much confidence as I could muster.

"He's not in today," the man said.

"I'm . . . I'm picking up some papers," I improvised.

"Ah, well, Harry's office is down this hallway, all the way to the end. You can't miss it. It's the big one in the corner. You'll see his secretary, Miss Foxworth, at her desk right outside his office. I'm sure she'll be able to help you with whatever you need."

"Thanks," I said, heading off in the direction he'd indicated.

I slowed when I approached the end of the hallway. I didn't need to be introduced to Miss Foxworth to recognize her. Her desk, set up squarely in front of the door marked Harrison Dempsey, was larger than any of the other secretary's desks I'd passed. She didn't notice me at first. I watched from a distance, shielded by a small forest of fig trees in large, gilded pots.

Clearly, the Dempsey Corporation was a darn sight busier than Dex's little operation. The secretaries here didn't need books to read to fill in their days. There was always a phone ringing somewhere, the rings punctuated by the clatter of a half score of typewriters. People were running here and there, and I wondered what they all were doing. Developing this, architecting that; I still didn't have a clear idea.

There was a large clock over Miss Foxworth's desk. From where I stood I could see it was nearly five o'clock. Which gave me an idea.

I approached the desk cautiously. "Excuse me," I said, and she looked up, seeing me for the first time. Her eyes narrowed while she judged me and decided where I fit.

"Temp?" she said. Her voice had a hoarse quality, like she smoked too many cigarettes. A full ashtray at her elbow confirmed the idea.

I nodded.

"For who?"

"Uh . . . Everett Slacum."

It was her turn to nod. "Down this hallway, you'll see the door marked about midway to the far wall."

I looked at her blankly.

"The powder room," she said, eyeing me curiously. "I thought that's what you were looking for."

"Oh, yes. Of course. Sorry. I mean . . . thank you," I said, forcing myself to shut up and putting my feet in motion before I said something even dumber.

I found the ladies' room without a problem and tucked myself into one of the stalls. Like I figured, after a few minutes an ever-increasing number of women came to freshen up before heading out in little clusters to begin their way home. I tried to listen to the snippets of conversation that they let loose once they were in the relative freedom of the bathroom, but there were too many of them to follow, and in any case I didn't know the people they were talking about.

"Sara-Beth thinks she might be in the family way."

"*Really*? Should you be repeating that? I know they've been married awhile, but with him gambling and having so much trouble getting work, that *can't* be a good thing. And you know that if she is, she'll get fired for sure."

"Of course she will. It's not like she could work once they start a family. But maybe a baby would settle him down," said a third voice.

"Or shake him up," said still a fourth, and then the sound of laughter receding.

I heard only one thing that had any meaning for me, and even that was kind of foggy.

"Harry's not here again today, huh?"

"Frisco, last I heard."

"Huh! How do you like that? He hiding from the missus?"

More laughter. "Wouldn't *you*?"

Finally, after perhaps fifteen minutes had passed, there were no more voices, and I figured it was now or never. After all, *her* day had to end sometime too. And with her boss out of the office, I figured there'd be less than usual for her to do. When I saw her desk was empty, I thought I'd figured right. I headed for the elusive door behind her desk, "Harrison Dempsey" emblazoned on a large square of frosted glass.

But just as I reached Miss Foxworth's desk, I noticed a cigarette smoldering in the ashtray.

In the same moment I heard high-heeled footsteps heading down the nearest corridor. Heading, that is, toward me.

I made a most unladylike rush for the door, not thinking about the fact that it might be locked until my hand touched the knob. I was grateful when it opened.

I didn't look behind me. I couldn't; I hadn't the time. So when I slipped through the door of Harrison Dempsey's office, I didn't stop to admire the corner view of the burgeoning young city, or the book-lined walls, or the zebra skin rug in the center of the floor. I just leaned against the heavy oak door and willed my breathing to come evenly again, instead of the heavy *pant-pant-pant* that was now pushing through me. And I willed at the same time that Miss Foxworth had *not* seen me.

So I waited in that position, my back against the door, for a few minutes, while I caught my breath, anticipating discovery. I was breathing normally before very long, but the office door never did burst open, and after a while, I assumed a more normal stance and allowed myself a look around.

The house on Lafayette Square had been a hint. It was the house of a swell. Why would I have expected any less of his office? And yet somehow I had. I'd expected something more dreary perhaps. More in keeping with my idea of a man whose background I'd thought was somewhat shady; someone who owed great sums of money to men like Lucid Wilson.

But though I'd been born with wealth and raised with it to a certain age, and though my friends had been among the young elite of California, both south and north, nothing had prepared me for the personal inner sanctum of Harrison Dempsey.

There was no decor, really. That is, the office was not done in a certain style. It looked as though if a decision had been needed between two items, Dempsey had chosen the more expensive one. And that's when I realized what was different between the surroundings of my childhood and that of my pals and what I found here and at the house on Lafayette Square. This, I decided, was what new money looked like. My father had tried to explain this to me when I was a child, but it hadn't made sense to me then. It didn't now either, but I figured I had a hint.

The Aubusson rug under the Regency sideboard and next to Dempsey's modern glass-and-chromium desk? I could not think of the circumstance that would have brought them together. They shrieked that they belonged apart. I knew that for the cost of the rug, Marjorie, Marcus, and I—and perhaps Dex as well—could eat for a year. And the cost of the breakfront? That would buy a new house.

And that was the point. It had to be. Not how one item complemented the other or completed the look. But that this piece was expensive, and that? So much more.

There was a davenport-type contraption in a corner under one of the windows. Though it was nothing so mundane as a davenport, I felt sure. A recamier, I decided, or perhaps a chaise. It had beautifully carved legs that came to the floor, with the paw of a griffin clutching a ball. The settee itself was the color of wine, and the fabric was fine, but not so fine that it didn't look inviting.

I allowed myself to sink onto this piece of furniture, though I kept one eye on the door. I was ready to jump to my feet and hide at the slightest sound. But I needed a few moments just to gather myself and to work through my thoughts. Here I was, after all. Yet I knew I'd not thought it through fully, and if I hadn't known it fifteen minutes ago, I knew it now. It wasn't as though I'd had a plot or a plan going in. Just to come here initially. Test the water, test the air. Beyond that . . . and now here I was.

Back at Dex's office, I'd just felt that something was missing. I still did. Something about the picture Dex and I had put together was incomplete. More and more I felt that the only part of the picture available to us that we *hadn't* examined was right here in the Banks-Huntley Building, in the office where Harrison Dempsey had spent most of his time.

There was a hammered gold clock on the breakfront. When it read five thirty and no one had come into the room, I got off the recamier and quietly started to work. I only hoped that I'd recognize what I was looking for when I found it.

CHAPTER THIRTY-NINE

HARRISON DEMPSEY'S OFFICE was a wonder. Or it would have been on a day when I could just indulge myself and enjoy it, the way you enjoy a walk through a museum or even a zoo. The office was filled with many fine things. Objets d'art and beautiful books, the latter probably chosen more for their bindings than for what was between two covers.

A quick look through the desk revealed nothing out of the ordinary, nor did it do much to illuminate the nature of Dempsey's business, at least not to me. The center top drawer was locked, and I resolved to keep a lookout for the key, though I doubted I'd come across it. The top right-hand drawer held a bottle of good scotch and four clean glasses. I wondered if that were the universal booze drawer, because that's where Dex kept his office stash as well.

The two bottom desk drawers held files. At a glance, they all seemed to be plans of one kind or another: a house at Lake Tahoe, an office building in Long Beach, and some sort of gambling palace in the desert. Whether these were plans for clients or for Dempsey himself, I couldn't tell. In any case, nothing about any of these files struck me as off or wrong. I realized that didn't rule them out. On the other hand, since I had no means of either duplicating or removing possibly incriminating files, I really had no choice but to move on.

A file marked Personal at first didn't reveal much of interest to me. The receipt for the green Packard, a bill for a new hat from a haberdashery in San Francisco. One thing stuck out though. Something that hit me like a jolt of recognition. It was a bill from a dressmaker addressed to "Mr. Harrison Dempsey,

the Banks-Huntley Building, 630-634 S. Spring Street, Los Angeles." The bill was for a "gold lamé dress in the style of Mainbocher" that had been "made to order for Mrs. Jergens" some
two months earlier. I could almost feel the room spinning as I
read this because it so altered my view of everything I'd
learned so far.

Try as I might, I could think of no good reason that
Dempsey—husband of Lila, lover of Rita, indebted to Lucid
Wilson—would have for buying a dress for Brucie, the wife of
the right-hand man of Lucid's archrival. I didn't know what it
meant, but a part of me just wanted to stop now. Just stop and
cry. Instead I filed the information mentally and pressed on. I
wanted to get out of there as quickly as possible, and even
though I didn't know exactly what I was looking for, it hadn't
been this.

The breakfront revealed a similarly eclectic assortment of
things. More glass, more booze—neither of which was surpris-
ing in that particular piece of furniture—and still more
benign-looking files. And though these seemed to do with finance, since none was marked "Large Amount of Money Owed
to Lucid Wilson," I had no choice but to keep going.

After another half hour, I began to feel really silly and not a
little afraid. After all, what I was doing could hardly be more illegal. And why was I doing it anyway? Maybe close proximity
to a private detective for a couple of years had made me over-
confident. And like a lot of employees, I suppose I'd been guilty
of watching my boss and thinking I could do what he did, only
better. I sat back down on the recamier with a quiet sigh and
thought about what to do.

That's when I again noticed the bookshelves that had
tempted me when I first entered the room. I moved across to
them and ran the tips of my fingers across the beautiful spines,
occasionally pulling a volume out more or less at random and
sampling the prose. I wished I could select a few to take with

me, but I wasn't about to add theft to my growing list of crimes.

I noticed that Dempsey had a copy of *The Seven Pillars of Wisdom* on the shelf. The binding was perfect, the spine uncreased; in fact, it didn't look like it had ever been read. I knew that the book I'd been reading, *Revolt in the Desert,* was an abridged version of this longer work. And, yes, I was on a mission. I had things to do and probably not a lot of time left to do them. But I wondered when I'd get the opportunity to see another copy of T. E. Lawrence's original work. Maybe not for a long time. Maybe never. And I'd been enjoying *Revolt* so much. It was impossible not to wonder about what I was missing.

That moment stands out. It was delicious. A stolen moment in a forbidden situation, and that tiny slice of time was intended just for me, to satisfy my curiosity about a book I'd been wishing I could lay my hands on. Now here it was.

I lifted the book off the shelf carefully, almost reverently, and before I could even open it, a piece of paper fluttered out. It landed on the thick rug, a pale white streak against an Aubusson sky.

I bent to pick it up. It was a receipt from the Los Angeles Steamship Company. What had been purchased was itemized. The week before, Dempsey had paid cash for two tickets for first-class passage on a south sea islands cruise aboard the steamship *City of Los Angeles.* One was in the name of John Harrison. The other was for Mrs. John Harrison. And both were dated for a ship that was due to depart tomorrow.

I tried to tell myself that the find was meaningless. That there were any number of reasons Dempsey would have tucked a recent receipt into a book that looked as though it had never been read. But I couldn't think of one. It seemed likely to me that the receipt had been secreted there. And if that was the case, the next question was why.

I replaced the receipt and resumed my search with renewed

vigor, checking book after book, but I didn't find anything else. At a little after six, when the sounds of the outer office had faded to practically nothing, I decided to call it a night.

When I peeked out, Miss Foxworth wasn't at her desk. I made the best of the situation and beat it out of there while I could, my heart rate approaching something like normal about the time I got back out onto the street. I hadn't known what I'd hoped to find, but I had the feeling I'd gotten more than I'd bargained for. Maybe much more.

CHAPTER FORTY

IF SOME GENIUS INTERIOR DESIGNER had been commissioned to create an office that was the polar opposite of the one that housed Harrison Dempsey's extensive operation, it would have looked like the place where Mustard did his business.

Over a garage on Alameda, you accessed Mustard's office by way of a narrow stairway that clung spiderlike to the outside of the building. Inside, the office was surprisingly tidy, with three wooden desks, each with its own phone. One wall was lined entirely with filing cabinets, giving the whole place the look of some low-rent accountancy firm. And though the office appeared clean—the floors swept, the windows not grimy, the ashtrays emptied when necessary—the smell of automotive excrement from the establishment below permeated the small space.

I'd never been here in full dark before, and the atmosphere wasn't helped by the absence of daylight.

"Hey, kid," Mustard said, putting down the phone as I entered. There was a racing form on the desk in front of him. It looked well thumbed. There was a notice for a fight to be held at Wrigley Field on Saturday night. Other than that the desk was bare. "This is sure a surprise. I don't see you down here very often. What's up?"

I took one of the empty chairs opposite his desk and wondered where to start. "You never told me how you know Brucie," I said without preamble.

He looked at me carefully before he replied. "I never did, did I?"

I shook my head.

"Why should I now?" he asked.

"I dunno. Maybe you're just interested in telling me."

"Am I, kid? Well, maybe I am. Since you seem to have an interest, and I've got nothin' to hide. Me and Ned, we went way back," Mustard said. I could hear him choosing his words. "We'd kind of fallen out of the habit of seeing each other since he married Brucie, but I'd met her all right. I was even there when they got married." His eyes looked past me, and I could imagine what he saw. "She was beautiful, even then. She kind of . . . she kind of took my breath away."

"Is that why you saw less of Ned?"

Mustard shrugged his broad shoulders. It was a motion that put me in mind of a caged bear. Like there was more to Mustard than what could be contained in an office or even in his well-cut suit. "In a way, but not really. Once he got married and then got in tight with Chummy, I guess our lives didn't really have room for each other anymore, you know? A job like the one Ned had? That's not like working in a gas station, Kitty. Not even like working in an office. You don't go home and just forget about it for a few hours. You live it an' breathe it and never really leave it behind. It's your life."

"But Brucie didn't mind the life?"

"Not that I could see. I'd see them out sometimes at different nightclubs. We'd smile and wave, maybe have a drink. I might even get Brucie to give me a dance, you know. Not real friendly, the three of us, but friendly enough."

"Like not *un*friendly?" I asked.

"Yeah," Mustard said. "Not unfriendly. But not a lot more."

Mustard didn't say anything for a while, but I knew he wasn't done.

"Something happened," I prompted.

"Well . . . no. That is, yes. Well, nothing really *happened*, Kitty. Just one day I saw them and I knew something had changed." He closed his eyes for a moment and I was frightened. He looked so sad. What if Mustard started crying, right here, right now? What would I do if Mustard burst into tears?

I needn't have concerned myself because, of course, he did not. But I saw the sadness on him just the same. That sadness was deep and velvety and familiar. Most of all, familiar. I recognized it when I looked. "And I . . ." His voice broke slightly, but he controlled it, dropped down to a whisper, and went on. "I was glad, Kitty. I was *glad*. Because I thought that meant maybe they'd break up, and if they did, maybe I'd have a chance with her."

I understood. "So when he died . . ."

"Right. When he died, I felt so bad, you can't imagine. It felt like my fault almost, you know?"

"But it wasn't," I said.

"You're not asking?"

I shook my head. "No. I'm not. I know it wasn't your fault. But who *did* kill him, Mustard? The story Brucie told . . . the park, the lake . . ."

"You don't think it was true?"

"It just didn't feel right somehow. Guys like that, they kill a guy like Ned Jergens, a guy used to handling himself, of knowing what's what . . ."

"But they don't get the missus? Yeah, I guess when you put it that way, it feels a bit fishy, all right. But Brucie . . . she's a sweet kid, Kitty. And it's like she just can't catch a break."

"Sometimes we make our own breaks."

"What's that supposed to mean?" Mustard demanded hotly.

"You ever hear anything about Brucie and Harrison Dempsey?" I said, not answering his question. Or maybe my question answered his too well. I avoided his eyes, looked instead out the window over his shoulder. I could see an oil derrick in the distance, lit from beneath. The easy rhythm of its rocking was hypnotic. Only right now I wasn't in the mood.

"What are you saying?"

"I'm not saying anything, Mustard. I just think maybe there's more here than we think."

"You're saying that Brucie was stepping out on Ned? That she was seeing Harrison Dempsey behind her husband's back?"

I thought about it. Was that what I was saying? I could see why the implication would be upsetting for Mustard. It would upset everything he'd believed about Brucie. More importantly, everything he'd believed about Brucie and himself. I pressed on. I just didn't have any other options.

"I found a bill at Harrison Dempsey's office."

"What were you doing *there*?"

"It was for a dress exactly like the one Brucie wore to the Zebra Room the other night."

"Exactly? C'mon. There must be a million dresses like that in the city. Two million." He said it with confidence, but I could tell he did not believe it to be true. Just in case, I set him straight.

"No, Mustard. Not a million. Probably not even a hundred. It was gold lamé, for cryin' out loud. And she told me it was a Mainbocher, but not a real one. That's what the bill I found said too: 'in the style of Mainbocher.' And the bill was sent to Dempsey, but it said it was made to order for a Mrs. Jergens."

"So he bought her a dress. So? That doesn't mean anything."

I didn't contradict him. I didn't have to. We both knew there was no reason for Harrison Dempsey to buy Brucie a dress.

"I think maybe it does mean something, Mustard. I'm just not sure what. Think about it. Lucid Wilson and Chummy McGee don't exactly pal around, do they?"

Mustard shook his head. I could see he'd thought of this already. "If anything, they hate each other," Mustard said miserably. "They're not at war, but you could say that their operations are close to that at any time."

"And Harrison Dempsey was into Lucid for a lot of money.

A dangerous amount. And he's buying dresses for the wife of Lucid's biggest rival?"

"Ned wasn't Lucid's biggest rival."

"No," I agreed, "but it almost amounts to the same thing, doesn't it? Ned was as close to Chummy as anyone, from what you've said." I paused for a minute, thinking. Then, "We need to talk to Brucie."

Mustard ran his hands through his ginger hair. "*I* need to talk to Brucie," he said finally. "You can just stay put. I'll drop you off at home on my way."

As Mustard drove, I protested, wanting to go along. But the look on his face deterred me in the end, even more than the fact that he'd pulled up in front of the house on Bunker Hill. His face was thunderous, even tortured. And I know one thing: a man looks like that, he needs to go his way alone.

CHAPTER FORTY-ONE

SOMETIMES I still miss my father, though I'm not sure exactly why. He abandoned me. He left me without resources, without recourse. He left me holding a lot of a mess that he'd created. It's like the gift of life he gave me was given under false pretenses. With one careless act he changed the picture of my life. Everything he'd taught me, every gift he'd given me, all of it turned into a lie.

I think about that sometimes. How could I not? I think about all the things he told me, about what was true and what was not.

I don't miss my mother. I can't. I miss not having had one, but I have no recollections of the woman who gave me life. Since I was old enough to understand what it meant, the word "mother" stood for a sort of lack of something. She was the void, the cold spot in my recollection. There only in absentia, always.

But my father . . . that was different. He could be demanding; he could be brooding; sometimes he could be absent even when he was there. But he *was* there, even when I was at school in San Francisco. He was the cornerstone of my life, the one I could depend upon.

And then he was not.

I thought about these things as I sat in my room that night. It had been late by the time Mustard dropped me off. I'd wanted to sit alone in my room, not be a part of the gentle hustle and bustle of a house full of boarders. Some nights it was soothing to be among them. Tonight it hadn't felt that way.

Marjorie said I looked wan, as though I was coming down

with something. She insisted on bringing a plate of food up to my room. The heel of a loaf of her good bread, some cheese, an apple carefully peeled and sliced. Simple food, but it was so good, an oasis in the storm that had been my day.

It was uncommonly cold for October. Not bitter cold, not freezing cold. Just a very real chill that no amount of warm clothing could chase away. Not in my room. Marjorie had felt the chill and insisted on starting the fire in the hearth in my room as she had in the days *before,* when my comfort had been one of the two most important considerations in the house.

She sensed my need that night, I think. Sensed that my spirit was low, perhaps near breaking, and that I needed looking after. And sure, maybe it wasn't just food I needed. Nor even physical warmth. Still both things went a long way toward restoring me to the cheerier place from which I usually greet the world.

Viewed from the safety of my own warm room, and with a plate of food and a cup of warm tea inside me, the events of the last few days seemed more manageable, if no more understandable. I could cope with these things, move beyond them.

I missed Dex. There were things afoot that his experience would help with. He'd know, for instance, what to make of the bill for Brucie's dress. And the steamship tickets that had been secreted in Dempsey's office. He'd know what to do with the questions I was asking, know whether to think Dempsey was dead or alive.

More than anything else, I found I missed his quiet assurance, even if that assurance was often tainted by his demons and his drink. And, yes, I was a modern woman. I didn't need the presence of a man to confirm my decisions or my place. But I felt I *could* be modern, could be independent, and yet I could still value another voice, one more experienced than my own. I valued not feeling lonely, and I didn't want to feel alone.

Acknowledging these things, combined with the food and

warmth, relaxed me. That night I gave myself up to my fate in a way. Allowed myself to realize that I couldn't always be in control of every situation, every aspect of my life. Some things are inherently not to be controlled.

After a while I stopped thinking big thoughts. I had a bath with bubbles, a mug of hot tea balanced on the edge of the tub.

When I went to bed, my hair was still damp from the bath. The room was warm; my tummy was full. And when I slept it was a dreamless sleep. Uncomplicated.

And it was good.

CHAPTER FORTY-TWO

IN THE MORNING, I approached the office door with some trepidation. The last two times I'd come down this hallway, things had been amiss. First the broken lock—Calvin—and then the window—parties still unknown. On this morning, however, all was as it should be. I found myself almost ridiculously relieved, though it was a relief I didn't allow to flood in fully until I'd entered the office and had a look around. We were on the fifth floor. A break-in that didn't come in the front door was unlikely. Still, the way things had been going, no thought seemed too outlandish.

I was disappointed not to find Dex in the office. I knew he probably wouldn't get back from San Francisco until later in the day, if even that early. Nevertheless, I had wished for his presence. The things that needed to be done on this day felt too big for me to deal with on my own.

I started out easy with the telephone.

Mustard answered on the first ring with a harried sounding "Hullo?"

"Mustard, it's me. What did she say?"

"She wasn't there, Kitty. Her and Calvin had cleared out."

"She leave anything, Mustard? A note? Anything?"

"Nothing, Kitty. Just . . . nothing. I'll let you know if I hear from her." But he didn't sound hopeful, and he rang off before I could say anything more.

It was not as easy to get Dr. Josiah Elway on the line. It took a series of misconnections and reconnections to place the long-distance call. Finally I got him. "Elway here," he said crisply. I felt relief at hearing his voice after spending half the morning trying to get him. And the line was clear and good, another reason for relief.

"Dr. Elway, I don't know if you remember me. This is Katherine Pangborn. I was in your office a few nights ago with my boss, Dexter Theroux."

"Right, of course. I remember you. Dex called you Kitty. And you lost your lunch in the crypt."

I grimaced at the reminder. "Yes, yes, that was me."

"Well, but . . . you've missed Dex, you know."

"Have I?"

"Yes. I saw him yesterday. With his lovely client, what was her name?"

"Lila Dempsey?"

"Yes, yes, that's right. They were horribly disappointed, of course. Or perhaps relieved, I'm not sure. You understand."

"No, Dr. Elway, I'm sorry. I don't."

"Oh. I thought Dex would call and tell you."

"Perhaps he did," I said. "I've been out of the office more than I've been in."

"Well, the body the two of you saw the other night? The one that made you lose your lunch? She hit the floor like a sack of spuds when she saw it."

"I can understand that, Dr. Elway. The body was in pretty bad shape." I could almost feel the nausea rise again when I thought about Dempsey's corpse. It would have been worse when Lila saw it. I didn't imagine it would have improved any since Dex and I were there.

"That's not the only thing that shocked her," Elway replied.

You could have knocked me over with a feather after what he told me next.

CHAPTER FORTY-THREE

I HAD PICKED UP A NEWSPAPER on the way to the office. I now spread it out on my desk looking for the departures list. It didn't take me long to find, or to discover that the *City of Los Angeles* was due to leave the harbor from berth 158 at three o'clock that afternoon.

Since I didn't have a car and it didn't look like the cavalry was going to rush in anytime soon, I needed to decide if I was going to go down there on my own. And if I *was* going to do that, I needed to leave pretty much right away so I could get to the harbor in San Pedro by Red Car with plenty of time to look around before the ship set sail.

I pondered a bit about it. And then I paced. I knew that, odds being what they were, I'd probably get down there and discover absolutely nothing. On the other hand, what if I didn't go? Would I forever wonder if a dead man had steamed away with a mystery partner? Would I think about chances missed and doors that were closed?

And I was anxious. Where was Harrison Dempsey and what was his connection to Brucie? Who had taken the fingerprints from the safe? Who was the stiff on Doc Elway's slab up in Frisco? And why did all of these unrelated things suddenly seem as though they were connected by some gossamer line?

I knew I should probably sit in the office all day and wait for Dex to show up, so he could be given all the facts and half facts I now had and use them to detect whatever could be detected. But if I did that, the *City of Los Angeles* would surely have steamed away. And it seemed to me there was a good chance I was wrong about the whole thing, that Harrison Dempsey would *not* be aboard and miraculously cured of whatever mishap had befallen him. Cured and with his beautiful mistress—or one of them—on his arm. I knew I *could* be wrong. But I really didn't think so.

Before I left the office, I scrawled a hasty note to Dex, telling him what I'd found and where I'd gone. I didn't think he'd get back before I did, but it seemed like the right thing to do, in any case. It's what a *detective* should do, I thought. And I wasn't one of those, but if I was going to act like one, I may as well get the procedure right.

Getting to San Pedro by streetcar was not an all-day affair, but it felt like it. When I finally got to the harbor, I resisted the urge to stand in line with the small well-dressed throng waiting to take the ferry out to Terminal Island in order to board the *Avalon* for passage to Catalina. Seeing them standing there reminded me of my own carefree past, and I felt a fleet but profound sadness. What would it mean, I wondered, to be without care and concern? A time like that seemed impossibly distant now. When I recalled my own trips to Catalina Island, it was like I was enjoying someone else's memories.

As I hurried past, I saw a small girl, beautifully dressed, tuck her hand into her father's and look up at him with excitement and anticipation. And happiness—that was the other thing I saw. I hoped I'd looked at my father like that. It was beginning to feel so long ago now; I couldn't be sure anymore. Maybe I never was.

I followed the signs to the Los Angeles Steamship Company's berths 155 to 158. En route, the docks were a zoo of departures. One of the "white flyers of the Pacific" that chugged up and down the coast between Los Angeles and San Francisco had recently arrived and was disgorging its passengers into the general melee.

People were coming and going in every direction. Stevedores were straining, porters were porting, and between them

were tearful good-byes, joyous hellos, and other expressions of
human emotion pushed to the extreme. My head swam with
the colors, the scents, and the sensations of travel.

I finally located the *City of Los Angeles* at the far end of
berth 158. And then I chided myself: how could I have ever
thought I'd miss it? I hadn't needed directions; I'd only needed
my eyes. The ship was the most beautiful one in the harbor. It
was creamy white with stacks painted red and trimmed in
black. I'd read about this boat, the largest steamer in American waters: 581 feet long, 62 feet across, with first-class ac-
commodations for over four hundred passengers. When the
steamship company purchased her, they'd added a gymnasium
and a swimming tank. Standing next to her on the dock was
like standing next to a floating hotel or a small well-trimmed
city. She took my breath away. I shook my head at the wonder
of it all, then realized that none of my gawking was bringing
me closer to my target.

My target. Truth be told, I wasn't even sure what that was.
When I thought about it, I was looking for a man I'd never
seen, traveling with a companion whose identity I wasn't sure
of. Just what, I thought, was I doing here? Yet in some very
real way—and even though I'd contemplated it—*not* coming
had never really been an option.

And then without really knowing anything at all, I suddenly understood *precisely* why I was there. Though it was difficult to see from the dock to where the passenger I'd spotted
was making her way across the deck of the boat, hers would
have been a difficult outline to ignore.

Unlike the people all around her, she wasn't waving down
to the crowd. Even though that's something you do when
aboard a boat. *Bon voyage.* Was she avoiding waving? I wondered. Trying to avoid being seen?

I was sure . . . well . . . almost sure. The flash of red hair,
the swivel in her hips as she moved away, the careless touch on

a dark and expensive-looking coat. Could it be anyone besides Rita Heppelwaite? Well, it could. But deep down, I felt certain that it was her.

My dilemma in that moment was huge. Though I had no proof, I believed that the boat was carrying Rita Heppelwaite and Harrison Dempsey—perhaps disguised as one John Harrison—away to some island in the South Pacific where they'd be safe from the law as well as whatever mobster mess Dempsey had managed to ignite. And it was one thing to think that—and to think that I *knew* that. And quite another to understand what to do. And I didn't.

I'd done everything I could to alert Dex by leaving a note at the office. But the chances of him seeing it and then thinking enough of the message to get here in time were slim. I found a phone box and tried to reach Mustard, but there was no answer. I thought about calling the police, but it brought the two flatfoots to mind again. And anyway, I really had nothing to tell them beyond some suspicions and uneasy feelings about things not fitting together properly. I knew that those weren't the circumstances that brought the police rushing to your aid. According to Dex, when it came to this matter and this particular man, it was hard to tell who was more crooked: the police or the dark characters Dempsey ran with.

In the end, though, I didn't call for help for one simple reason: what if I was wrong and neither Rita nor Dempsey was aboard? What if it was all some figment of my overactive imagination? Even then, I believed this to be a possibility. After all, how could even a fraction of the things I was imagining be correct? A world like that would make no sense. I wanted a world where one was one and two was two. I didn't want to be right about any of the things I was supposing. But I had to know.

There was an hour left before the *City of Los Angeles* was due to launch. I *had* to get aboard. The crew was watchful though. As if waiting for just such a move. Perhaps it was a sign of the times? I took a seat on a bench near the gangplank and just kept my eyes open for a while. Perhaps an opportunity would present itself.

After a while it did.

CHAPTER FORTY-FOUR

THE FAMILY was large and complicated. I could see a husband and wife, three children, and perhaps six servants. One of the children—a boy of maybe three or four—cried incessantly, an intensely loud cry that seemed designed to pierce the calm of even the bravest of sailors. The men nearby shuddered as the wails rent the air.

There was some confusion with the party's ticketing. The father bellowed at the man in charge. "Do you know who I am?" he said three or four times. The officer obviously did not, because it didn't seem to ease their progress. Perhaps, I thought from my safe distance, it even made things worse.

The woman—I took her to be the bellowing man's wife—kept clasping and unclasping her hands, looking as though she might say something, then holding back. The servants shuffled madly this way and that; one young woman in particular looked nervous about the whole venture and was already turning slightly green. And the child wailed on.

I slipped my hat off my head and pushed it into my handbag so I might be more easily taken as a servant. Then I joined the group as quietly as possible, just as the uniformed officer indicated they should go on aboard. Everything would be sorted out later, he assured them. I got the feeling he would have done anything to get the noisy kid out of earshot, and in any case, the group had been holding up the line.

One of the servants seemed to notice me join the group. She met my eyes and looked at me oddly. I thought for a second she was going to say something; then she seemed to change her mind, and she looked away. Bellowing employers don't do much to inspire loyalty in those who work for them.

I stuck with the group until we were deep inside the vessel. At the earliest opportunity I went left when they went right, ducking into yet another powder room to catch my breath, fix my hair, and replace my hat. The small glimpse I'd already had of the ship told me one thing: the *City of Los Angeles* was huge. I'd have my work cut out for me finding anything at all.

I'd taken perhaps six tentative steps away from the washroom when an employee of the line stopped me. Feeling guilty as I did, I was sure he was about to give me the bum's rush, but he smiled pleasantly and asked if he could be of assistance.

"Do I look that lost?" I asked, pleased that my voice came out sounding controlled when I didn't feel that way at all.

"I'm afraid you do," he said, nodding kindly. Under his peaked cap, he had an open face and kind blue eyes. "Getting lost is an easy enough thing to do on this ship, miss. I spent my first few weeks aboard just trying to find my way around."

"You did? Well, I'll try not to feel so silly then."

"What deck are you on?" he asked.

I looked around for a hint. "I'm afraid I haven't a clue. Don't *you* know?"

He looked at me blankly for a moment, then burst out laughing. "No, no. You're on C deck now, of course. I meant, on which deck is your stateroom?"

It was my turn to look blank. I really had no idea of what to say, which is what in the end I decided to tell him. "That's the problem, you see. I don't remember. Is there any way . . . that is . . . can you help me?"

"Yes, of course I can. Come with me." He led me back the way I'd come when I'd slunk past with the noisy family. He stopped at the purser's desk.

"I'm afraid this young lady is quite lost," my new friend said to the man behind the desk.

"Oh, ho," he said warmly, smiling at me. "Is she now?" I had the feeling this happened a lot. "You don't remember at all?"

I shook my head.

"Well, then, what's your name?"

Any second's hesitation was a hesitation too long. Yet I had to hesitate. I had to process quickly who I should be and where I wanted to be sent. I reasoned that the receipt I'd seen was for John Harrison and Mrs. John Harrison. I decided I looked more like Mrs. than John.

"Mrs. John Harrison," I said into the void. I told myself it had only *seemed* like long minutes had passed. In fact, it could only have been a few fat seconds.

"Harrison . . . Harrison. Let me see . . ." he said, running his index finger over the passenger list. "Here we are. You said John Harrison?"

I nodded.

"Good. Only Harrison this sailing, in any case. Right then, you're in one of the suites deluxe." He looked me over again, perhaps checking for signs of affluence he'd missed on the first take. There weren't any, so he went on. "Those rooms are all on the highest level, which makes them quite easy to find. Gill here can show you the way."

"If you'd just direct me," I said quickly, "I'd prefer to find my own way." Poor Gill looked somewhat crushed, so I hastened to add, "I've taken more than enough of his time already. And in any case, I think I'd like to look around before I go back up."

The two of them gave me careful directions, the purser adding to them with a small but well-crafted diagram. I assured them I wouldn't get lost and headed on my way.

The ship seemed immense to me. And immaculate. The pristine woodwork was carefully painted, beautifully maintained. Polished floors flowed underfoot, and everywhere you looked, the brasswork gleamed like so much spun gold.

I knew that at another time I would have delighted in exploring the craft—following the stairways, trying the food that was already being laid out. The ship was a wonder to me. A small, self-contained city preparing to make a journey to a different realm.

At the same time that my imagination told stories about this seagoing magic carpet, it tried to tell me others about the people I passed in the broad corridors. There, that stout woman. She was no doubt a dowager duchess abroad, looking for an unsuspecting king. That woman there? She must be a silent screen actress, left jobless because she didn't have a voice anyone wanted to hear. That tragic man there, with the dark eyes? He was a widower, of course. He had undertaken the journey in the hope of finding a new wife, one who could be mother to his children. The little girl in a pinafore. What disappointments lay in her future? And here I stopped myself. The game was becoming too dark.

Even with good directions, it took a while for me to find what I sought. That was just as well because I used the time to try to think about what I was going to do. By the time I reached the stateroom door, I'd come to no conclusions, and before I even knew what I was doing, my arm snaked out and I gave the door a firm knock.

CHAPTER FORTY-FIVE

THE EXPRESSION on Rita Heppelwaite's face when she pulled the door open told me she'd expected a more pleasant surprise. As it was, her eyes went all wide when she got a load of me. She stood there for a second or two just looking at me, perhaps trying to figure out where in her memories I fit. For her, I was out of place.

It didn't take long for her to figure out what part of her memory I belonged in though. I saw the recognition dawn on her face, and in almost the same moment she reached out with one gloved hand, fastened it on my wrist, and dragged me into the stateroom. She was stronger than she looked; I figured I'd have a bruise the next day where her hand had grabbed me. If I lived to bruise, that is. That wasn't a forgone conclusion at that moment.

As she closed the door behind us, I realized there was a third person in the cabin. Now it was my turn to shuffle through recent memories. I knew that I knew him, but his appearance was so altered by his grooming and clothing, I didn't recognize him at first. He was dressed in a good suit, a well-made fedora tilted at just the right angle on his handsome head. It was Calvin, Brucie's brother, considerably altered out of his country-boy clothes. And though I was certain he recognized me, he played as though he had not.

"What's goin' on?" he said.

"You know that shamus? Dex Theroux?" Rita asked. Calvin nodded. "This is his secretary."

"His secretary," the guy said. He made his voice show the shock Rita would have expected, but he wasn't so shocked that he couldn't reach under his jacket and pull his hand out with a roscoe inside. A big roscoe too. Big enough to put a hole or six into me without too much trouble.

Up close and personal like this, I realized I had made at least one mistake. It made sense to me that since Cal was here with Rita, Rita probably didn't know anything about Brucie. Cal would want to keep it that way, making the danger to me very real. Everyone knows there's only one real way to silence someone. I tried to swallow, but my throat had closed up. My heart was up to some odd shenanigans too.

And in between the attempts at swallowing and trying to get my pulse under control, I realized I'd made another miscalculation: whatever game was being played here, there were very few points that I'd gotten right. And I'd gotten enough of it wrong to put me in grave danger.

"I thought you told me that mook hadn't gotten wise," Cal said.

"He didn't. I'm sure he didn't."

"What's *she* doin' here then?" He waved his gun at me most disconcertingly as he said this, the motion oddly like déjà vu. I forced the swallow I'd been working on, but didn't say anything.

"I don't know, Cal. I just don't know." She looked honestly perplexed.

"We'll have to croak her." It wasn't a question. He looked a challenge at me. I wasn't sure he was smart, but he was wily, like a fox with distemper. However this went down, he was holding the gun. In this particular game of poker, Cal was the one who held the best hand.

Rita Heppelwaite nodded, as though he'd said they'd have to plant roses or buy a new car. "We will," she agreed. "But not now. The gun would make too much noise. We'll wait until tonight. We'll be under power, and we can get rid of the body then too."

The mook nodded his understanding. "Good thinking. We'll just take her outside, croak her, then slip her into the drink."

There were things I could have been saying at this point. Things I *should* have been saying. Things that would help my situation, perhaps ease my plight. I'm quick with the tongue. I always have been. Too quick sometimes, if my teachers at school were to be believed. Yet in that instant, in the confines of the stateroom deluxe, with Rita Heppelwaite's beautiful eyes on me and Cal's secrets and his impatient-looking gun, I couldn't make myself say boo, let alone the clever, witty, and persuasive things I knew myself capable of dreaming up. I just stood there and watched them, feeling like a deer caught in headlights. The forest was near—so near—yet I hadn't the courage or the wherewithal to make a single move.

Just as I figured I'd be pushing up daisies in no time flat, there was a ruckus at the cabin door. The knock came triple time—and hard. I saw Cal's and Rita's eyes meet over my head, but neither of them made a move. Then both sets of eyes went to the doorknob as it turned. The door opened, and Harrison Dempsey burst into the room without so much as a how-do-you-do. And this time I *knew* it was Harrison Dempsey. It was in the way he stood there, his legs spread just slightly apart, like they were his roots and he was an oak. And it was in the way he looked at the three of us, sizing up the situation as though seeing where he fit. Where we all did.

He was about the same build and coloring as the man we'd found in the bathtub on Lafayette Square, and the features were not dissimilar, but there was something about the set of his face that spoke volumes about the glimpses of the life Dex and I had gotten over the past few days. And maybe a whiff of something that came off him; the smell of success and corruption in his own special blend.

Dempsey stood in the doorway for a long moment, drinking

in the scene. His eyes slid over me and looked coldly at Cal, but they stopped at Rita like they'd hit a wall.

"So this is how it is, huh?"

"Harry . . ." Rita's voice was as small and girlish as I'd ever heard it. "It's not what it looks like. It's not what you think."

"And what do I think, Rita? That you double-crossed me? That you agreed to go away with me, then fed me to Lucid's torpedoes?"

"It's not like that Harry. . . ." Her voice was plaintive now.

"It was a nice setup, Rita. You get me to buy the tickets . . . get me to put up the dough for the trip . . . for a life. Then you get rid of me so you can run off with *this* boob."

"Hey!" Cal said, shifting the gun uncomfortably from one hand to the other and targeting first Dempsey, then me, then Dempsey again, as though he couldn't quite decide whose presence represented the biggest threat. I could have told him, but he didn't ask.

"Yeah, you heard me, you dumb palooka," Dempsey went on. "Look at the broad you chose. Think about the game she's playing, chum. She doesn't care for you any more than she cared for me. First chance she gets, she'll throw you over for something better, because that's what her kind does."

Now Cal seemed to have three people to watch carefully. Me, Dempsey, and Rita. Of the three, there's no doubt I seemed the least likely to try anything funny.

"We was . . ." Cal cleared his throat, went on. "We was gonna go away together."

"A lonely island in the Pacific, right?" Dempsey said. "Yeah, poor sap. We were gonna go there too, weren't we, sweetheart?" he said, addressing Rita again. "How much you get for me? Was it enough?"

"Fifteen G's," Rita said quietly.

Dempsey whistled. "Not bad, not bad. With the fifteen I'd already given you to hang onto for the South Pacific, you were gonna be set up pretty good. You and pretty boy here," he said, cocking his thumb at Cal. "Too bad those looks ain't brains or you'd be dangerous."

"Hey!" Cal said again.

"You figured I'd take it lying down, Harry?" Now there was a white heat on Rita's face. She didn't look beautiful anymore. "You think I didn't know you were carrying on with that Jergens broad? I've got eyes, Harry."

I flashed a look at Cal's face at the mention of Brucie's name. What I saw there was anything but brotherly. If I hadn't been sure before, I was now: no one in this room knew the whole game. Probably not even Cal.

"People talk," Rita added.

"They talk too much," Dempsey sniffed.

"She wanted what I had." Rita seemed not to have heard Dempsey at all. "And when she tried to take it, I realized I wanted more. I wasn't gonna be *that* girl, Harry. I wasn't gonna be the girl you left behind because you found someone new."

"So you . . . what? You cooked up this cockamamy plan to go off with *him*? And with my lettuce? I don't think so, Rita. I don't think so at all."

While Dempsey spoke, I could feel something like tension rise in the small room, or maybe it was just the heat from under his collar. It can't have felt good to come to understand how he'd been both duped and used. As he became aware of just how deep this treachery had gone, I could see the anger rise in Dempsey's face. I watched while a deadly light dawned, and though his expression never changed, the tension around him did. After a while I felt that if I reached out, I'd be able to touch it. And I'd get burned.

When with a flinch and a shrug a weapon seemed to appear in Dempsey's hand, I was almost not surprised. Or maybe I *was* surprised—that it had taken so long to happen. How much had either of this pair thought he would endure before he'd snap?

Dempsey pulled out the gun and aimed it levelly at Cal. Not to be outdone or undone, Rita reached into her handbag and brought out a tiny pearl-handled derringer. In another situation, that gun might have been laughable. In the confines of the tiny quarters, however, I figured she could make any one of us pretty good and dead.

I let my eyes slide over these characters one by one, situated now like some weird Mexican standoff. Cal with his roscoe trained on Dempsey. Dempsey with his gun aimed almost casually at Rita, while Rita stood pointing her little weapon with great care in Dempsey's general direction. The room felt like a powder keg. I didn't figure it would take much of a spark for it to go off.

"What I wanna know, doll," Dempsey said to Rita, "is why? We had us a pretty good plan. If the P.I. would've seen what we meant for him to see . . ."

"Yeah," Rita retorted, bolder now. "*If.* If you weren't married. If your wife hadn't come back from her mother's in Pasadena sooner than expected so's we had to get the body out of the house. If you didn't have an eye for a pretty skirt. If the shamus hadn't got it into his fool head to go to Frisco, seeing the corpse and then fingerprintin' it. If, if, *if.* But the biggest if of all has nothing to do with fate or the universe, Harry. The biggest if of all was Lucid Wilson. It was stupid to try an' play him. He'd have found us sooner or later; then I'd have ended up dead too." She finished on a wretched sigh, then raised her weapon. The other two raised theirs as well.

There was a shot. Maybe two. But I didn't hang around to see who fell. In the heat and the noise, I took the only break I figured I was going to get and headed out the cabin door, running like hell and screaming blue murder. I could have saved the screams, I guess. By the time I hit the corridor, uniformed sailors—or were they steamers? I wondered maniacally—were heading toward me. My friend Gill, from earlier in the day, was at the head of the line.

"What's going on?" he asked naturally enough, his pleasant face not so calm now.

I let them know all hell had broken loose in one of the staterooms and led the way back, though they hardly needed me; the smell of cordite was rich in the air.

By the time we got there, Harrison Dempsey was dead—really dead this time—shot through the chest, just as the body in the tub had been, the body Dex and I had found at Lafayette Square.

All of us could see the small but deadly popgun still smoking in Rita's hands. She looked at the tiny pearl handle with something like wonderment on her face. Perhaps she hadn't expected that the little gun was actually capable of a mortal wound. It was.

There was no sign of Cal, which didn't surprise me. He'd seemed like someone who would take care of himself first. Would he slink over the side and paddle the few feet back to shore? Or hide in some gangway and then sneak back off the boat when the coast was clear? Or, as I was increasingly suspecting, was Brucie holed up in a stateroom on this very ship, waiting for Cal to join her, perhaps with thirty large in hand?

Either way, I figured we'd seen the last of him. His type is catlike: they land on their feet until one day they finally hit the ground too hard. That's the thing about cat lives; they only get the nine.

"What did you do this time, kiddo?" At the sound of his voice, my heart filled with relief.

"Dex!" I said, wheeling around, pleased but not surprised to see he had Mustard in tow. "What are you doing here?"

"Your note, for one. Plus the fact that Lila Dempsey couldn't identify her husband's body."

"Because he wasn't dead," I said. "Elway told me when I called him this morning looking for you."

"I take it she could identify him now?" Mustard said, indicating the fallen man through the stateroom doorway.

They didn't let us stand around much longer. A P.I. license will get you only so far. There wasn't room for the three of us in the tiny cabin, not with Dempsey's corpse taking up space and an ever-increasing stream of people trying to get into the room to either clean things up or figure things out. Besides, there suddenly didn't seem to be any reason to hang around.

It took us a while to find our way off the ship, but when we did we met O'Reilly and Houlahan coming up the gangplank.

"Hello, boys," Dex said casually. "What are you two doing here?"

"A little bird downtown told us Harrison Dempsey was dead and on this tub," O'Reilly said. "Considering the shenanigans this body has been gettin' up to, we figured we'd better get down here quick and check it out for ourselves. How many times can one man die?"

"It's Dempsey all right. This time it's Dempsey for sure. And when you two are finished here, you swing by my office. There's more of this tale I need to tell."

I looked at Dex as we continued on our way, but he didn't say anything. Maybe he would have, but just as we were about to move away from the ship, I spotted another passenger coming down the gangplank. It was Rita Heppelwaite, being escorted by two uniformed officers. She was handcuffed and managing the gangplank only awkwardly, hindered by high heels and a fur coat that kept wanting to slip off her shoulders.

As we watched her make her careful way, I realized I may inadvertently have saved Rita's life. If all I now suspected was true, it was possible that Brucie and Cal would have slipped Rita into the drink along with me once the ship was motoring toward Hawaii. Just as this thought flitted through my head, I saw Rita's eyes slide over the three of us—me, Mustard, and Dex—as though she hadn't seen us at all. That's when I realized another thing: I may have saved her life, but right this moment I wasn't sure she'd thank me.

"You know, it's a damned shame and even kind of a waste," Dex said. "A woman like that, she seems to so love her clothes, wouldn't you say, Kitty?"

"I guess," I replied, unsure where this was going.

"I wonder how she'll like the more limited wardrobe she'll have in prison."

"I don't think she'll like it much. For one thing, the prison blues will clash with her hair."

"I expect you're right, Kitty," he said thoughtfully, watching as they led her past us. "I expect she won't like it at all."

CHAPTER FORTY-SIX

"WHAT I DON'T UNDERSTAND"—Houlahan's voice held a slight slur—"was why she double-crossed him."

"Too many players," Mustard piped up. "Which she? Which he? I'm havin' trouble keepin' 'em all straight."

Houlahan looked piercingly at Mustard, as though he didn't quite understand. And I guess he wouldn't have understood it all in any case. Not now. Not yet. That would have to come.

"Well, why would Rita double-cross Dempsey? It seems like she had a pretty sweet setup. They both did. They'd have gotten away with it all, and no one the wiser."

Dex, always the perfect host, reached into his desk and pulled out a bottle of bourbon. He reached across the cluttered surface, topping glasses as necessary. He did it with the air of a man who was using this simple act as a touchstone while he thought. I could see why; it was a confusing enough tale.

Dex and I had pulled every available chair into his office. Now Dex was behind his desk, and O'Reilly, Houlahan, Mustard, and I sat around him. I was pleased to be included in the group, not relegated to my own desk and instructed to type. I'd expected the order when we'd parked in front of the office, but it hadn't come. O'Reilly and Houlahan didn't need impressing on this day. And Dex knew that my part in the matter had been vital and foolhardy. He'd told me about both in the car in no uncertain terms.

"Near as I can figure," Dex said now, "in the end the double cross was because of a girl."

"Ain't it always?" Houlahan said with a smirk.

Dex nodded, but said, "It ain't always, but it is often enough that it makes you think."

"Brucie," Mustard said. Maybe I was the only one who could hear a slight note of sadness in his voice. Disappointment. What might have been.

Dex nodded, and like a couple of German shepherds, the flatfoots were instantly alert.

"What's that?" O'Reilly said.

"Nothin'," Dex replied. "It doesn't matter now." He sighed deeply and ran his hands through his hair. It was a familiar enough gesture, and I knew exactly what it meant. The flatfoots had to be told about Brucie and about how she fit into all this. They needed all the details if justice was to be done. But they didn't need it right this second, not with Mustard sitting right there and looking as miserable as I'd ever seen him. "OK," he said finally, "it *does* matter, but there are a few pieces I'm still putting together. And there's a client I need to talk to before I can spill the whole thing."

"Tomorrow morning?" O'Reilly said. "At the station."

"Sure. Sure thing, fellas."

"Scout's honor?" Houlahan said.

Dex nodded. "Scout's honor," he said, though I was fairly confident he'd never been a scout.

O'Reilly maybe had the same idea, and he narrowed his eyes at Dex, but didn't pursue the matter. Instead he drained his glass, then held it out for more. "The girl said there was another man in the cabin at first," he said, while Dex poured. "But we couldn't find any trace."

"The girl is Miss Kitty Pangborn here," Dex instructed, pointing at me.

"Katherine," I corrected.

"And she said the guy was a torpedo named Cal," Dex said.

"How'd she know he was a torpedo?" Houlahan asked.

"Your mouth is moving, but your head is pointed in the wrong direction," I said pertly. "I'm sitting right here."

"OK, sister," he said, addressing me for the first time. "How'd you know he was a torpedo?"

I shrugged. "It fits, is all. He talked about killing me, calm as you please. He would have done it too, I'm sure. He said they'd wait until dark, then 'slip' me 'into the drink.' " There was more I could have said. Stuff about Brucie. Brucie and the brother I suspected wasn't. But I held onto it for now. I needed to talk to Dex. Alone. What I had to say shouldn't be said in front of Mustard; he shouldn't hear it that way first. Besides, the way I figured it, there was no hurry. The *City of Los Angeles* would be seven days on the water. Plenty of time to work out how best to handle the matter, how to finally tell the police and have them wire down there so the authorities at Hilo could apprehend Brucie and Calvin when the ship docked.

"Slip you into the drink, huh? Nice. Wouldn't even have had to waste a bullet." Mustard said it jovially, but belated concern for me etched his brow.

I grinned back at him. "That's right, Mustard. No use wasting perfectly good bullets when there's no call."

"Here's another thing I don't get," Dex said, interrupting the exchange. "You said you locked the fingerprints we took in San Francisco into the office safe, right?"

I nodded. "That's right. Before Cal and I headed out to . . ." I shot a look at Mustard, knowing his place in Venice was his secret. Or at least it had been until he took Brucie there and I inadvertently dragged along her lover.

"Out where?" Houlahan insisted now.

"Out to Venice," Mustard finished. "We'd stashed Brucie out there." I could almost feel the flatfoots perk up again at the name, but then they settled down. Either the booze was softening them up, or they realized Dex would deal with them straight later. Maybe both.

"Right," I said. "I locked the fingerprints in the safe that day. Before we left. And I've racked my brain about it too, Dex, because who would have broken in and taken them?"

"Because who would have known they were there?" Dex added.

"Right. The only thing I can figure is this: when I opened the safe, Cal was there in your office. Sleeping."

Dex arched a single eyebrow. "*My* office."

"Sorry but . . . yeah. I didn't know what else to do with him. And don't forget, at the time I was sure he was Brucie's brother. The only thing I can figure is that maybe he *wasn't* sleeping. Maybe he saw me open the safe and put something in there— maybe he even had some idea what the something was—and later on he checked in with Rita, who told him—or someone— to come back and glom the envelope."

Dex kicked back a bit and looked thoughtful. "I guess that's as good an explanation as any," he said at length. "And the way things have turned out, it looks like it might be the only one we get."

Mustard drained his glass, put his head in his hands, and rubbed his ginger hair. "What a business," he said distractedly, into the table. "What a mixed-up business the whole thing has turned out to be."

"You got that straight," I said. "Which reminds me . . . we now know for sure that Dempsey wasn't the one killed at the house on Lafayette Square. So if not Dempsey, who was killed there?"

This the flatfoots had already worked out. "We won't know for a few days yet, but we're figuring it was G. Eddie Powell. He'd been working for Dempsey for a few months, and his wife reported him missing three days ago."

"What's the G stand for?" Mustard asked distractedly.

Houlahan shrugged. "Gregory? Gorgeous? Graham? It doesn't matter. What *does* matter . . ."

O'Reilly picked up the story as if he and Houlahan were an old married couple: "What matters is G. Eddie was probably hired because he looked a lot like Dempsey. Same build, similar coloring, good-looking guy. Dempsey and Rita probably had this cooked up for some time."

Dex took up the story. "So they killed G. Eddie at Dempsey's house. I was supposed to witness the whole thing. Only I was sleeping when it went down, and missed all the action."

"Remind me not to hire you to do any P.I. work," O'Reilly chirped.

"That's too bad," Dex replied dryly. "I could have made a small fortune off the two of you."

"But why take the body to San Francisco?" I asked. "Why not just dump it into the river, let the sharks here take care of things?"

"It wasn't the sharks, kiddo," Dex replied. "It was the distance. The way I figure it, Dempsey wanted the body found so Lucid Wilson and his boys wouldn't go off looking for him. Dempsey and Rita didn't just want to leave a cold trail, they wanted to leave *no* trail. Frisco was perfect because it's far enough away to make identification difficult. It would just give them that much more time to get away."

"Is that why Rita was in San Francisco? When I saw her at the club with Morgana?" I asked.

"That's what I was thinkin'." Dex nodded. "Dempsey was probably holed up someplace—maybe even in the city—while Rita made sure the body got found and ID'd as Dempsey, in time for the two of them to get away clean."

"But they'd probably hoped for a couple more days before the body turned up," Mustard said. "If he'd been more decomposed, it would have been that much harder to identify him. Hell, a few weeks in the drink, no one would have been able to identify him at all."

"He was plenty decomposed," I said with a gulp, remembering. In an effort to calm myself, I took a tentative sip of the whiskey Dex had insisted on pouring for me. It burned going down. I could feel myself relax, though I wasn't sure if the whiskey helped or not.

It was over. It was done. And I was glad.

CHAPTER FORTY-SEVEN

WHEN I GOT HOME it was late, and I was so tired I just wanted a bowl of soup and my bed. Marjorie caught up with me on the stairs.

"Mrs. Jergens was here earlier," she told me. On a certain level I wasn't surprised.

"She's not here now though." I didn't need to ask.

"No, that's right. She's not. She had a young man with her. He loaded her trunk and her boxes into a car, and she told me she wouldn't be back."

I was saddened but not entirely surprised by this, either. What she said next, however, *did* surprise me.

"She left this for you," Marjorie said, reaching into the pocket of her housedress and pulling out a creamy envelope. "And she apologized, though I'm not sure for what. And she didn't ask for the month's rent back." Marjorie didn't have to tell me that she was relieved about that part. Empty rooms didn't fill any soup pots.

I took the letter into what had, for an instant, been Brucie's room—she'd not spent even a single night there. The room was unoccupied again, and no sign of Brucie had been left behind. Even the flowers I'd bought for her had been cleaned up, and not a single dead leaf remained.

I sat in one of the wingback chairs and looked out the window and over the city. It was full dark, but downtown Los Angeles was ablaze with lights. Marjorie had said that my mother liked to sit in this very spot and read when she was with child. What did she think about at those times? Did she think about me? I imagine she did. She would have thought about the phantom me, kicks increasing as I readied myself to come into the world.

What would my mother have said about all of this? I wondered. But I had no reference for discovery. After a while I knew I couldn't delay any longer. I sat more deeply in the chair, preparing myself for what was to come.

Dear Miss Katherine, the letter began, a nod, I knew, to the one evening we'd shared in the house, and her mirth at the way Marjorie still addressed me. I realized that I'd never seen Brucie's handwriting before this instant. It was tidy. Neat, but with flourishes. Like an artist might write. Like a bird trying to find her way out of her cage.

By now you'll know a great deal. What a mess I've made of everything. You mustn't think too badly of me. The lies I told were never against you, and I hoped none of them would hurt you. In fact, if I were allowed only one regret— and I have more than one, believe you me—it's that we didn't get to become friends. I know that if things were different, we should have done.

There are things that I could tell you, details that would make things more clear, but to be honest, I'm not sure I have clarity myself.

I'm going far away. I'm going to find someplace where they've never even heard of Lucid Wilson or Chummy McGee. And I'm going to be better there, Kitty. I'm going to be the me I've always wanted to be.

Please give my regards to Mustard. Another regret or six. But he deserves a better girl. A girl whose heart is as pure as the one he thought he saw in me.

Thank you for taking me into your home, and sorry again for all the trouble I caused.

And it was signed, simply, *Brucie*.

I read the note once all the way through, and then I read it again trying to find the things she hadn't said. They weren't there, or if they were, I couldn't see them.

When I thought things over, I realized that if half of what I suspected was true, even though everyone had been playing everyone else, Brucie had been the puppetmaster who had, in the end, controlled all the strings. Somehow the description didn't seem to fit the merry young woman I'd met. But there you have it. Sometimes, as they say, appearances can be deceiving.

I wondered if she'd orchestrated the death of her husband so that the way would be clear for her to manipulate Dempsey. And then, with Dempsey dealt with, she could run away with Calvin. It was even possible that Calvin was also merely a means to an end. Malleable and handsome, he would have played the part of pawn quite well.

I knew I'd probably never have the answers to all of these questions, and it made me a little sad. Brucie, the bright, beautiful smiling girl. Brucie of the big brown eyes and the seal-sleek hair. Those are the things I'd seen, but now I knew there'd been so much more.

She'd asked for my forgiveness, but I didn't know that it was really in my power to grant it. For what it was worth, I could forgive Brucie. She'd done terrible things, but none of them had been against me. Her demons though—well, I doubted they'd forgive her anything. Because forgiveness—real forgiveness—must come from within.